MURDER IN THE MUSEUM

Later that afternoon, shortly before the museum closed, Daisy asked Smith Woodward about the Piltdown Man controversy.

He took her to see it again, but this time he contemplated it in silence for a minute, before sighing, "It really is very troublesome. Fossil fish are really my field, you know. I believe I may say I am accounted something of an authority on fossil fish. Do let me show you my Arthrodire."

He had been so kind that Daisy let him off the hook. She could always ask someone else about Piltdown. He limped at her side across the gallery, and they entered the hall leading to the fossil reptiles, with the dinosaur gallery beyond, wherein the fishes occupied their modest place.

Somewhere in front of them a voice rose in triumph and contempt, the words indistinguishable. The bellow that followed held a note of surprised agony, like that of a wounded bull. Then came a tremendous crash.

With a gasp, Smith Woodward stopped, rooted to the ground. Daisy ran through the arch ahead.

Sprawled on his back, immobile amidst a litter of smashed Pareiasaurus bones, lay Pettigrew. And across his white shirtfront and pale grey waistcoat seeped a crimson stain . . .

Daisy Dalrymple Mysteries by Carola Dunn

DEATH AT WENTWATER COURT

THE WINTER GARDEN MYSTERY

REQUIEM FOR A MEZZO

MURDER ON THE FLYING SCOTSMAN

DAMSEL IN DISTRESS

DEAD IN THE WATER

STYX AND STONES

RATTLE HIS BONES

TO DAVY JONES BELOW
(coming soon)

Published by Kensington Publishing Corporation

RATTLE HIS BONES

CAROLA DUNN

KENSINGTON BOOKS
Kensington Publishing Corp.
http://www.kensingtonbooks.com

KENSINGTON BOOKS are published by

Kensington Publishing Corp.
850 Third Avenue
New York, NY 10022

All Kensington Titles, Imprints, and Distributed Lines are available at special quantity discounts for bulk purchases for sales promotions, premiums, fund-raising, and educational or institutional use. Special book excerpts or customized printings can also be created to fit specific needs. For details, write or phone the office of the Kensington special sales manager: Kensington Publishing Corp., 850 Third Avenue, New York, NY 10022, attn: Special Sales Department, Phone: 1-800-221-2647.

Kensington and the K logo Reg. U.S. Pat. & TM Off.

First St. Martin's Press hardcover printing: June 2000
First Kensington mass market printing: March 2003

10 9 8 7 6 5 4 3 2 1

Printed in the United States of America

ACKNOWLEDGMENTS

My thanks are due to John Thackray, Archivist of the Natural History Museum in London, who patiently answered my many questions and showed me around the private areas of the museum; also to his assistant, Clare Bunkham. Errors, omissions, additions, and alterations are all mine.

Dr. (later Sir) Arthur Smith Woodward is the only genuine museum staff member amongst my cast of characters. I trust I have done him justice. (The Director in 1923 really was Sir Sidney Harmer, but Daisy—perhaps fortunately—never meets him.) All other employees of the museum, police, et al., except for movie special-effects man O'Brien, are entirely fictional.

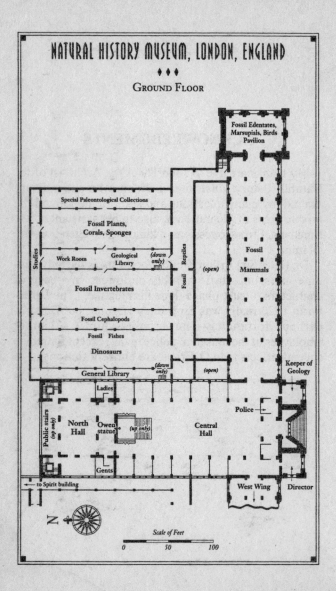

NATURAL HISTORY MUSEUM, LONDON, ENGLAND

♦ ♦ ♦

GROUND FLOOR

Fossil Edentates,
Marsupials, Birds
Pavilion

Special Paleontological Collections

Fossil Plants,
Corals, Sponges

Studies

Work Room | Geological Library | *(down only)*

Fossil Reptiles

(open)

Fossil Mammals

Fossil Invertebrates

Fossil Cephalopods

Fossil Fishes

Dinosaurs

General Library | *(down only)* | *(open)*

Keeper of Geology

Ladies

Police

Public stairs *(up only)*

North Hall

Owen statue | *(up only)*

Central Hall

Gents

West Wing

Director

← to Spirit building

N

Scale of Feet

0   50   100

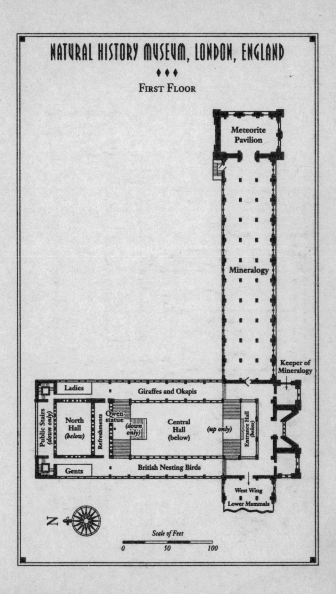

NATURAL HISTORY MUSEUM, LONDON, ENGLAND

♦ ♦ ♦

FIRST FLOOR

Meteorite Pavilion

Mineralogy

Keeper of Mineralogy

Ladies

Giraffes and Okapis

Public Stairs *(down only)*

North Hall *(below)*

Refreshments

Owen statue

(down only)

Central Hall *(below)*

(up only)

Entrance Hall *(below)*

Gents

British Nesting Birds

West Wing Lower Mammals

N

Scale of Feet

0   50   100

The road it is rough, and the hearse has no springs,
And hark to the dirge that the sad driver sings—
Rattle his bones over the stones . . .
—THOMAS NOEL

One

He hurried up the stairs from the basement and unlocked the door which kept the public from wandering down into the private areas of the museum. Pushing it open a crack, he heard voices in the North Hall. He froze, still as a rabbit mesmerized by a stoat, nerves aquiver.

"Regular maze down there, Sarge, innit?" The constable must have just come up the stairs on the other side of the hall. "Proper sinister, the pipes gurgling away up by the ceiling, and all them pillars with their shadows moving when you walk past with your torch. And all full of bones and dead things—ugh! Like a cata-thingummy."

"Catacomb. It's live people you're looking out for, Jones. Anyone in the offices downstairs?"

"Nah, they don't work late, mostly, these light summer evenings."

"There's a bloke in one of the Bird Rooms, stuffing a bird of Paradise. Lovely thing."

"One of them taxi-whatsits," suggested the constable.

"-Dermists. Taxidermists. Couple of chaps in the libraries, too, noses stuck in their dusty old books. Me, I'd rather be outdoors smelling the roses."

"Wouldn't mind being out on the beat, nice day like this."

"No kettle on the beat," observed the sergeant. "Let's go brew up. Twitchell'll be down in a minute."

Their voices receded, accompanied by the clink of the sergeant's great bunch of keys and the thunk of police boots on the mosaic floor, echoing hollowly in the vast spaces of the museum.

The listener hesitated. The third policeman, Constable Twitchell, would probably descend by the main staircase after completing the night's first patrol of the upper floors. Even if bad luck brought him down these stairs, he would think nothing of meeting another late worker, like the taxidermist in the Bird Room, the readers in the libraries.

Still, better not to be seen unnecessarily. He stayed where he was, ears straining for a third set of footsteps.

Only his own breath soughed in his ears. The massive Victorian building absorbed even the heavy tread of three policemen, relaying no hint of their whereabouts. Two would have reached the police post by the main entrance by now, but had the third come down to join them yet? Vital minutes ticked away while he listened.

Surely Twitchell *must* have gone down the main stairs by now.

Rubber-soled shoes silent on the stone steps, he sped upward again. Now he was committed, at least to the extent that he had no legitimate purpose above the ground floor.

Slightly out of breath, he reached the first floor. Instinct shrieked, "Go with care!" but to be caught peeking around the corner would instantly arouse suspicion. He stepped out boldly. No one in sight in the long gallery ahead.

As he passed the head of the main staircase, keeping well back, he glanced that way. From the corner of his eye, he caught a glimpse of a still figure standing on the broad half-landing. His heart jumped.

Sir Richard Owen did not stir, being bronze. But footsteps sounded down in the Central Hall.

The tread of heavy boots, not a scholar's shoes—all three coppers accounted for. Tempted nonetheless to look over the balustrade to make sure it was the third policeman, not a stray museum employee, he made himself move on along the window side of the gallery. Between him and temptation marched a silent, motionless parade of giraffes and okapi.

Four steps up, then the stairs to the second floor, bridging the central hall, rose on his right. The heavy black wrought-iron gate to the Mineral Gallery barred the way to his left, and Pettigrew's private office lay straight ahead. The Keeper of Mineralogy had just started his annual fortnight's holiday.

It was a shadowy corner. He had not reckoned on being silhouetted against the frosted glass door-panes, all too visible from the giraffe gallery and the stairs.

Crouching below the level of the glass, he fumbled in his trouser pocket for the key.

His discovery that the key of the Keeper of Geology's office also opened Pettigrew's directly above had been purely fortuitous. He happened to be present that day last year when Dr. Smith Woodward, having—typically—mislaid his own keys, borrowed Pettigrew's. From that chance had developed his present brilliant plan. The old man's forgetfulness of anything not directly concerning his beloved fossils had made it easy to borrow the keys and have the important ones copied.

The door-key copy grated in the lock and his heart stood still. He glanced round, but only *Giraffa camelopardalis* watched him, with a glassy-eyed stare.

The key clicked round. Taking out his handkerchief, he wiped his suddenly damp forehead, then used the cloth to turn the door handle. The door swung open. He stepped through and closed it quickly behind him . . .

. . . Leaving the blasted key on the outside.

That was the sort of stupid mistake which could get him caught. All the same, he decided to risk leaving it there for a few minutes. He must find Pettigrew's keys very soon, or he might as well give up. Of course, if the Keeper of Mineralogy had taken them home, the whole thing was off.

As he put away the handkerchief and took out his light summer gloves, he scanned the spacious room. The two large windows admitted plenty of light in spite of the trees outside and the late hour.

On a row of pegs behind the door hung a silk scarf in a brown and blue Paisley pattern. The keys were not conveniently hanging next to it, nor under it—he checked.

On a work-bench to his left, under the east window, lay various tools and a dozen or so pieces of rock, of varied size and colour but undifferentiated and uninteresting in his eyes. Pettigrew apparently liked the view of trees and the omnibuses, hansoms, motor taxis, and horse-drawn vans in the Cromwell Road, for the government-issue pedestal desk faced the south window. Against the right-hand wall stood a filing cabinet and a bookcase.

Desk, cabinet, and bookcase, appropriate to the grade of keeper, matched Smith Woodward's in the office below. Whether they were keyed alike he was about to discover.

He crossed to the desk and pulled open the centre drawer to find paper, envelopes, a book of penny-ha'penny stamps, blotting paper to fit the pad on top. The first drawer on the left held an old fountain pen with a cracked cap, a bottle of blue-black ink and another of India ink, a paper knife, and other odds and ends. The second drawer down was locked.

Smith Woodward's desk key turned in the lock. So much for government standardization! The drawer slid open to disclose a plethora of keys.

For a moment he stared, scarcely able to believe his luck. There they lay, the big iron key for the iron gate and three rings of small brass ones for the display cases. The latter even had tags with the numbers of the cases they opened.

He began to feel a sense of inevitability. Everything seemed to conspire to help him: the keys falling into his hands; Pettigrew's absence when short summer nights made a betraying torch unnecessary; one lucky coincidence after another. Dame Fortune favoured those with the guts, brains, and patience to take advantage when opportunity offered.

Long patience had made tonight possible, but for the next few hours time was of the essence. He picked up the keys, stuffed all but the large one in his pockets to stop them jangling, and hurried to the door.

Now caution was called for. He had crossed the line; if he was caught coming out of Pettigrew's office laden with Pettigrew's keys no excuse would serve, his goose was well and truly cooked. Opening the door a crack, he peered through the narrow gap.

The view was singularly uninformative. Eyes shut, head cocked, he listened. His heart thundered, but no whisper of external sound reached him.

Pull the door open; step through; close it, gently; lock it and take the key. He tiptoed ten long yards to the iron gate. Set in a grid which filled the archway, it was backed by a wood and glass screen and door which kindly limited the view of the interior, as did the double row of rectangular pillars within.

The clumsy key turned silently. Not a creak escaped the well-oiled hinges. And the door opened with equal ease. He was inside the Mineral Gallery.

He cast a long, yearning look at the Colenso diamond, but a hundred and thirty carats of crystallized carbon was too conspicuous, too recognizable. The rest of the diamonds he passed with a disdainful sneer. They were all paste copies of famous stones, including the uncut Cullinan, a monster at over three thousand carats.

Without a jeweller's lens, the heavy lead glass invented centuries ago by Herr Strasser was virtually indistinguishable from the real thing. They were all inanimate objects, unchanging, never alive, their value artificial, one very like another in all but size. Studying them taught nothing. What did it matter whether the public gaped at genuine gems or counterfeits?

Moving on, he opened case after case. His inside breast-pockets filled with amethysts, sapphires, garnets, topazes, aquamarines, rubies, emeralds. Kind of Sir Arthur Church to bequeath his splendid collection to the museum!

He hesitated over the Transcarpathia ruby. It was an uncommonly large stone, famous half a century ago, but few colored jewels achieved the lasting notoriety of the largest diamonds. Weight for weight, though, a large ruby was more valuable than a diamond. He pocketed it.

Under the arch to the meteorite pavilion stood the case of precious stones mentioned in the Bible. Superstitiously, he left it untouched.

The rear exit was close by, with little-used stairs right down to the basement. He had the key to the door. Alas, the innocent wood was backed by another of solid steel, and only the police had the key to that. No choice but to return the way he had come.

He started back along the north aisle, glancing from side to side to check that he had closed all the cases. Had he locked the iron gate behind him? In a sudden flash of panic he could not remember. The patrolling constable probably tried it every time he passed.

The constable might even now be on his way upstairs after his cup of tea. The gate was two hundred feet away, nearly the whole length of the gallery.

His immediate impulse was to run. Sweating again, he tried to force himself to be calm, to think. The urge for speed won.

Feet thudding dully, he loped towards the entrance. The keys clinked in his bulging pockets. Suspiciously bulging—so many details he had not envisioned! But it would take too long to return Pettigrew's keys to his desk.

As he approached the entrance he slowed, and stopped, panting, to one side of the arch. Craning his neck, he could see through the glass that the gate was still closed. No police countenance frowned back at him. Bent double, below the level of the glass panes, he crept forward and reached for the handle of the inner door.

He had locked it, quite unnecessarily. Dammit, he cursed under his breath, what a waste of time! Fumble for the key, open a crack to listen, reach through to try the gate.

It, too, was locked. All that panic for nothing.

The big key turned easily. A moment later he was out, feverishly locking door and gate behind him while straining for the sound of boots.

The nearest stairs were in a nook just around the corner from Pettigrew's office. He had avoided them before because, on the ground floor, they opened to Smith Woodward's office, right beside the police post. Now, time slipping away, he unlocked the door at the top and tiptoed down the narrow, gloomy stairwell, heart in mouth, clutching his pockets to keep the keys quiet.

On the ground floor, only a wall and a yard or two separated him from the police.

Back in the basement at last, in the dim light beneath grumbling pipes, he leant weakly against the yellow brick wall and blotted his brow. He would not use those nerve-racking stairs again.

Just a little farther, to the staff cloakrooms, and he was safe. He had left his hat and attaché case there. From here on, he was just a late-working employee on his way home.

As on any ordinary day, he left the museum by a door at the rear of the basement. The usual staff entrance, it was secured with a Yale mechanism. Every employee had a key, though he did not need one to exit. He walked along the arcade to Queen's Gate and turned south towards South Ken tube station. There, he showed his season ticket at the barrier, and plunged into the depths, breaking into a trot as a subterranean rumble warned of a train's approach. Emerging onto the platform in its chasm, open to the darkening sky, he automatically turned to the west-bound side.

Then he remembered he was not going home. He had

told them he had been invited to give a lecture in Cambridge and it would be easier to stay the night there. Swinging round, he made for the east-bound platform. The first train to come in was on the Inner Circle, but he took it anyway. The sooner he escaped the vicinity of the museum, the happier he would be. He could change at Mark Lane onto a District line train to Whitechapel.

A rosy dawn stained London's sooty skies when he returned to Kensington. He was tired and hungry—he had felt conspicuous enough walking down the street among the bustling Hebrew population of Whitechapel without venturing into one of their cafés to dine. Besides, he had no idea what sort of weird, foreign concoctions they ate.

He was also hurried. All too soon an army of housemen would arrive to sweep, scrub, dust, and polish. He had to be gone before then.

Haste and lack of sleep must not lead to carelessness, he thought, yet caution must not slow him. If he was seen, no conceivable excuse could explain away his presence at that hour of the morning.

Slipping in through the basement door, he made for the west end of the west wing, where stairs led all the way up to the second floor. That was the safest place to cross to the central block at this time in the morning. The constable on duty upstairs would be busy later keeping an eye on the housemen. At this dead hour, he was probably to be found with his colleagues in the police post on the ground floor, drinking endless cups of tea to stay awake. If he made occasional patrols, he might not even bother to go above the first floor.

In the dim dawn light, the Upper Mammal Gallery on the second floor was an eerie place. The gorillas, lurking in their artificial jungle, seemed about to pounce. Once or twice he could have sworn a chimpanzee or a monkey turned its head to watch as he trudged wearily past.

The human skeletons on the other side sent atavistic shivers down his spine. If they affected *him* so, he told himself, no uneducated boor of a policeman was likely to enter the gallery unnecessarily until full daylight drove the ghosts away.

Guarding the top of the main stairs, the massive marble statue of Sir Joseph Banks was a friendly figure in comparison. In Sir Joseph's shadow he stopped to listen.

The huge, sound-deadening mass of the building weighed oppressively on his nerves now. He felt as if an officer could creep up silently behind him and tap him on the shoulder before he became aware of his presence.

Utter bosh! Police boots could be heard a hundred yards off, he reminded himself. He crossed to the stair head, stared down into the shadowy depths. Nothing moved.

Another shadow, he tiptoed down, turning right on the half-landing. More monkeys watched, a terra cotta troupe climbing the arch over the stairs, chattering at him silently.

Twenty minutes later, he returned by the same route and let himself out by the basement door.

The cleaners who polished the glass cases in the Mineral Gallery, their every move scrutinized by the constable on duty, noticed nothing amiss. Nor did the public, when they wandered in later to ooh and aah at diamonds and sapphires before moving on to the meteorites.

Naturally; nothing *was* missing. Yet.

That was Monday night and Tuesday morning. The following Friday he went out to Whitechapel after work, to make sure everything was proceeding according to plan.

Satisfied, he did not return until the Friday after, fortunately a sunny though cool and breezy day. He went at midday, setting off from the museum with his attaché case, as if to eat his luncheon sandwiches in Kensington Gardens. Only that day, the case contained no sandwiches. It was stuffed with banknotes, every last remaining penny of his nest-egg.

Sitting in the Tube, as it joggled its rattling way beneath the West End and the City, he wondered if he was crazy. He could turn around now, open a new Post Office savings account, and redeposit his few hundred. No one would ever know what he had already done, what he planned to do tonight.

But he could not bring himself to abandon hope. Not when he had already paid over half the price, with no chance of recovering the money.

Besides, what he had to do tonight was no riskier than what he had already accomplished—if anything, less. He was cleverer than the police, cleverer than the museum authorities, cleverer than Pettigrew. He had the cool daring to complete the business, the patience to wait for time to cover his tracks.

Pettigrew always returned from his holiday laden with rock specimens. Until he had studied them thoroughly, he had little interest in anything already classified, catalogued, labelled, and locked away. Weeks, if not months, would pass before he discovered that the jewels in his display cases were all as false as the Cullinan "diamond."

Stepping off the train at the Whitechapel station, he went up to the noisy, anonymous street.

The strass glass gems were ready. They looked to him just as good as the real jewels. Having—that night two weeks ago—taken photographs and minutely precise measurements of the originals, and matched the colours against dozens of samples, the old man swore he had made perfect copies.

"Better qvality you vill novhere get," he declared. "Vunce zese stones are beautifully set, only an eggspert can ze difference tell. Your vife vill be proud to vear. You vant I tell you ze address mine cousin's, can make rings, necklaces, bracelets, vhat you like?"

"No, thank you!" He lifted his attaché case onto the work table and opened it. "My wife has her own favourite jeweller. Here you are."

Peering through thick spectacles, the old man watched him count out every note. Then he tenderly tucked each of his creations into its own little chamois bag. The exchange was made. Another bridge crossed.

He left it late, until even the most dedicated of his colleagues had surely gone home. It couldn't be helped that that made his own presence the more questionable. He must not be seen!

This time, he had to put the keys back in Pettigrew's desk. The gods were assuredly on his side. As he left the Mineral Gallery, nothing moved among the giraffes and okapis. Nothing moved on the stairs. No footsteps echoed. Turning left, he sped to the Keeper of Mineralogy's office.

The key which had grated, he had taken to a locksmith to be smoothed. Now it rotated in the lock as easily as a spoon in a soft-boiled egg. He was in and out of the office in no more than ninety seconds.

He intended to leave via the giraffes and the back staircase at the north end, but as he came abreast of the main stairs to the second floor, he changed his mind. If he *was* spotted, the farther from the Mineral Gallery the better. It would be safer to go along the far side of the Central Hall. The stairs tempted him, arching over the hall below, but he resisted—far too exposed. Back he went and around, past the iron gate and Pettigrew's office, past the entrance to the Lower Mammals: stuffed everything from aardvark to zebra.

The stairs rose on his right, now, and ahead four steps led down to British Nesting Birds.

A shadow moved. His heart stood still.

"I weren't asleep, sir," protested a thick voice. From his seat on the steps, a stout police constable lumbered to his feet. An elderly man, he blinked bewilderedly as he moved forward, straightening his jacket. "Jest resting me pins a minute. The knees ain't what they was."

"I shan't report you, Officer." He had to force the words through his constricted throat.

His one thought now was to get away without doing anything which might fix him in the man's memory. His head averted, trying not to scurry, he carried on between the glass cases, scrutinized as he passed by the beady eyes of plover and pigeon. The policeman would surely presume he had come from the Lower Mammals, or perhaps down the stairs from the second floor. Anyway, the fellow would not mention seeing him, for fear of his unauthorized nap coming to light.

The door to the stairwell closed behind him. Down the stairs he ran, past the ground floor and on down to the basement.

An old man, confused with sleep, the constable would not remember whom he had seen—probably had not recognized him. The police seconded to the Natural History Museum could not know every employee by sight. No prompt outcry would make him recall the incident, for the substitution of paste for precious stones would not be discovered for ages. *Should* not be discovered.

With an effort, he slowed his stride. The gloomy corridor seemed endless. At last he reached the still-gloomier pillared cavern beneath the east wing. He was halfway across when he heard the approaching tramp of police boots.

He froze behind a pillar. A regular patrol? Or had the constable upstairs reported his presence?

The officer passed no more than ten feet from him, swinging an electric torch so that its beam probed the darkest corners. If it was a search, it was far from systematic—but nonetheless alarming.

His heart pounding, palms sweaty, he ducked around the brick pillar. Suppose the old man was suspicious, had called down to his colleagues in the Central Hall. Suppose they put a guard on the basement exit? He dared not try to leave carrying the jewels.

Better to lock them in his office overnight and take them home tomorrow at midday, at the end of the short Saturday workday, when he was one of a swarm of departing employees.

No, he did not want to keep them at home. He did not know how long it would take to find a buyer, and when the paste gems were discovered, the police might search everyone's residences. And what if the theft was somehow detected before tomorrow noon? It would be safer to hide the real stones somewhere in the museum until the furor died down. Then, if they were found, there would be nothing to link them to him.

The torchbeam bobbed away, the footsteps faded. As he let out the breath he had unconsciously been holding, the answer came to him.

Perfect! He could hide the jewels tomorrow morning, before the museum opened to the public, and no one who saw him would ask what he was doing. No one else would conceive of looking there, however long he left them. When the moment was right, he could retrieve them with ease.

He should never have doubted himself. Not only was his plan brilliant to start with, but he was quite capable of improvising brilliantly when advisable. He was going to outwit the lot of them.

Two

Through grey drizzle, Daisy peered up Brompton Road towards Knightsbridge. She was sure she felt her shingled curls frizzing in the damp air, in spite of the protection of her blue cloche hat and cheerfully pillar-box red umbrella.

Among the drays and horse-lorries, taxi-cabs and ancient hansoms, chauffeur-driven motor-cars and damp errand-boys on bicycles, towered at least half a dozen omnibuses. Like honeybees, they swooped to taste the queues of nectar-people at the flower-stops.

A Number 30 bumbled towards the corner where she stood, closely followed by a 96. She stepped back to make room for descending passengers.

Ah, there was a 74. Daisy hurried to meet it. Alec had assured her his daughter, Belinda, was perfectly capable at the age of nine of getting herself and Derek from St. John's Wood to Kensington, but she was still anxious. They did not have to change 'buses, true. But brought up in the country herself, with occasional visits to London a matter of train and cab, she recalled her confusion over where to get off when she first came to live in town.

The 74 stopped. Three or four people stepped down, the conductor assisting an elderly woman who stood on the pavement struggling to open her black umbrella. Daisy suppressed an impulse to help, and addressed the conductor.

"I'm meeting two children, two nine-year-olds. A little girl with ginger pigtails—"

"Aunt Daisy!" Derek thundered down the winding stair. "Aunt Daisy, is it true a gentleman goes first down the steps?"

"Yes."

"I told you so!" Belinda scampered down behind him.

"And then he turns to help the lady down into the street," said Daisy.

"Oh!" Already on the pavement, her nephew swung round, grabbed Bel's hand, and tugged her off the platform.

Belinda landed safely, protesting, "Not like that, silly!"

"That's not quite it," Daisy agreed, laughing. "We'll practise later, but come along now. I've got an appointment with the Director of Geology. You had better both try to squeeze under my umbrella. Why on earth did you sit on top in this rain?"

"You can see better," Belinda pointed out, and Derek added, "It's more fun. Besides, it's not raining very hard and it's warm—after all, it's summer—and I'm not very wet, but I shall be if we all try to share the umbrella 'cause I'll get drips down my neck. You ladies can have it," he said grandly. "And I'll carry that for you, Aunt Daisy. What is it?"

"A tripod for the camera. Be careful, won't you? It's Lucy's."

The 'bus moved on down Fulham Road. The policeman on point duty held up the traffic with white gloves and whistle, and they crossed the street towards the Brompton Oratory. Belinda, the Londoner, pointed it out to the provincial Derek.

"It's a sort of church," she explained knowledgeably, "RC, I think. And that great big building next door is the Victoria and Albert Museum. We went there from school—not the church, the museum. Didn't you write about that one, too, Aunt Daisy?"

"That's right," Daisy assured her stepdaughter-to-be.

"I'm doing a series of articles on London museums for an American magazine."

As they walked down Cromwell Road past the smoke-begrimed Italianate church and neo-Renaissance museum, she listened to the children's chatter. Derek's stay with the Fletchers seemed to be going well, in spite of Belinda's grandmother's antipathy towards the boy's aunt.

Old Mrs. Fletcher, in agreement with Daisy's mother, the Dowager Lady Dalrymple, strongly disapproved of the daughter of a viscount marrying a middle-class Detective Chief Inspector. Daisy suspected that Alec had occasional qualms, fearing that she would regret stepping outside her own class.

She herself had no doubts whatsoever. She was a working woman. Her father dead in the flu pandemic—like Belinda's mother—and her brother killed in the trenches of Flanders, she had chosen not to sponge on the cousin who inherited the title and the Gloucestershire estate. As for living in the Dower House with her mother, nothing could persuade her. She and Lady Dalrymple had not seen eye to eye for years.

So the Honourable Daisy Dalrymple worked for her living, and this morning she had a business appointment.

"Come along, you two, don't dawdle."

They crossed Exhibition Road. Behind the railings rose the long façade and towers of the Natural History Museum. The soot-blackened building was liberally adorned with murky terra cotta in elaborate friezes and tracery around the windows, the world's flora and fauna petrified. Beastly gargoyles topped the downspouts, and statues of beasts posed between the windows of the top-most story.

Climbing the steps to the entrance, Belinda asked, "May we go and see the birds and butterflies, please, Aunt Daisy?"

"Butterflies!" Derek groaned. "We have plenty of birds and butterflies at home. Just like a girl! You'd be just like all the rest if your father wasn't a Scotland Yard 'tec. You said there's dinosaurs and whales here. Who wants to look at butterflies when there's dinosaurs and whales?"

"There's all sorts of horrid insects, too," Bel told him, "the kind boys like."

"You'll have plenty of time for all of them," Daisy promised. "You can go off without me, but stay together. Go to the butterflies first, and we'll meet in the Dinosaur Gallery at quarter to one. I'll treat you to lunch in the refreshment room."

"Gosh, honestly?" Belinda breathed, eyes shining. "Spiffing!"

Accustomed to restaurant meals when his parents visited his prep school, Derek was less impressed. "Good," he said with uncharacteristic brevity, taking off his damp cap and stuffing it into his pocket as they passed between bearded Darwin and bewhiskered Huxley, seated in marble majesty. "Bel, look, there's stone monkeys climbing up those pillars."

"They go all the way up and over the arch," said Belinda. "Come along, you can see from here."

"Oh yes!" Derek nearly fell over backwards craning his neck to look up at the vaulted roof, part glass, part flower-painted panels, seventy feet above. "Crikey, it's big!"

Like a cross between a cathedral and a mainline terminal, Daisy thought, but cleaner than the latter, at least. Inside, the ubiquitous terra cotta was the honey colour of Cotswold stone, patterned with a slate grey which matched the wrinkled skin of the huge African elephant looming in the centre of the hall.

Derek had to take an admiring turn around the elephant. Then the children went off to the west wing to hunt for birds and butterflies, while Daisy presented herself to the Keeper of Geology.

Dr. Smith Woodward's neat, pointed white beard and moustache were no match for Darwin's magnificent hirsuteness. A slight, elderly man, almost entirely bald, he looked up from a desk covered with papers to view Daisy with some perplexity through studious pince-nez. "Miss . . . ?"

"Dalrymple. Daisy Dalrymple. I'm a journalist."

"Ah yes." The paper he had been reading still in his left hand, he came around his desk to shake her hand. He walked with a limp, a relic—Daisy guessed—of one of his adventurous fossil-collecting expeditions.

Until she rang up to make an appointment, Daisy had assumed geology was all about "rocks and things," as she said to her house-mate, Lucy. At the Natural History Museum, the switchboard girl told her, rocks and things were the province of the Keeper of Mineralogy, and geology was all about fossils.

"I'm delighted to meet a young lady who is interested in palæontology." He spoke with a slight North Country accent. "I flatter myself I was instrumental in admitting ladies to the Geological Society. It was after all a lady, Mrs. Mantell, whose discovery of Iguanodon teeth led to one of the first important studies of dinosaurs, and Mary Anning found the first plesiosaur and ichthyosaur. What can I do for you?"

Daisy had already explored the museum and framed her article, aimed at American travellers visiting London who had an odd afternoon to fill in. Now all she wanted was to ask a few questions, and to request permission to take photographs of some of the more spectacular exhibits.

Dr. Smith Woodward, plainly enamoured of his subject, answered the questions with such a flood of information that Daisy was hard put to take it all down in her idiosyncratic version of Pitman's shorthand.

He was particularly impassioned over the skull of Pilt-down Man, *Eoanthropus dawsoni,* as he called it. Sure that Daisy must be eager to take a photograph, he took her to see it in the Fossil Mammal Gallery. Daisy did her best to produce murmurs of enthusiastic appreciation. To her the controversial relic was no more than a couple of scraps of brown-stained bone.

"I'll mention it, of course," she said doubtfully, "but I'm afraid a photograph wouldn't quite—"

"Mooning over your musty old bones as usual, eh, Woodward?" boomed an approaching figure, a tall, robust man who strode down the gallery as if he owned the place, scattering members of the public before him like autumn leaves in a brisk breeze.

Smith Woodward uttered a muted groan.

"You ought to let 'em crumble in peace," said the newcomer scornfully, eyeing Daisy with interest, "instead of fabricating imaginary creatures around 'em. Lot of balderdash, if you ask me."

"I didn't," pointed out the Keeper of Geology with slightly querulous dignity. As the man showed no sign of moving on, he continued resignedly, "Miss Dalrymple, allow me to introduce our Keeper of Mineralogy, Dr. Pettigrew. Miss Dalrymple is writing an article about the museum."

"She won't want to write about fusty old fossils, my dear chap. They're a waste of her time—and yours. Jewels are what the ladies are interested in. *They* know what's truly valuable. I'm off to see the Director now, Miss Dalrymple, but I shall be in my office upstairs in half an hour. Come and see me, and I'll show you precious stones worth a king's ransom."

"Thank you, this afternoon, if I may?" Daisy put business first, though she had taken an instant dislike to the boorish Keeper of Mineralogy. "I'm rather concentrating on fossils this morning. Actually, I find these old bones simply fascinating."

"Well, it's your funeral, dear lady." With a contemptuous laugh, Pettigrew took himself off.

Daisy and Mr. Smith Woodward exchanged a glance.

"Thank you," said the Keeper of Geology simply. "I fear Mr. Pettigrew has a greater respect for worldly values than for the value of pure knowledge." He sighed. "I expect the mammoths and the larger reptiles will be most suitable for your photography. Let us go and find the appropriate curators. Ah, there is Witt now."

Farther along the gallery, two men stood inside the rope barrier fencing off one of the mammoth skeletons. One was short and scrawny, his face fringed with a yellowish beard and whiskers, his tie askew. He was talking eagerly to his companion, with much gesticulation, and constantly pushing his horn-rimmed spectacles up on his nose.

The other, younger, taller, slim rather than skinny, and nattily dressed, appeared to listen with calm courtesy. However, as Daisy and Smith Woodward approached the pair, she thought she detected a trace of hidden amusement behind the gravity of his decidedly good-looking face.

"Ah, Witt, can you spare me a moment?" said Smith Woodward.

They both turned. "Certainly, sir," said the younger man politely, his voice pure public-school and Oxbridge. "Mr. ffinch-Brown is going to lend me several flints to make some experiments. Excuse me a moment, ffinch-Brown."

"Miss Dalrymple, this is Calvin Witt, our Curator of Fossil Mammals." Smith Woodward explained Daisy's project. "Her article is sure to bring us visitors from America, so I wish her to receive every facility. And when you have answered her questions, be so kind as to take her to see Mr. Steadman."

Witt bowed his dark, sleek head in acknowledgment. Dr. Smith Woodward departed, head bent to read the paper still in his hand, heedless of the people hastily stepping out of his way.

"He's going to have another accident," said Witt with exasperated affection. "Break the other arm or leg, likely as not."

"Is that why he limps?" Daisy asked, disillusioned.

"He walked into a display case. He wouldn't spare the time to go to the hospital, insisted on setting it himself."

"Good heavens!" Seeing the scowling ffinch-Brown

open his mouth, Daisy went on hastily, "I don't want to interrupt your discussion, Mr. Witt."

"We're quite finished, ma'am, aren't we, ffinch-Brown? I believe I understand perfectly what you wish me to undertake."

"You're sure? Good, good." The little man rubbed his hands together. "I'll be popping in quite often to see how you are getting on."

A shadow of irritation crossed Witt's face. "It may take some time to see results," he said.

"No reason why it should," ffinch-Brown objected, hands beginning to wave again. "After all, the hunters must have worked quite quickly."

Daisy foresaw a long wait for Witt's undivided attention, and besides, her curiosity was piqued. "Do tell me what experiments you are planning," she said.

"Allow me to introduce Mr. ffinch-Brown," said Witt resignedly, "from the British Museum, of which we are, of course, a mere branch. Mr. ffinch-Brown is an anthropologist. He means to investigate the marks made by the weapons of primitive hunters on the bones of slaughtered mammoths, by comparing them with marks made now on butcher's bones."

"Witt refuses to lend me any of his marked fossil bones." Not attempting to hide his disgruntlement, ffinch-Brown glowered, his whiskers bristling.

"My dear sir, as we have already agreed, fossils are a great deal rarer than flints, and fragile, to boot." He smiled at Daisy. "However, Miss Dalrymple cannot wish to hear our debate on the subject rehashed. I have promised to take the greatest care of your spearheads and knives."

"We ought to have some of those fossils in our Prehistoric room," the anthropologist said discontentedly, pushing his specs up again, "the ones marked by the tools of man. They are artifacts, not mere natural objects. As are the cut gems in the Mineral Gallery. It's disgraceful that that blackguard Pettigrew refuses to hand them over."

"A matter for your Director to take up with ours," Witt pointed out. "Now I hope you will excuse me, sir. I must not keep Miss Dalrymple waiting any longer. So you want to photograph the mammoths, ma'am?"

"And the giant armadillo, perhaps."

"Ah, the Glyptodon. Right-oh."

Witt summoned the commissionaire on duty in the Fossil Mammal Gallery. Sergeant Hamm's bottle-green uniformed chest boasted not only well-polished brass buttons but an impressive array of military medals. Despite lacking an arm, he helped Witt move aside the rope barrier around the mammoth skeleton, while Daisy unfolded the tripod.

She was trying to work out where best to set it up when Pettigrew reappeared.

"Witt!" he hallooed. "Come along, I've something to show you."

"I'm afraid I'm busy just now."

"Come along, come along, man," the Mineral Keeper repeated impatiently. "I found some flints in a cave in Cornwall, and I want your opinion on whether they have been worked or not. I know you're hand in glove with that little pipsqueak, ffinch-Brown."

"Mr. ffinch-Brown is the man you should consult."

"Bosh! He'll only try to take them away from me." Pettigrew seized Witt's arm and practically dragged him along.

Witt glanced back, his smooth façade ruffled by a grimace which combined anger, embarrassment, and an apology to Daisy. "Help Miss Dalrymple, Hamm, there's a good chap," he called as he was borne away by the irresistible avalanche.

"Whatsoever a man soweth, that shall he also reap," Sergeant Hamm muttered forebodingly.

"Mr. Pettigrew doesn't seem frightfully popular," Daisy observed.

"Huh!" snorted the commissionaire, waving away a couple of boys who were approaching the mammoth too closely. "The destruction that walketh at noonday, that's 'im. I could tell you some stories, miss, as 'd curl—Don't touch, if you please, madam! Big but fragile, them bones. . . . As I was saying, miss, Ol' Stony, he's a roaring lion seeking whom he may devour, like it says in the Scriptures. Made Sergeant Underwood cry, 'im as was third up the ridge at Vimy."

"Good heavens!" Daisy inserted a plate in Lucy's camera, wondering whether she need mess about with a magnesium powder flash or if the grey light coming through the window was sufficient.

"Underwood was on duty in the Mineral Gallery, see, and 'e didn't ∍p to it quick enough for Ol' Stony's liking. Well, stands to reason, 'e's a bit slow, only got one leg, though 'e does 'is job right enough. Same as what I do and I'd like anyone to say the cont'ry," said the sergeant belligerently.

"I'm sure you do."

"But Ol' Stony, out of his mouth went a sharp two-edged sword, which is to say, 'e told Underwood 'e was bloody useless—pardon the language, miss—and only 'ired for charity's sake."

"How beastly," Daisy sympathized, peering through the viewfinder. "I think that's all right. What happened?"

"Oh, Mr. Wright, as is Superintendent of House Staff, his anger was kindled, like it says in the Good Book. 'E stationed Underwood in Fossil Plants, Corals, and Sponges, where it's nice and quiet, and sent Pavett up instead." Hamm grinned. "Young Pavett were a gunner. Deaf as a post, 'e is, or near as makes no odds. Been no trouble up there since."

Laughing, Daisy asked, "Hasn't Dr. Pettigrew complained?"

"'Asn't 'e just! But 'e might as well be a voice crying in the wilderness for all the good it does 'im. Sir Sidney 'Armer, that's our Director, 'e says non scientific staff is Mr. Wright's business and 'e's got better things to do with 'is time than sorting out Dr. Pettigrew's petty problems."

The flow of gossip continued, interrupted by occasional admonitions to members of the public who tried to take advantage of the absence of the rope barrier. Going about her photography, moving on to a lifelike, life-size model of a shaggy mastodon, Daisy listened with half an ear. It sounded as if the Keeper of Minerals had managed to alienate half the museum staff, including his own assistants.

Daisy had not realized the museum had so many scientific staff working behind the scenes. If she had, she would have supposed scientists were too engrossed in their work to squabble like ordinary mortals. On the contrary, it seemed they simply added personal spats to professional disagreements and jealousies. Even if she discounted half of what Sergeant Hamm relayed to her with such relish, scientists were human after all!

The commissionaire accompanied her to the pavilion at the end of the gallery, where the Glyptodon awaited her. The twelve-foot, armoured creature with the medieval morningstar tip to its tail would make a spiffing illustration to her article. She was setting up the camera when Witt returned, looking harassed.

"Look here," he said, "I'm most frightfully sorry, Miss Dalrymple, but Pettigrew's thrown me right out. There's some work I simply must get done before lunchtime."

"That's all right," said Daisy. "Sergeant Hamm has taken very good care of me, and I'm nearly finished here. Just a couple of quick questions . . . "

"Perhaps you'd allow me to take you to lunch, and we could talk at leisure?"

"Thanks, but I've brought two children with me." The way his face fell made her want to laugh. She asked her questions and thanked him, and he went off, promising to tell Mr. Steadman she would like to see him.

As Daisy folded up the tripod after finishing the Glyptodon's portrait, a plump man scurried up to her. He wore a long, dusty, white lab coat with frayed cuffs. His greying fair hair curled wildly above a round, pink face adorned with straggling eyebrows and an incongruous hooked nose.

"Miss Dalrymple?" he asked, speaking very rapidly. "Allow me to introduce myself. I am Mummery, Septimus Mummery, Curator of Fossil Reptiles. I want to make quite sure you understand that the Archaeopteryx skeleton really belongs among the reptiles, with the pterodactyls. Witt is utterly unreasonable about it, simply refuses to give it up. I hope any reference to it in your article will point out the misplacement."

"I'll remember," Daisy promised cryptically, as she mentally deleted from her article a passing mention of the early bird. Wondering whether Archaeopteryx in its day had breakfasted on worms—she had rather ignored the fossil invertebrates—she went on, "I was just going to the reptile gallery. Will you tell me a bit about the pterodactyls and those sea monsters?"

"Leviathan that crooked serpent, and the dragon that is in the sea," muttered Sergeant Hamm.

"Superstition!" Mummery's wild eyebrows quivered in annoyance. "Ichthyosaurs and plesiosaurs. Fascinating creatures. I shall be more than happy to assist you, Miss Dalrymple. Allow me," he added, taking the tripod and camera from her.

He walked as fast as he talked. Daisy trotted at his side through the passage to the fossil reptiles.

Their gallery was half the width of the mammals'. On the left-hand wall hung slabs of stone, each with the skeleton of a prehistoric monster half-embedded. Poor, pathetic things! Mummery started to expound, in detail, upon the painstaking process of extracting a fragile fossil from the matrix where it was found. Daisy began by taking notes, but he went too fast and used too many technical words. Her attention wandered.

The opposite wall was pierced at regular intervals by the rounded arches typical of the museum, narrow alternating

with wide. The first was Special Palæontological Collections. Next came the wide entrance to Fossil Plants,
Corals, and Sponges—that was where the one-legged Underwood had ended up, wasn't it? Some of the plants were
quite pretty, Daisy recalled, but not interesting enough for
her article. The third arch had a closed door with a sign,
GEOLOGICAL LIBRARY.

Between the arches stood mounted skeletons, impressive in their way but less spectacular than dinosaurs. She
hoped Mr. Mummery would not expect her to photograph
them. Regretting having encouraged him, she drifted along
after him from display to display.

Another arch divided the long reptile gallery in half. Beyond it were the entrances to the invertebrates and to
cephalopods—*What* were cephalopods?—and then the dinosaurs Daisy was aiming at. As if on guard outside the
last, a squat, massive monster some ten feet long lurked on
splayed legs. Though armoured with bony back-plates and
armed with spikes on its blunt, heavy head, it made Daisy
think of a giant bulldog.

Mummery noticed the direction of her glance. "Ah, you
are admiring the Pareiasaurus," he exclaimed, moving towards it. "From South Africa, and one of the finest things
in my collection."

"A fearsome beast," said Daisy.

"No, no, not at all, a peaceful herbivore." He leaned
across the rope barrier and fondly patted his pet's hefty
haunch, then gestured along its length. "All this is defensive, purely defensive. A splendid chap, isn't he? A
complete skeleton, too. Not a single one of those bones is
plaster of Paris."

A tall, lanky man emerging from the Dinosaur Gallery
gave Mummery a sour look, but turned to Daisy.

"Miss Dalrymple? Witt tells me you want to take some
photographs? I'm Steadman, the dinosaur curator."

"Oh yes, thank you. Dr. Smith Woodward said I may photograph the dinosaurs, and I have some questions for you."

"Dinosaurs are just another branch of Reptilia," grumbled Mummery.

"*Just* another branch," Steadman protested. "You might as well agree with Pettigrew that fossils are 'just another branch' of Mineralogy."

"Not likely! Why, the rotter thinks they're utterly worthless."

"Unless they have usefully metamorphosed into coal or petroleum," said Steadman dryly. "This is your equipment, is it, Miss Dalrymple?"

Mummery meekly handed over the tripod and camera, his claim to the dinosaurs dissipated in shared dislike of Pettigrew. He glanced wistfully from the camera to his pet Pareiasaurus. "If I can be of any further assistance, Miss Dalrymple," he sighed, "you will find me in the work room behind the Geological Library. Or if I'm not there, one of my assistants will find me."

Daisy thanked him, somewhat absently. Libraries and work rooms—she pondered the possibility of expanding on the travel article to describe the scientific work of the museum for the interested layman. One of the weightier magazines might buy it.

Avoiding over-technical information would be easy. All she had to do was leave out anything she didn't understand. The girls' boarding school she had attended had been absolutely free of any masculine taint of science. The school motto should have been *Ignorance Is Bliss,* but a minimal grounding in the basics might at least have let Daisy understand what Pettigrew, Mummery, and Steadman were arguing about.

Three

Mr. Steadman ushered Daisy into the Dinosaur Gallery. Over half its length was taken up by the Diplodocus, eighty-five feet from nose to the whiplash tip of its tail, thirteen feet high, with its tiny head perched at the end of a long, slender neck.

"I'd like to take the Diplodocus," Daisy said, "but it's so huge I don't think I could do it justice. Besides, it's American, isn't it?"

"The Iguanodon is home grown," said Steadman with a smile, smoothing back his thinning hair. "Do you want to try that? It's smaller, of course, but still quite dramatic."

About to agree, Daisy heard the gallery's commissionaire say sharply, "No running, *if* you please!" She looked round to see Derek and Belinda approaching at a sort of compromise between a run and a walk.

Derek skidded to a halt, eyes only for the Diplodocus. "Crikey!" he said, scanning it from end to end. "Crikey! Is it real?"

"Course it is, isn't it, Aunt Daisy?" Belinda said scornfully. "Everything here is real."

"You'd better ask Mr. Steadman here," Daisy advised. "He's the museum's dinosaur man. My nephew, Derek, Mr. Steadman, and . . ." She could hardly introduce Bel to the curator as her future stepdaughter, particularly as he was now looking rather disgruntled. She shouldn't have troubled him with the children. "And Belinda," she finished.

"Please, sir, is it *real?*"

"In a sense, it's real, Master Derek. Miss Belinda is correct in that we don't have imaginary animals in the museum. Creatures like this did exist millions of years ago. But I'm afraid this particular skeleton is a model made from casts of the real bones."

"Oh," said Derek, disappointed. Steadman grimaced. Daisy gathered his disgruntlement was with the plaster model, not the children. "Oh well," said Derek, "it's still spiffing, isn't it, Bel? You can see what it was like, even if it's not quite real."

"You mustn't mind," Bel said kindly to Steadman. "Did you lose the bones?"

"No, no! The Diplodocus was found in America, and the Americans sent casts to various museums all over the world. Shall I tell you a secret?"

"Yes," breathed Derek. "Please!"

"Promise not to tell?" They both nodded, wide-eyed. Stooping to their height, Steadman whispered, "They used the wrong feet by mistake. The front feet of this model are really the back feet of a Camarasaurus!"

"Really and truly?"

"Really and truly."

Derek dragged Belinda off to study the erroneous feet. Daisy and Steadman went over to the Iguanodon, a heavily built beast about twenty-five feet long. It stood more upright than the Diplodocus, perhaps twelve or fourteen feet tall, its forelimbs more like arms than legs, with huge claws on the thumbs. It would be a bit easier to fit into the viewfinder, Daisy agreed.

While she prepared to take the photograph, she asked several questions about the creature, and then said, "Wasn't the Iguanodon the one Dr. Smith Woodward said was discovered by a woman?"

"That's right. At least, Mrs. Mantell found the teeth."

"And there was someone else—Ann something?"

"Mary Anning, a highly talented fossil hunter of the last century. I believe she unearthed the first complete ichthyosaur and plesiosaur both. Mummery could tell you more about that."

Bother, thought Daisy. The female aspect sounded like a good idea to widen the appeal of her article, but it would mean applying to Mummery, whom she didn't much care for.

"Are many dinosaurs found in England?"

"A few. The best hunting-grounds are elsewhere, however, chiefly Africa and the American West." He glanced discontentedly around his collection. "The American museums and universities bag all the best."

"Even the African ones?"

"They have the money to send out their own expeditions, as well as to buy the best from independent finders. Our trustees have been debating setting up an expedition since 1918. Smith Woodward is pushing for it, but five years and still no decision! The poor old fellow will die of old age before it happens. But I don't want to bore you. Is there anything else I can tell you?"

"What else would you suggest I photograph?"

"Megalosaurus," he said promptly. "It's English, and actually the first dinosaur genus ever named or described in detail, just a century ago. We haven't a complete skeleton, but a photograph of its head showing the dentition would be worthwhile, I believe."

Dentition—dentist—teeth, Daisy worked out. Latin was another subject the girls at her school had not been subjected to, but French *dent,* a tooth, helped.

Derek had already found the Megalosaurus skull and was gazing with bloodthirsty awe at its vicious, carnivorous grin. Steadman explained to him the functions of the various types of teeth in far more gruesome detail than Daisy considered necessary. Belinda had already gone off in disgust to look at some innocuous fossil fish on the other side of the gallery.

Apparently the description of a dinosaur meal, even as it destroyed Daisy's usually hearty appetite, had aroused

Derek's. Having politely thanked Mr. Steadman, he reminded her that they were to have lunch in the refreshment room.

After lunch, the children decided to go with Daisy to the Mineralogy Gallery. From the cafeteria on the first floor, a glassed-in room with a view to the Central Hall on one side and the North Hall on the other, they walked past the giraffes and okapis.

Derek had recently seen live giraffes at the zoo, near Belinda's home in St. John's Wood. He was more interested in hanging over the arched and pillared balustrade to see the people walking below.

"Come along," said Daisy crossly, grabbing the back of his jacket, her temper ruffled by the prospect of her interview with the unpleasant Pettigrew. "What am I to say to your mother if you fall and break all your bones to bits?"

"There's lots of people here," Derek pointed out, "who spend all their time sticking bones back together."

"Not always right," Belinda reminded him. "S'pose they stuck dinosaur feet on you?"

This struck both of them as the height of wit. Guffawing, Derek started to walk as he imagined a dinosaur might. Daisy shushed them and thrust them still giggling into the Mineralogy Gallery, while she went on to Pettigrew's office.

Over his door, the architect's whim had placed a terra cotta medallion of a strutting buck. Its combative stance reminded Daisy all too clearly of the Keeper.

However, Dr. Pettigrew greeted her courteously and answered her questions painstakingly, if with a heavy patience which suggested ill-disguised scorn for her ignorance. She finished by asking about the rock samples strewn on the work-bench under one window.

"Just some bits and pieces I picked up in Cornwall, on

my summer holiday. Nothing of great value," he added, but he rose from his desk chair and went over to the table.

"Isn't that gold?" Daisy enquired, following, as a yellow gleam caught her eye.

"No, I'm afraid not. There is a little gold in Cornwall, but that's just iron pyrites. Often known as fool's gold."

Daisy laughed. "I see why. And the others? What are those green crystals?"

"Polished up nicely, hasn't it? That's torbernite, a phosphate of copper and uranium. These blue crystals are azurite, a copper ore. Both copper and uranium are mined in Cornwall. It's an area rich in useful minerals, zinc, lead, arsenic, wolfram, and tin, of course, which the Phoenicians came to trade for. This is its ore, cassiterite. Then there are the building stones, granite, sandstone, and slate; and mica; and the pigments ochre and umber. Useful stuff," he repeated insistently, "not like those ancient, crumbling bones downstairs which absorb so much money and effort."

Fearing a tirade, Daisy hastily finished scribbling shorthand hieroglyphics and said, "I'd better be getting along. I left two children in the gallery. Thank you for all your help."

"Children? Maybe they would like a piece of pyrites each. Here—no, I'll come along."

They found Belinda and Derek entranced by the display of opals. Pettigrew actually unlocked the case and allowed each of them to hold one of the iridescent stones while he lectured them on the subject. Though he was rather condescending, it was kind of him, Daisy thought. She decided Ol' Stony was not so stony-hearted as he was painted, in spite of his rudeness to Smith Woodward—unless the story of his brutality to the one-legged commissionaire was true.

She looked around. Between the rectangular pillars embossed, oddly enough, with sea creatures, she caught glimpses of a commissionaire's uniform. The youngish man patrolling the aisles appeared to have a full complement of limbs. Of course, she couldn't tell whether he was deaf, and even if he was, it would not prove Sergeant Hamm's tale.

Pettigrew locked away the opals and gave the children the two small chunks of fool's gold. He was starting to explain them, when the sound of the commissionaire's footsteps nearby made him look round.

He frowned irritably. Then he looked beyond the approaching commissionaire and broke into a furious scowl. Abruptly deserting Daisy and the children, he stormed off towards a figure bending over one of the cases.

"There's that damn fellow again. Hi, you!" he shouted. "What have you come back for?"

All over the gallery heads turned—except the undoubtedly deaf commissionaire's. The object of Pettigrew's ire straightened and swung round. Daisy saw that he was a slim young man, whose longish fair hair, parted in the middle and carefully slicked down on top, matched a sweeping cavalry moustache.

The most notable aspect of his appearance, however, was his dress. His uniform would not have disgraced a foreign grandee in a Gilbert and Sullivan production, the Duke of Plaza-Toro, perhaps, or Prince Hilarion. The pale blue tunic with crimson facings was lavishly frogged and laced with gold, and bore the ribbons, stars, and sunbursts of at least a dozen orders. A crimson sash topped cream breeches, which descended into knee-boots with gold tassels.

The plumed helmet and ceremonial sword required by such a costume were absent. Daisy wondered whether he had left them in the cloakroom or had balked at wearing them in public.

On the other hand, he could hardly appear in public with a bowler, a soft felt, a topper, or a cloth cap to crown that get-up!

"What's that uniform, Aunt Daisy?" asked Derek, who had a vast collection of lead soldiers at home.

Daisy's confession of ignorance was drowned.

"I told you there's nothing doing!" Pettigrew's angry voice rang from end to end of the eighty-yard-long gallery.

The stranger's was not as loud but reached Daisy and the children. *"Dieser Rubin*—dis ruby—belong mine family," he said in a determined tone, his solid, obstinate jaw jutting.

"Oh, a foreigner," said Derek dismissively.

"Used to belong, *used* to belong," corrected Pettigrew. "It's mine now—the museum's."

"I ask for it to return."

"You haven't a hope in hell!"

"I ask de king, mine cousin."

"Your sixteenth cousin fifteen times removed," Pettigrew snorted. "In any case, the old queen gave it to the British Museum. You're out of luck. Get out of my gallery."

"Here is public place, *nicht wahr?*" the young man demanded sullenly. "I may at mine ruby look."

The Keeper glared but gave in. "I've got my eye on you," he threatened, then retreated to bellow at the commissionaire to keep an eye on the interloper. There, too, he was defeated. Daisy saw him writing down instructions.

"May we go and look at his ruby?" Belinda asked. "It must be extra special."

Half the people in the gallery had the same notion, but she and Derek got there first. The gaudy stranger looked somewhat disconcerted when they bobbed up on either side of him.

Daisy apologized. "We could not help overhearing," she said, enunciating clearly in deference to his foreignness. Close to, he seemed very young, not much more than twenty, she guessed. He had a long nose, and brown eyes set a trifle too close together, spoiling an otherwise handsome face. "The children are eager to see your . . . the ruby."

He pointed dramatically. "Dere it is, de largest here and de last hope of mine contry."

Between the children's heads as they pressed forward, Daisy glimpsed several rubies of varying sizes and shades of red.

"It's not as big as the opals," said Belinda, disappointed, "and not as pretty either."

"Your country?" Daisy enquired quickly.

"Excuse, please!" Recollecting his manners, the young man took a pace backwards, clicked his heels, and bowed. With a glance around at the people with pricked ears politely but unconvincingly studying the contents of nearby cases, he lowered his voice. "I am Rudolf Maximilian, Grand Duke of Transcarpathia, at your service, *gnädige Frau.*"

"Fräulein," Daisy corrected, that being about the only word of German she knew. It was not at all proper to introduce herself to a strange gentleman met in a public place—her mother would have fainted at the thought—but Daisy was now dying of curiosity. In order to hold her own with a Grand Duke, she used the courtesy title she usually omitted. His stiff expression relaxed a little as she said, "I am the Honourable Daisy Dalrymple. How do you do? I'm afraid I'm not very sure where Transcarpathia is."

"Mine contry is between Moldavia and Transylvania and Bukovina," he informed her, leaving her little the wiser. "Now is mine contry not existing. De Russians have take it. Instead of Grand Duke is Red Commissar. Mine family is exile, penniless, and mine pee-ople suffer under de Russian boot. Wizzout dis ruby can I for them nodink."

The splendid uniform was threadbare, Daisy noticed, the cuffs frayed, the gold braid unravelling. Given his youth, either the Grand Duke Rudolf possessed no other clothes, or he had inherited the outfit from his father.

"How exactly does the ruby come to be in the Natural History Museum?" she asked.

"Mine *Grossvater* has de ruby to Qveen Victoria presented. You understand, in dose days vas de family rich. Dey visit to England and make gift to cousin of magnificent precious gem. But now ve have need, cousin vould give back, *nicht wahr?*"

Daisy rather doubted that most cousins would be so generous. The museum's trustees were even less likely to oblige. However, she said soothingly, "I am sure King George will sympathize and do what he can for you."

With a despairing gesture towards Pettigrew's back as the Keeper stalked out of the gallery, the Grand Duke groaned, *"Dieser viehische, schreiende Kerl* vill everysink spoil."

"Please, sir, what's . . . what you just said?" Derek queried. He and Belinda had long since stopped admiring the ruby—which, however large and precious, just sat there—in favour of listening to Rudolf Maximilian's story.

"And what will you do if you get it back?" asked Belinda.

To fend off a translation, which she suspected was better not delved into, Daisy seconded Bel's question. "Yes, what would you do?"

"I use to raise an army of loyalists, naturally. Mit mine pee-ople behind me, ve zrow out de Red Army and make peaceful again."

Though not much of a newspaper reader, Daisy knew the Red Army had proved virtually impossible to throw out once having steamrollered in. The Transcarpathian loyalists were more likely to be slaughtered wholesale than to succeed. That an entire army of loyalists could be raised on the proceeds of even the most valuable jewel was another dubious proposition. Transcarpathia must be somewhere in eastern Europe. The common people of that part of the world were Slav peasants little better than serfs, with no reason to feel loyalty towards their German-speaking rulers. Unless the Grand Dukes' reign had been singularly benevolent, Rudolf Maximilian was probably headed for bitter disappointment even if he recovered the ruby.

Which was unlikely—but disillusioning the ardent young man was none of Daisy's business, and she still had business to be done.

"Enough chatter, children," she said. "Come along, time is passing and I want to take a photograph of the Melbourne meteorite with you two on each side to show how enormous it is. I wish you the best of luck, sir."

Instead of shaking the hand she held out to him, Grand Duke Rudolf bowed over it, heels clicking, and raised it to his lips. "I sank for your much sympazy, *gnädiges Fräulein*," he said. "You lift to me de courage. I fight on!"

Bel and Derek were much more excited by the Grand Duke's story than by the three-and-a-half-ton meteorite. They wove a wonderful tale about a wicked sorcerer called the Red Commissar and a magic ruby with the power to raise an army overnight. Pettigrew's place in the narrative was a source of much argument. Derek had him as an ogre who had stolen the jewel, while Belinda insisted he was not an ogre, because he had been nice to them, letting them hold the opals and giving them fool's gold.

"Not real gold," Derek pointed out. "It'll prob'ly turn into dead leaves overnight. I bet he's in league with the Red Commissar, and he's just trying to buy us off."

They were still elaborating their make-believe when Daisy put them onto a bus back to St. John's Wood— inside. Though the rain had stopped, the skies had darkened ominously. As she walked home through South Kensington and Chelsea, the photographic equipment and her notebook seemed to grow heavier and heavier. It wasn't far to Mulberry Place, but she had been tramping around the museum for hours. Hard floors and city pavements were much more tiring than fields and woods.

When she reached the "bijou residence" she shared with Lucy Fotheringay, she went straight through the house and down to Lucy's mews studio. Lucy, tall, dark, smart, and fashionably flat fore and aft, was just seeing a client out of the alley door. Turning, she asked, "How did it go, darling?"

"Not too bad," said Daisy, plopping down on the nearest chair, "except for my poor feet. The children were good and everyone was frightfully helpful."

"I mean the photos," Lucy said impatiently.

"I can't tell, darling, till you develop them for me. Be an angel and do them right away."

"Tomorrow," Lucy promised. "Binkie's taking me to see *The Prisoner of Zenda* tonight."

Daisy burst into gales of laughter. "I've just met him!" she gasped.

"Who? Ramon Novarro? Where? Not at your stuffy old museum!"

"Not Ramon, a Ruritanian prince." She told Lucy about the Grand Duke Rudolf Maximilian.

"Darling, how too, too romantic!" Lucy, who prided herself on her hard-headed practicality, was at heart far more of a sentimentalist than Daisy, as witness her choice of films. Her amber eyes glowed. "And how sad. Is he good-looking?"

"Not as handsome as Ramon Novarro, and much too young for you, darling. A good five years younger than us, at a guess."

"And no money," said Lucy mournfully.

"Even less than Binkie, I should think, and no job."

"Darling, grand dukes simply don't take *jobs,* like mere mortals. Especially reigning grand dukes."

"He hasn't got anything to reign over," Daisy pointed out. Lucy sighed.

As good as her word, she developed the plates next morning. They were all absolutely hopeless.

"Never mind, darling," she consoled Daisy. "I'm going down to Haverhill this weekend for Grandfather's birthday—can't miss it, it's his eightieth, the old sweetie—but next week I'll go to the museum with you and get some good shots."

* * *

While Lucy was toasting the start of the Earl of Haverhill's ninth decade, Daisy joined the Fletchers for Sunday dinner, her nephew having by then gone home to Kent. Mrs. Fletcher actually unbent enough to commend Derek as a nice-mannered child.

"Spoilt, though," she added hastily, as if horrified to find herself praising anything associated with Daisy, "but what can you expect, his father being a lord."

Daisy, Alec, and Belinda escaped for the afternoon by taking Bel's new puppy, Nana, for a walk on Primrose Hill.

During Lucy's absence, Daisy also typed up her notes and started to get her article into its final shape. The quantity of excess information reminded her of her idea for a more scientific article. She popped into the nearest W. H. Smith's and found several suitable magazines, surreptitiously scribbling down their addresses and editors' names without buying anything but the *Daily Chronicle*. Letters of enquiry went out by the second post on Monday.

Soon after Daisy's article and Lucy's splendid photographs set sail across the Atlantic, two magazines replied, expressing their total lack of interest. A third wanted the complete text before deciding, and a fourth requested resubmission at a later date, as the next fifteen issues were already filled. Slightly disappointed, Daisy went off to Shropshire to do the research for the next article in her series on minor stately homes for *Town & Country*.

Much as she might wish to, she could hardly visit that part of the world without staying a night or two with her mother, at the Fairacres Dower House. She found the Dowager Lady Dalrymple as disapproving as ever of Alec's middle-class background and distasteful profession, yet making plans for an elaborate—and expensive—wedding in St. George's, Hanover Square.

"Who is to pay for this, Mother?" Daisy asked, exasperated.

"I dare say your cousin Edgar can be brought to understand his obligation, since he so cruelly exiled us from hearth and home."

"Mother, you know Edgar had no choice but to succeed to the title," Daisy could not help saying for the thousandth time, "and he offered us a home."

"As though I should accept that man's charity! A schoolmaster, so underbred, and the way Geraldine puts on airs is quite shocking." Lady Dalrymple counterattacked: "When are you and Mr. Fletcher going to set the date? I disapprove of long engagements, and the church must be booked months in advance."

Daisy at once started to think about registry offices. She also wondered, rather dolefully, whether Alec could get a guaranteed leave of absence from the Metropolitan Police to be married, or if a sudden complex case might tear him from the altar—or the registry office equivalent. Frightful thought!

Her mother always had a depressing effect on her spirits but she revived as soon as she left Fairacres. Her recovery was completed when she reached Mulberry Place. On the table in the tiny hall, an extravagantly vast bouquet of chrysanthemums awaited her, and Alec's card with a note saying simply, "Missing you."

Beside the vase was a heap of letters, accumulated during her absence. Daisy flipped through them, recognizing the handwriting of her sister, two friends, a cousin. Then a business-size, typewritten envelope. Another rejection, no doubt.

But it wasn't. *Dilettanti* magazine wanted her article, as long as she could let them have it by the end of September. If so, would she please telephone as soon as possible to confirm.

"Lucy?" she called up the stairs. No response.

Only three weeks! Still, it was not like starting from scratch. She already had a good start on the research, and she had made the acquaintance of all the people she would need to interview. Reaching for the telephone she and Lucy had had installed just a month ago, Daisy confirmed.

She was dying to share the news with someone who would appreciate it, but she always tried to avoid phoning Alec at the Yard, and he was often out of his office anyway. Mrs. Potter, the charwoman who "did" for Daisy and Lucy and took a deep, admiring interest in their work, had already gone home. Daisy rang through to Lucy on the studio extension, but there was no answer.

Three weeks—she had better get cracking. She telephoned the Natural History Museum and made appointments to see the Keepers of Zoology and Botany in the morning.

That done, she dropped her hat on the table, her coat on the chair, and leaving luggage strewn about the hall, hurried to the tiny back parlour which was her study. She already had a rough draft of the stately home article, typed on the portable machine on semi-permanent loan from her *Town & Country* editor (How her mother had moaned at the evidence of her daughter's occupation!). It wouldn't take long to finish it up on the massive, ancient Underwood typewriter which sat incongruously on the elegant Regency writing table from Fairacres.

The Underwood saw a great deal of her that week. Each day she returned from the museum with reams of notes and typed long into the evening. The museum's business was far more complicated than she had realized.

In the private offices, studies, and work rooms where she was now introduced, the preparation of specimens for display was a minor aspect of the work in progress. From all over the world, unknown plants and creatures were sent to be classified. Daisy had never previously heard of Linnaeus, but she was soon as familiar with his system as with the map of the London underground. The museum staff produced not only minute descriptions but painstaking drawings and even paintings of each specimen.

That was in the Zoology and Botany departments,

where specimens normally arrived with all their parts intact. In the Geology Department, imagination played a greater part. As Mummery had explained to her, few fossils were found complete; the missing bits had to be guessed at. At least, it looked like guesswork to Daisy, though Mummery insisted it was educated deduction.

His position was undermined by the iconoclastic Ruddlestone, Curator of Fossil Invertebrates, a jolly North-countryman who rivalled Alec's sergeant, Tom Tring, in size and baldness.

"Guesswork is more like it, though we have advanced a bit since Waterhouse Hawkins," Ruddlestone admitted to Daisy.

"Waterhouse Hawkins?"

"He built life-size concrete dinosaurs for the Crystal Palace exhibition of 1851, all as bulky and firmly four-footed as elephants or hippos. Believe it or not, he gave a dinner party inside one half-completed model. Then there were the Americans, Cope and Marsh: bitter enemies, brilliant in many ways, but Cope stuck the skull of an Elasmosaurus on the end of its tail! Marsh never let him forget it." Ruddlestone roared with laughter.

"Mr. Steadman told me his Diplodocus has the wrong feet."

"Poor Steadman, it rankles badly that his prize exhibit is made of plaster of Paris. A load of real bones the Americans sent over during the War was sunk by a German submarine. A great loss, whatever that ass Pettigrew said." The curator was no longer amused.

"What did he say?" Daisy asked, though she had a good idea.

"That the loss of mere fossils was trivial. In his view, a cargo of munitions would have been a great loss. But munitions can be replaced and fossils cannot! I'm afraid affairs like the controversy over Dr. Smith Woodward's Piltdown skull play into the hands of ignoramuses like Pettigrew." Ruddlestone cheered up. "But it illustrates what I was telling you: They can't all be right, so someone's 'educated deductions' have to have gone far astray!"

Later that afternoon, shortly before the museum closed, Daisy asked Smith Woodward about the Piltdown Man controversy.

He took her to see it again, but this time he contemplated it in silence for a minute, before sighing, "It really is very troublesome. Fossil fish are really my field, you know. I believe I may say I am accounted something of an authority on fossil fish. Do let me show you my Arthrodire."

He had been so kind that Daisy let him off the hook. She could always ask someone else about Piltdown. He limped at her side across the gallery, and they entered the hall leading to the fossil reptiles, with the dinosaur gallery beyond, wherein the fishes occupied their modest place.

Somewhere in front of them a voice rose in triumph and contempt, the words indistinguishable. The bellow that followed held a note of surprised agony, like that of a wounded bull. Then came a tremendous crash.

With a gasp, Smith Woodward stopped, rooted to the ground. Daisy ran through the arch ahead.

Sprawled on his back, immobile amidst a litter of smashed Pareiasaurus bones, lay Pettigrew. Across Ol' Stony's white shirtfront and pale grey waistcoat seeped a crimson stain.

Four

"Help!" squawked Daisy. She did not want to go near that bloody body, but unlikely as it seemed from this distance, Pettigrew might still be alive. Someone must check his pulse.

Someone must also go for the police, though surely it could not be murder, not in a museum of all places! The Keeper of Geology must have had some sort of fit, fallen against the Pareiasaurus, and been stabbed by a shard of bone.

Through the chest, when he was lying on his back?

"What was that?" A plump, grey-haired woman appeared under the arch to the dinosaurs. "Good gracious! Stay there, children, don't come any further." She spread her arms in a barricade, behind which bobbed five youthful, inquisitive faces.

"What's happened, Granny?"

"Never you mind, Arthur Stubbs. Take the others to look at the dinosaurs, do." She moved a few steps towards Daisy and asked in a lowered voice, "Is he dead?"

"I think so. I don't know. I haven't . . ."

"You leave it to me, dear. I used to be a nurse. If there's a pulse, I'll find it." Bustling forward, she stooped to clear the bone fragments from a patch of floor and knelt at Pettigrew's side.

"Don't touch anything you don't absolutely have to," Daisy warned.

"What . . . what . . ." came a weak voice from behind her.

"Dr. Smith Woodward, will you please go and tell the police there has been a . . . an accident?"

"Police? Surely a doctor . . ."

"Too late for that. He's gone," pronounced the grey-haired woman. She looked down with grim compassion at the crimson bloom on Pettigrew's chest. "And the young lady's right, it looks like it could be a police matter."

"Police, yes, at once." Smith Woodward fled.

"Give us a hand up, dear. I must get back to the grand-kiddies, though what I'm to tell them I'm sure I don't know. What is the world coming to?"

"You won't leave, will you? I mean, the police . . ."

"There's no way out I know save through here, and I'm not about to let the children see this." She started back to the dinosaur gallery. A boy of twelve or thirteen was peering round the corner. "Shoo, shoo! Back you go this instant. You'll be all right, dear, will you?" she asked, turning her head.

"Y-yes," Daisy said doubtfully.

As long as she didn't actually look at the dead Keeper of Mineralogy, she wasn't going to faint, or be sick, or anything like that. She had to stay on the spot, though, until the police came, to stop anyone touching what might turn out to be clues.

Was it really murder? Alec would be furious that she had "fallen over" another body, got herself mixed up in another case—as if she wanted to, or could help it. It was awful of her to be worrying about that when poor Pettigrew lay dead. He had been helpful to her and pleasant to Derek and Belinda, whatever his faults. All the same, how was she going to explain to Alec that once again someone she knew had been killed practically in her presence?

Perhaps she could keep it from him. Perhaps the museum police would sort it out quickly and not need to call in Scotland Yard. Where were they?

Daisy glanced at her wristwatch, a recent present from Alec. She was startled to see how few minutes ago she had

decided there was time enough before the museum closed
to ask Smith Woodward about the Piltdown fuss. It felt like
an age since he had scurried off. Maybe he was having
trouble persuading the police of the need for speed.

"Hoy!" The dinosaur commissionaire lumbered out of
his gallery. "What the bloody—'scuse me, miss—flippin'
blankety blank's going on here?"

"Dr. Pettigrew's dead," Daisy said tersely.

"That's what the lady said, miss. Blimey, will you look
at what Ol' Stony's done to that pariosaurus! Mr. Mummery's going to have forty fits."

"Never mind about the blasted Pareiasaurus! Dr. Pettigrew's been killed."

"Who by?" asked the commissionaire.

"I don't know. And goodness knows where he's got to
by now. Are there any other ways out besides through the
mammal gallery?"

"Two lots o' private stairs to the basement, miss, and
one lot going up. Reckon they oughta be watched?" Looking around, he demanded, "Where's Harry? Gawd, you
don't think he done it? Nah, not Harry!"

"This gallery's commissionaire?"

"That's him when he's at home." Skirting the corpse and
the scattered bones by a respectful margin, he stuck his
head into the invertebrate gallery and yelled, "Hoy, Bert!
C'mere, and get a move on!" He moved on to stand under
the arch between the two halves of the reptile gallery and
roared in parade-ground tones, "Harry!"

Receiving no apparent response, the commissionaire
hurried back between Daisy and the remains, saying, "Tell
you what, miss, I'll go to the General Liberry stairs. You
tell Bert to hop it over to guard the ones by the Geological Liberry, and send Harry to the up-stairs at t'other end.
Prolly too late, but mi's well. Right?"

Again without waiting for an answer, he disappeared
through the door in the arch at the end of the gallery.

Daisy had just started to wonder whether he or Bert

might be the villain, when Bert arrived from one direction and a police sergeant from the other. They both stopped dead, and while they stood for a moment gaping at Pettigrew, Harry came through the dividing arch.

His concern was all for the Pareiasaurus. "Cor, that's put the cat among the pigeons, and how! Mr. Mummery won't half hit the ceiling!"

Bert nodded solemn agreement.

The police sergeant rounded on Harry. "Where were you, Boston, when this here incident took place?"

"Just popped through to have a word with Reg Underwood, di'n't I?" Harry Boston said in an injured voice. "See he was orright, like, and did he need a hand wiv anyfing."

"It's a foot he needs more like," said Bert. He snickered, then cast a sidelong, half-guilty glance at Pettigrew.

"And where were you?" demanded the sergeant, a stocky, blue-chinned man of perhaps forty.

Bert stiffened to attention. "In my place," he said loudly, "back there with the fossile inverbitrates like I was s'posed. Wilf Atkins'll tell you."

"Atkins was with you?" asked the sergeant. "Where is he now?"

"If Atkins is the dinosaur gallery commissionaire," said Daisy, "he went to guard the stairs to the basement from the General Library. He suggested these two should watch the other stairs from this part of the building."

"Prob'ly too late, miss," the sergeant said despondently, "but they might as well. I've got a man on the main entrance," he continued, as Bert and Harry hurried off, looking relieved, "and one on the entrance to the fossil mammals. The other two I sent down to the basement, but there's three back doors. They can't cover 'em all, nor the stairs to the Spirit Building, besides."

"The Spirit Building?" Daisy exclaimed, intrigued by a sudden vision of the Natural History Museum's collection of ghosts. Then she realized he must be referring to the place where one of the zoologists had taken her to see specimens preserved in spirits. He had not mentioned the annex by name.

"Out the back, 'cause of the fire hazard," the policeman confirmed her guess. "I haven't got enough men for summat like this, miss, and that's the truth, though luckily the next shift'll be arriving any moment. I rang up the station. They'll send some fellows round double quick, too, but meantime our murderer's prob'ly done a bunk."

"I'm afraid so," Daisy agreed, not quite liking the "our."

"I s'pose you won't be able to identify him, miss? You saw what happened?"

"No, only heard. Dr. Smith Woodward and I were out there, in the through hall, coming this way. By the time I got here there was no one in sight except . . . except Dr. Pettigrew. At least," she corrected herself conscientiously, "for a bit all I looked at was the . . . the mess. I should have looked around. I'm sorry."

"Can't be helped, miss." The policeman patted her arm. "Musta been a horrible shock. By the way, miss, Sergeant Jameson's the name, and right sorry I can't let you go, but the detective officers'll want a statement when they get here."

"Of course. They will be local detectives?"

"It's up to the Chelsea Division super, miss, whether to call in the Yard." He took out his notebook. "'Spect I'd better get your name and address down. It's Miss Dalrymple, isn't it, that's writing about the museum? How d'you spell it?"

Daisy gave him the information, and told him about the woman who had declared Pettigrew dead. "I'll go and keep her grandchildren out of the way," she offered, "and send her to give you her name, if you like. You'll want to stay here and see that no one interferes with the scene of the crime, won't you?"

"That's right, miss. You know a bit about police procedure, I see. Read detective stories, I dare say," he added—to Daisy's relief, as she was kicking herself for revealing her familiarity. Gratefully, he went on, "Yes, miss, it'd be a help if you could send the lady to me."

Daisy retired into the dinosaur gallery. Mrs. Ditchley, as the ex-nurse introduced herself, went to see Sergeant Jameson, happy to leave her daughter's children in Daisy's charge. "I'll be that glad when they go back to school next week," she confessed.

Aged from six or so to the thirteen-year-old Arthur, they gathered excitedly around Daisy.

"What happened, miss?" Arthur asked. "Gran won't tell."

"Someone was hurt," Daisy temporized, "one of the museum staff. He fell against the Pareiasaurus skeleton and smashed it all to pieces."

"Cor, really? Which one's that?"

"It's the fat one," a girl of perhaps ten told him knowledgeably. "Isn't it, miss? Not as big as the dinosaurs, but its bones look awf'ly solid."

"That's right," Daisy told her. "But fossil bones are often pretty fragile, even the big ones."

"Told you so, Arthur, nyah, nyah, nyah. That's why you're not allowed to touch. I'm going to dig up fossils when I'm grown up, miss."

"Good for you."

"Girls don't do stuff like that," Arthur objected.

Daisy told them about Mary Anning and Mrs. Mantell. The girl, Jennifer, was thrilled.

"Who cares about stupid old fossils?" was Arthur's reaction.

"My nephew thought the dinosaurs were pretty exciting, just because of their size," Daisy said. "Have you looked at them properly?"

"Not much."

"Did too! You were looking at the Megalosaurus."

"The one with the big teeth? Well . . . I say, miss, what happened to the man who got hurt? Someone hit him over the head with a fossil?"

"Sort of. Did you see anyone cross the gallery?"

Daisy was sure she would have seen anyone going through the main entrance to the dinosaurs, straight across from the hall where she was when she heard the crash. But halfway down the gallery, a door on the left led to the General Library, and an arch on the right to the fossil cephalopods (what *were* cephalopods? She still had not found out). If Wilfred Atkins had been with Bert in the invertebrates beyond, the murderer could have fled unseen through the mysterious cephalopods and crossed the dinosaurs to the library.

The children glanced at one another and shook their heads.

"No," Arthur admitted, disappointed.

"But we might not've," Jennifer insisted. "You were too looking at the Megalosaurus, like anything. He was, miss, honestly. And talking about its teeth. We might not've seen anyone, nor heard footsteps neither."

"Here comes Gran." The littlest child ran to meet Mrs. Ditchley. "Gran, I want to go home. I don't like it here."

"Well, no more do I, Katy. Such goings on, and in a museum, too. And all these bones, it's not natural. I don't hold with it. But the policeman says there's nothing he can do till he gets reinforcements. . . ."

"I don't like policemen."

"They're just doing their job, duckie, so we'll have to make the best of it, won't we? Let's sing a nice, cheerful song."

So Daisy found herself standing among the skeletons joining a rousing chorus of "I Do Like to Be Beside the Seaside," followed by "Pack Up Your Troubles in Your Old Kit-Bag." They were *Smile, smile, smiling* for all they were worth when the door to the General Library opened and Mr. Mummery burst forth.

"What the deuce is this horrible racket?" he howled. His round face was red with fury, his wild hair and eyebrows bristling like an upset hedgehog. Marching up to the silenced singers, he gabbled, "Madam, it is after six o'clock. Peace and quiet should by now have descended upon this august institution. Kindly remove yourself and these bra— children immediately. If, as is no doubt the case, you find yourselves locked in, the solution is not to caterwaul among the dinosaurs but to find one of our admirable police guards and request egress. Do I make myself clear?"

Katy buried her face in her grandmother's skirt and burst into tears.

"Mr. Mummery, please!" said Daisy. "Let me explain—"

"Oh, it's you, Miss Dalrymple. I had not observed you. Are these people in some way assisting you in your research? The effect of loud noises on a dinosaur's otic ossicles, perhaps? I must say, I had thought better of you. I cannot—"

"Mr. Mummery," Daisy interrupted, taking a firm hold of his sleeve and leading him, resisting, towards the gallery's entrance arch, "you must listen to me. Mrs. Ditchley and the children can't leave because the police won't let them. There's been a . . . an apparent murder. Dr. Pettigrew is dead."

Mummery threw back his head and guffawed. "Pettigrew murdered? He had it coming! If anyone did, I mean," he said sobering. "But you can't be serious, my dear Miss Dalrymple. True, we deal daily in death, but it is ancient death." His sweeping gesture embraced the dinosaurs and all the fossils beyond. He turned tetchily reproachful. "I cannot believe this jape is your notion. It must be Pettigrew's, of course, simply to bedevil me. Why you should support—"

"Come and see, then." She had intended to warn him of the destruction of his pet reptile, but she was now too annoyed with him. "Come along."

Two more uniformed police officers had joined Sergeant Jameson, another sergeant and a constable. Mummery scarcely spared them a glance as, with a screech of rage, he strode past them.

"My Pareiasaurus! He did this on purpose!"

Jameson and the constable caught his arms.

"Keep back, sir, if you please."

"My Pareiasaurus! It will take months of work to stick those bones back together, if indeed it can be done. I'll kill him!"

"He's already dead, sir," Jameson said reprovingly, and with a touch of suspicion, "if it's Ol' . . . Dr. Pettigrew you're referring to. I can't let you touch the skellington, and I'll have to ask you to remain on the premises until you have given a statement to a detective officer."

Mummery visibly deflated. "A detective? Miss Dalrymple mentioned murder."

"Looks that way, sir, but it's not for me to say. We'll have a detective here soon as can be."

"In the meantime, I suppose I may go back to the library and continue my work?" he asked with querulous dignity. "Miss Dalrymple, be so kind as to find some quiet diversion for those horrible brats." With a last, desolate stare at his ruined Pareiasaurus, he stalked back into the dinosaur gallery.

"He might as well be there as anywhere," said Jameson. "Well, Miss Dalrymple, do you think the old lady'll be willing to bring the kids through here? If so, you can all go up to the refreshment room and wait in comfort, now I've enough men to guard all the exits."

"Thank you, Sergeant. I'll see."

Past the dead Keeper, Daisy led a string of children with their eyes shut, while Mrs. Ditchley marched Arthur with her hands over his eyes. The newly arrived Constable Neddle went with them.

At the arch from the fossil mammals to the Central Hall, they found another constable on guard duty. A young couple stood nearby, hand in hand, looking disconsolate. A scrawny, bewhiskered man in horn-rims, vaguely familiar to Daisy, was arguing excitably with the guard.

"My dear chap, whatever the trouble is, it's nothing to do with me. I don't work here."

"Then you're a member of the public, sir," the constable said patiently.

"No, no, not at all. I work at the British Museum."

"This *is* the British Museum, sir, Natural History branch."

"Exactly! And I'm from the main institution in Bloomsbury, so I haven't a key to the back stairs. So just be a good fellow and let me through."

"I can't, sir. I've me instructions, haven't I. And it's no good going on asking me why, 'cause I haven't been told, not proper, not so's to be able to tell you."

"Hello, Mr. ffinch-Brown," Daisy intervened, recognizing him instantly when he pushed his spectacles up on his nose. "I don't expect you remember me—Daisy Dalrymple. Mr. Witt introduced us. Did you come to see him?"

"I did," said the anthropologist testily, "but I finished my business with him some time ago. Do you know what all this to-do is about? Why won't they let me leave in peace?"

"I can let you leave the gallery now, sir," said the guard, who had spoken briefly with Constable Neddle, "but I must ask you to go to the refreshment room upstairs and wait there. You two, too," he added to the young couple.

With an air of utter bewilderment, they meekly followed Mrs. Ditchley and the children out into the Central Hall. Shepherded by Neddle, ffinch-Brown followed not at all meekly, with Daisy.

"The refreshment room!" he exploded. He really was remarkably like Mummery in temperament. His voice did not get quite as loud, perhaps because he worked off surplus energy by waving his arms. "Wait in the refreshment room? For what, may I ask, for what?"

Daisy glanced back at Constable Neddle, who rolled his eyes. Taking this as permission, she outlined the situation.

"No great loss," said ffinch-Brown contemptuously. "Any fool can polish up rocks, but Ralph Pettigrew had the unmitigated gall to think he could make flint tools that I—

I!—would be unable to distinguish from the genuinely primitive article."

"The ones he claimed he found in a cave in Cornwall?" Daisy asked as they started up the main staircase towards the statue of Sir Richard Owen.

"No, no, those don't remotely resemble worked implements." He rubbed his hands in remembered glee. "You should have seen his face when I confirmed Witt's verdict. That was when he swore he could deceive me with flints he had chipped and flaked himself. Ha!"

"Impossible?"

"Impossible," affirmed ffinch-Brown, but with a trace of uneasiness. Then, cheering up, he said brightly, "Well, now we shall never know, shall we?"

Suppose Pettigrew succeeded in deceiving him, Daisy thought. The mineralogist would never have kept quiet about it. In that case, to what extent would the anthropologist's reputation suffer? And what had he been doing since he finished his business with Witt? Quarrelling with Pettigrew?

Ascending the second flight, Daisy glanced up at the bronze bust of Captain Fred Selous, big-game hunter, bronze elephant-gun in hand. It was hard to believe primitive man had hunted big game with nothing but flint weapons.

"How is Mr. Witt's experiment going?" she asked. "Has he duplicated the marks on the mammoth bones?"

"Not just mammoths, my dear young lady. I was contemplating certain grooves on the giant sloth's tibia when—"

"Fräulein? It is Miss Dalrymple?"

Daisy swung round. The Grand Duke of Transcarpathia was coming up the stairs behind them.

"Hello, where have you sprung from?" she asked with a smile.

"I have not *gesprungen!* I walk."

"It's just an English expression. Where have you been?"

"I vas de Irish elk regarding. Irish, pah!" he said angrily. "In mine contry also vas once dis magnificent beast, but de English dey must all take to self, de elks, de jewels, everysing!"

"So you were in the fossil mammal gallery? I didn't see you there."

The Grand Duke turned sullen. "Dis de police also say. Lurking dey say, vhy you vas lurking behind de elk? Vhat is lurking, *bitte?*"

"Er, sort of hiding," Daisy explained.

"Hiding? I not hide, but if I am not seen vhen de police come, I not at once rush out. To myself I remind, here in England I am not Grand Duke, only a damn foreigner!"

Rudolf Maximilian had a grudge against the world, Daisy thought as they entered the cafeteria, but also good reason to loathe Pettigrew. Having bumped him off, he could easily have nipped along the reptile gallery, through the hall at the far end, and into the mammal gallery.

Mr. ffinch-Brown, who had gone ahead into the refreshment room and was glowering disgruntledly at the CLOSED sign on the counter, claimed to have been in the end pavilion looking at the sloth. He would not have seen the Grand Duke. What about the young couple, who had also apparently been among the mammals when Pettigrew was killed? They were now ensconced at a corner table, heads close together, whispering, eyes for nothing but each other. Add their self-absorption to the giant mammals and wide pillars, and they would probably have remained unaware of anything short of a bomb blast.

They would not have noticed when ffinch-Brown went through into the pavilion, either. The Grand Duke just might have seen him, though, and might have some idea of the time. Daisy was tempted to ask.

She really must stay out of the investigation, she reproved herself. True, she had been the first on the scene, but her alibi, along with Dr. Smith Woodward's, was impeccable. Though she had to give a statement, and would no doubt be called to give evidence at the inquest, the Chelsea district detectives would resent any attempt to add her twopenn'orth.

The detectives were a long time coming. Mrs. Ditchley, defiantly determined, went behind the counter and found milk and biscuits for the tired, hungry children.

"Put on a kettle for tea," suggested Mr. ffinch-Brown. "I'll pay for the lot." He put a half-crown on top of the till.

Constable Neddle had left them. With main entrance closed, none of them could leave the building if they tried. No one else joined them. Daisy wondered whether Mummery was the only member of the scientific staff, apart from Smith Woodward and Pettigrew, who had not gone home at half past five. There might be others tucked away in offices, work rooms, and libraries, not yet winkled out, or left to work in peace until needed.

So far, Mummery, ffinch-Brown, and Grand Duke Rudolf were the only suspects Daisy knew of.

The only ones she was ever likely to know of, she tried to persuade herself. She was *not* going to get involved. She went to sit with Mrs. Ditchley and the children.

At last a tall young man appeared and announced himself as Detective Constable Ross. "We'll take Miss Dalrymple's statement first," he said. "Would you come this way, please, miss?"

Mrs. Ditchley arose in wrath. "What about my grand-kiddies?" she demanded. "And their mum come home from work and waiting for them and not knowing where they've got to? I'm sure I'd have no objection to Miss Dalrymple getting to go first if it wasn't for the kiddies, but you wouldn't mind, would you, dear, if I took your turn?"

"Not at all," said Daisy.

D. C. Ross, with Mrs. Ditchley advancing upon him, caved in. "All right, madam, all right. I s'pose it won't matter that much."

"Come along, children."

But there the constable drew the line. He hadn't been told nothing about bringing no children along.

"I'll take care of them," Daisy offered.

Mrs. Ditchley was only gone a few minutes, fortunately, as Katy was growing tearful and Arthur obstreperous. Upon her return she gathered her flock, wiped noses, and saw coats buttoned as Ross escorted Daisy from the room. Daisy wondered whether she ought to mention that the children had told her Mummery could have crossed the dinosaur gallery without their seeing him. She felt the detective in charge ought to have spoken to them himself, but perhaps he planned to at a later date, or maybe he already had information clearing Mummery.

In any case, she was *not* going to get involved.

She followed D. C. Ross through the Central Hall to an office at the front, tucked away to the right of the entrance as Smith Woodward's was to the left. A sign on the door read SIR SIDNEY HARMER, DIRECTOR.

Ross opened the door and stood aside, announcing, "Miss Dalrymple, Sergeant."

Behind Sir Sidney's desk rose a very familiar figure, vast, suited in ghastly tan and yellow check, with a luxuriant greying walrus moustache counterbalanced by the shining dome of his hairless head.

"Mr. Tring!" cried Daisy.

Five

"Good evedig, Biss Dalrybple," said Alec's favourite sergeant, coming round the desk to shake her hand. "Do sit dowd, please. Excuse be a bobet." He turned his back and harumphed hugely into a large white handkerchief. "Ah, that's better."

"So they did call in Scotland Yard." Daisy sat down in one of the red leather armchairs before the desk. "But where's the Chief?"

"Detective Chief Inspector Fletcher is out on another job and took young Piper with him. But seeing it involves some outdoor business and I've got this bit of a cold, he left me to clear up some paperwork at the office."

"I expect you'd rather have gone with them than getting stuck with desk work," Daisy said sympathetically.

His little brown eyes twinkled at her. "Isn't that the truth! At least, it would be if it wasn't for this affair coming up. The Chelsea division detectives are all out already, and my super hadn't got an inspector to spare, so he sent me along."

"I'm very glad he's put you in charge." Though *bang* went any chance of keeping it from Alec.

"He thought it was a simple little case I'd be able to clear up tonight." Tom Tring sighed gustily. "Don't suppose he has any idea what a regular rabbit warren the place is. Well, Miss Dalrymple, what have you got to tell me? Stop staring, Ross, and get your notebook out. Yes, this is *that* Miss Dalrymple."

Ross and Daisy both blushed, Daisy wondering whether she was notorious simply as Alec's fiancée, or as the Assistant Commissioner for Crime's bête noire.

"I've been doing some research here for an article," she said hurriedly. "This evening at twenty to six I went to Dr. Smith Woodward's office—he's the Keeper of Geology—to ask him about Piltdown Man."

"Exactly twedty to six? Excuse be." Tring pulled out his hankie, turned his head, and produced another explosion.

"Roughly. You know how you look at a watch and you don't so much notice the exact time as how long you have till . . . well, in this case till the museum closed. I saw I had about twenty minutes left and I decided it was long enough."

Tring nodded. "And then?"

"We walked round to the Piltdown skull, just around the corner in the fossil mammal gallery. Dr. Smith Woodward looked at it for a minute and decided he'd much rather talk about fossil fish. So we crossed the gallery—I didn't notice anyone there, but I wasn't really looking. There was no one in the hall leading to the reptile gallery, I'm sure of that."

"That would be here?" The sergeant pointed to a large sheet of paper on the desk in front of him.

Leaning forward, Daisy saw it was a plan of the museum. "That's right," she said. "We must have been about halfway along when we heard someone ahead speaking loudly, then a sort of roar, and then the most frightful crash." She hesitated. "Thinking back, I'm pretty sure it was Dr. Pettigrew's voice, though I didn't recognize it immediately."

"What did he say?"

"I couldn't catch the words. This building's so solid it muffles sounds. We would have seen, though, if anyone had entered the dinosaur gallery through this arch." She showed him on the plan.

"Yes, that all agrees with Dr. Smith Woodward's statement. That lets him out."

"And me," said Daisy.

Tring's moustache waggled above a half-concealed grin. "And you," he acknowledged. "What next?"

"I dashed into the reptile gallery, and saw Pettigrew lying . . . I'm afraid I was rather too aghast to notice if anyone was running off. I'm most frightfully sorry." More affected by the memory than she had been by the actual event, Daisy suddenly felt cold and horribly sick.

Always light on his feet despite his size, Tom Tring was round the desk in a flash, his hand on her shoulder. "Here, put your head down on your knees. Ross, quick, pour a drop of whatever it is Sir Sidney keeps in that decanter. That's the ticket. Take a good swallow, Miss Dalrymple."

Head whirling, Daisy only half heard him. Expecting water, she gulped whisky. It hit the back of her throat like a lighted squib. As she choked and spluttered, tears pouring down her face, a comforting warmth spread through her middle. At least it had settled her stomach.

Tring thrust a handkerchief into her hand. "Here, it's a clean one. The missus sent me out with half a dozen. Feeling better?"

"Yes, thank you," Daisy croaked, mopping her eyes. "I *think* so. Gosh!"

"Cad you . . . Half a tick." He found another hankie and trumpeted into it. "Can you go on? You sent Dr. Smith Woodward for the police?"

"It sounds frightfully pushy, put like that, but I suppose I did. Mrs. Ditchley turned up first, though. You've seen her."

"I want it in your words, please. You know the Chief's methods."

Tears pricked at Daisy's eyelids. How she wished for Alec's comforting presence, even if he was angry with her. But Tom Tring, dear Tom Tring, was now enveloped in a rosy haze, like a mammoth cherub. He needed her help. Blinking away the tears, she suppressed a giggle and tried to concentrate.

"Mrs. Ditchley," prompted the mustachioed cherub.

Daisy told him about Mrs. Ditchley's failure to find a pulse, her return to her grandchildren, and the dinosaur commissionaire's subsequent arrival on the scene. At that point she got Wilf Atkins's name hopelessly muddled, and she could not pronounce "Pareiasaurus" to save her life, though by articulating with extreme care she managed to substitute "skeleton."

"Wolf Catkins—you know who I mean—said Mr. Flummery would have forty fits when he saw the smashed ske-le-ton. He did. He threatened to kill Pet-ti-grew, but he was too late."

"Yes," said the cherub, his face wavering in and out of her vision, "so Sergeant Jameson says. I think the rest of your statement had better wait till morning, Miss Dalrymple."

"Sorry. Seem to be fearfully tired all of a sudden." Daisy's eyes closed of their own volition, and she couldn't get them to open again.

Distantly, she heard the constable's incredulous voice: "Sozzled?"

"A whacking slug of whisky on an empty stomach," Tring rumbled. "Our Miss Dalrymple's not one of these cocktail-bibbing Bright Young Things, you know. I can't escort her home now. Help me move the chair over into that corner."

Briefly Daisy flew through the air. An overcoat was tucked around her and she slept.

When she awoke, Daisy was sure she had not been dead to the world for more than a few minutes. She was still slouched in a leather armchair with a coat draped over her. No headache, thank heaven, but she felt decidedly lethargic.

It was not only lassitude that kept her immobile, her eyes closed. If Detective Sergeant Tring knew she was awake, he might think he ought to send her from the room. With Tom Tring in charge of the case, she abandoned her attempt to curb her curiosity.

Mummery's strident outcry had roused her. (Had she dreamt it, or had she really referred to him as Flummery? Too shaming! She only hoped she could rely on Tring not to tell Alec she had been tiddly, and to silence Ross.) After that brief explosion, Mummery was now explaining, using a great many lengthy scientific terms, what he had been doing in the General Library after working hours. Come to think of it, Flummery suited him rather well. He sounded as if he was taking malicious delight in befuddling the poor uneducated coppers. Daisy wondered how the note-taking Ross was coping.

Tom Tring was unruffled. After listening in massive silence until Mummery ran down like an underwound gramophone, the sergeant said politely, "Thank you, sir. It's kind of you to take so much trouble to give me all the details when my Chief Inspector will likely be asking you to repeat it tomorrow. Very particular he is. Now, what time did you go to the library?"

Mummery claimed to have been there from shortly before five until he burst forth to rebuke Daisy and Mrs. Ditchley for the singing. Several others were there when he arrived—he named a couple—but he thought all had left at half past five, at the end of the working day.

"I cannot be certain," he said condescendingly. "No doubt you are unaware, Sergeant, that academic libraries contain a great many tall bookshelves, which tend to conceal the occupants from one another."

"Is that so?" Tring spoke with such ponderous gravity that Daisy was sure he was amused. "Well, well, that's a great pity, sir. Thank you, sir, that's all then . . . for the moment."

"For the moment?" squawked Mummery.

"Tonight, I'm just trying to get everyone's movements clear, sir. You are at liberty to go home. Tomorrow, the Chief Inspector will no doubt have a number of questions to put to you, 'specially as Sergeant Jameson reports you threatened the victim."

"But he was already dead!"

"Ah," said Tring inscrutably. "Good night, sir."

There was a blank silence, then a mutter from Mummery, the sound of a chair pushed back, and a door opening and closing.

"One up to you, Sarge," Ross exclaimed. "But I didn't get much of it down, the scientific stuff."

"That's all right, laddie. It was mostly obfuscation"— Mr. Tring was by no means the ignoramus some took him for—"and I wouldn't give him the satisfaction of asking him to spell out the long words for you. The Chief'll sort him in the morning."

"You think the Super'll give the case to Mr. Fletcher?"

"Bound to, when he knows who's got herself mixed up in it. Right, let's have Mr. Witt in next."

Blushing, a tendency she deplored as positively Victorian but was unable to overcome, Daisy heard the door open and close again. To distract herself from Superintendent Crane's probable reaction, not to mention Alec's and, eventually and inevitably, the A. C.'s, she pondered Witt's appearance on the list of suspects.

"You can open your eyes now," said Tom Tring.

"Oh!" Daisy did. He had turned Sir Sidney's swivel chair and was regarding her quizzically, in the shadowy corner where he had put her. "I didn't want to interrupt your interview," she excused herself.

"Much obliged, I'm sure. Feeling better now?"

"Yes, much, thanks."

"Ah." He ruminated. "Still, I wouldn't want to send you home alone, not after . . ."

"Mr. Tring, you *won't* tell the Chief?"

Tring chuckled. "What, that his young lady was under the affluence of incohol, as they say oop north? When it was me poured the stuff into you? You don't tell, I don't tell. And I'll keep young Ross mum, never fear. But what am I going to do with you now? I can't spare a man to escort you."

"You could just leave me here," said Daisy innocently. "I expect I'll fall asleep again."

"Ho, pull the other one! All right, you know the place and you know at least some of the people. You can stay, if you swear not to tell the Chief I let you, and to keep your eyes and your mouth shut."

"Cross my heart and hope to be fossilized," Daisy said, and closed her eyes just in time as the Director's door opened.

"Mr. Witt, Sergeant."

"Good evening, Sergeant." Witt's voice, smooth and well-bred, reminded Daisy of how helpful he had started out to be, and how he had had to pass her on to the equally helpful one-armed commissionaire assigned to his gallery.

Sergeant Hamm—all these sergeants were getting confusing—ought to be able to confirm ffinch-Brown's and Grand Duke Rudolf's movements. If he himself had been where he was supposed to be. Could a man with one arm have inflicted the fatal wound on Pettigrew?

Daisy realized she did not know exactly how the Keeper of Mineralogy had been killed. It was not a subject she cared to speculate about. She refocused her attention on Witt's interview.

"Yes, ffinch-Brown left my office at about twenty to six, perhaps a few minutes earlier. My office is at the back of the building, here." Daisy pictured him leaning forward to point at Tring's floor-plan.

"I see, sir."

"You will observe, there are private studies behind the galleries, accessible through doors at the end of each gallery. Ffinch-Brown went out through the cephalopod gallery. I could have followed him to the reptile gallery and there met—er, the *corpus delicti,* shall we say?—in his pre-*corpus* state. However, I did not. I remained in my office, writing letters. Alone, alas."

"*Sine alibi,* as you might say, sir."

Witt laughed. "One might indeed, Sergeant."

"Very good, sir. Thank you for your cooperation.

Chief Detective Inspector Fletcher will have some more questions for you tomorrow, I'm afraid."

"C'est la vie, Sergeant, or rather, *c'est la mort."*

The door opened and closed, then Ross said, "Cheerful sort of bloke, Sarge! I got your joke—*sine alibi* like *sine die* in a court adjournment, right? But I didn't get that last bit of Latin down."

"French that was, but that's all right, laddie. Fetch Mr. Steadman now, will you?" Tring paused while the constable departed, then said, "Well, Miss Dalrymple?"

"A cheerful sort of bloke," Daisy echoed the constable, "but he had good reason to dislike Pettigrew. They all did."

"Mr. Steadman too? No, you'd better go into that with the Chief."

"Right-oh," Daisy sighed. "Who did you talk to while I was . . . out for the count?"

Tring reached back for the list on the desk. "Mr. Chardford and Miss Fellowes."

"The young couple who were in the fossil mammals?"

"That's right. And another visitor, a bloke who claimed to be the Grand Duke of Transcarpathia, wherever that might be. Very offended because one of the constables accused him of lurking behind a giant deer, just because he didn't rush out to see what was going on. Funny people, these foreigners. We'll go into the visitors' backgrounds, of course, but they're just members of the public who happened to be here, like Mrs. Ditchley and her brood, no reason to connect them with the deceased."

"Oh, but there is! Grand Duke Rudolf—I'm pretty sure he really is—loathed Pettigrew."

"Did he, now?" Tring exclaimed. He made a note against the name. "You won't forget to tell the Chief about him. Let's see: There's the commissionaires I've had a go at. They were all off chatting to each other, it being the end of the day and not too many visitors about."

"Sergeant Hamm was with someone, not in the mammals?"

"With Underwood and Boston in plants, corals, and sponges, if my memory serves."

"I'm sure it does, Mr. Tring." If Underwood had done in the Keeper, Daisy thought, Boston and Hamm might conceivably give him a false alibi, considering Ol' Stony's behaviour towards the cripple. But a one-legged man was unlikely to attempt to tackle the hefty victim, and surely could not have got away before Daisy arrived on the scene.

"Then there's a couple of assistants, who were together the whole time in the work room behind the Geological Library. And Mr. Gilbert ffinch-Brown, two small *f*'s, from the British Museum, who went from Mr. Witt's office straight through the . . . er, cephalopods, is it? and along through the reptiles to stare at a ground sloth in the east pavilion. No alibi and swears he didn't see Mr. Pettigrew on the way. Peppery gentleman, like Mr. Mummery."

"Peppery's just the word!" Daisy agreed. "Peppery Mummery—it sounds like a tongue-twister nursery rhyme. Anyone else?"

"That's all I've seen, and just three to go. Ah, here's Mr. Steadman."

Daisy hastily resumed her feigned torpor as Ross ushered in the dinosaur man.

"I was on my way home hours ago," said Steadman crossly.

"Yes, sir, I'm sorry we've had to keep you. Won't you sit down? I hope you've managed to find something to fill the time."

"There's always work to be done. I . . . I suppose you want to know where I was when . . . it happened."

"Exactly, sir," said Tring affably, accustomed to putting nervous suspects at their ease, "if you'd be so kind."

"When . . . ?"

"Let's start from five o'clock."

"I was in the work room, looking at some bones I've been trying to classify. I'm the dinosaur curator, by the way. We often—usually, in fact—get incomplete skeletons, frequently of hitherto unknown species. Sometimes the discoverers misidentify other reptilian fossils as dinosauria, pure wishful thinking. I realized that was the case in this instance, at which point I decided to go home."

"What time would that be, sir?"

"Time?" said Steadman vaguely, a slight tremor in his voice. "I couldn't tell you exactly. I know it was after five-thirty, because several assistants left the work room on the dot. The official work day ends at half past five, you know. I went through the Geological Library to the stairs and down to the staff cloakroom in the basement. That's where we all keep our outdoor clothes, of course."

"Of course, sir. So you put on your coat and hat, two minutes, shall we say, or three."

"A little longer than that, I'm afraid. I was there for several minutes, er . . . hm . . ."

"Answering the call of nature, sir?"

"Yes, yes, that's it," Steadman said gratefully. Having heard him discourse freely on the disgusting eating habits of the Megalosaurus, Daisy was amused by his delicacy. "Then I went to the usual exit at the rear of the basement, where I found a police officer barring the way. I was horrified to learn of Dr. Pettigrew's . . . death." Again his voice shook.

"A nasty business, sir, and a bit different from your dry old bones, eh? Well, that'll be all, thank you."

"That's all?"

"For now, sir. My chief will have some questions for you tomorrow, I expect."

"Oh! Oh, I see. Yes. Well, I'll be on my way, then."

"Good night, sir. If I were you, sir, I'd have a stiff drink when you get home, and put the whole thing out of your mind until the morning." The door closed behind the squeamish dinosaur man. "Dr. Bentworth still asleep, Ross?" asked Tring.

"Yes, Sarge, sweet as a baby."

"Leave him for last. I'll take Mr. Ruddlestone next."

Daisy had a feeling something was wrong with the list of people Tring was interviewing, but she could not quite put her finger on it. She did know someone he had missed, though.

As soon as Ross was gone, she asked, "What about the children, Mrs. Ditchley's grandchildren? Are you going to talk to them tomorrow?"

"That's up to the Chief. Mrs. Ditchley told me you'd asked them if they saw anyone crossing the dinosaur gallery, which they hadn't. Not much help there. It doesn't incriminate Mr. Mummery, nor let him out, neither."

"No," Daisy admitted.

"You fancy Mr. Mummery for our villain, do you?" Tring enquired teasingly.

"Gosh, no! Not more than the others, anyway. He has quite a temper, but as far as I know, he only had the same general reason to dislike Pettigrew. A running feud over the respective importance of palæontology and mineralogy hardly seems adequate cause for murder!"

"You never can tell," said the sergeant sagely. "Be about the same as a bloke doing in a nagging wife, or vice versa, I reckon. You'd be surprised how often they think that's a reasonable excuse when trying to explain a corpse on the kitchen floor. 'But Officer, he went *on* and *on* at me,'" he mimicked in a squeaky falsetto.

Daisy swallowed a half-shocked giggle as Ross showed in Mr. Ruddlestone. Eyes shut, she pictured the two large, bald men confronting each other like a couple of boiled eggs on the breakfast table.

"Sorry to keep you so late, sir," said Tom Tring.

"That's quite all right, Sergeant." Ruddlestone's distinctly Lancashire voice sounded as if he was beaming his wide, jaunty beam, positively bubbling with enthusiasm. "I might well have stayed till now anyway. I found some fascinating stuff I hadn't come across before."

"Where was that, sir?"

"In the Special Palæontological Collections. That's the

stuff presented to the museum over the centuries by collectors like Sir Hans Sloane, Gustavus Brander, and William Smith. Most of the specimens are filed away in drawers, and one tends to forget they are there, but something drew my attention to . . . Oh, but you won't want to hear about that. Here, I was here in this easternmost gallery."

"Thank you. From what time, sir?"

"Time? It must have been about four. I had tea and a biscuit in my office. Several biscuits, to tell the truth, Sergeant," Ruddlestone said confidentially, sharing amusement, one outsize man to another. "Then I went through to the special collections and I was still there, quite forgetful of the time, when a constable came and told me what had happened. He kindly let me stay there until just now. I'm more than ready for my dinner now, I can tell you, as I'm sure you must be."

"Ravenous!" Tring agreed. His eyes must be twinkling, Daisy would have bet on it. "Now, I see there are doors from this gallery here to the . . . let's see . . . Fossil Plants, Corals, and Sponges, and to the reptiles."

"The reptile gallery is where it happened, isn't it?" the invertebrate curator said, now grave. "It's shocking to be so cheerful when a man lies dead, even a man like Pettigrew. But I have had such an invigorating evening." His gravity already vanished, he spoke with a joyful earnestness. "Most people can't see the fascination of corals and sponges, echinoderms, arthropods, mollusks, cephalopods, and so on, especially fossilized ones, but I assure you, when one really gets to know them they are quite wonderful."

"I'm sure they must be, sir. A bit like police work—lots of people can't see why anyone'd want to do it."

"Exactly! You are an expert in your field as I in mine. As an expert, you take the same pleasure in your business as I take in the study of invertebrates. On the scale of mere mass, dinosaurs outweigh them, to be sure, but only look at age, numbers, and diversity! Invertebrates came first, and there have always been far more of them than of vertebrates, both in numbers of species and in numbers of individuals. Where would we be without earthworms, I ask you?" ·

"I, er, couldn't say, sir," Tring admitted.

Ruddlestone laughed. "An unfair question, and rhetorical, I assure you. But you must have questions for me. I am holding up your investigation. I ought to have warned you not to let me mount my hobby-horse, Sergeant."

"It's been very interesting, sir. Given me a bit of an eye-opener, you might say. You didn't set foot outside that gallery after you went in, sir?"

"Not until one of your officers came and told me what had happened. Poor Pettigrew, he was his own worst enemy. I don't know about his private life, but in his professional life he succeeded in alienating one and all."

"Ah," said Tring. "Well, Detective Chief Inspector Fletcher will want to hear all about that tomorrow, sir, but for now, I'm done, thank you. I'll warn the Chief to keep you off your hobby-horse, sir."

"Do that, Sergeant!" Ruddlestone laughed again. "Good night to you, and I hope you get your dinner soon."

Her eyes still shut, Daisy noted that, whatever their similarity of build, his departing tread had none of Tring's lightfootedness.

"A nice gentleman, Sarge," was Ross's verdict, "shaking your hand and all."

"So he seemed, laddie, so he seemed, but if you want to get on in our business, it doesn't do to judge a book by its cover." Tring heaved a heavy sigh. "All that talk of dinner, and the missus was making steak and kidney pud tonight. It's not the same warmed over. Still, finishing up Miss Dalrymple's whisky seems to have cleared the tubes and knocked my cold for six. All right, let's have Dr. Bentworth in."

"So that's what happened to the rest of the whisky," said Daisy tartly, hearing the door close.

"Waste not, want not," Tring responded in a mock sententious tone, which switched to injured as he continued, "I couldn't very well put it back into Sir Sidney's decanter, could I? Young Ross poured with a heavy hand, like it was beer."

"I'm glad it's cured your cold, if only temporarily. Gosh, I could do with some of Mrs. Tring's steak and kidney pud! I only got one biscuit with my tea."

"You can leave if you want. You sound *compos mentis* enough now to get yourself home."

"You *are* making a parade of your Latin today!" Daisy teased. "No, I'll stay, though I'll be very surprised if you get anything useful out of Dr. Bentworth."

"Oh?"

"Wait and see. Here they come."

Dr. Bentworth had retired as the Curator of Fossil Plants some eighteen years ago. Since then he had been working on a magnum opus on fossil ferns, coming in to the museum five days a week and pottering about the collections and the Geological Library . . .

". . . And I fear I may have drifted off," he said in his thin, old voice, "taken a nap, forty winks or so, in the library, the Geological Library, though Palæontological would be more accurate, more descriptive, altogether more appropriate."

Daisy did not bother to close her eyes, knowing that Bentworth had a very fuzzy view of the world through the thick lenses of his gold-rimmed glasses. Gnomelike, he sat there opposite Tring, leaning forward anxiously with his ropy hands on his knobbly knees.

"So Dr. Pettigrew is dead, has been killed, *murdered,* you think? It is shocking, quite dreadful, simply disgraceful. Nothing like this happened in my day, when I was employed at the museum, when I was in charge of fossil plants. No, I saw no one, no one at all, not a soul, but then, my sight is not what it was, alas, very poor, presbyopia they say, and cataracts, though I see quite well close to, for reading and writing, for examining specimens, you know. But I fear I may have drifted off, nodded—"

"Thank you very much, sir," Tring interrupted, having come full circle. "I'm very sorry to have kept you so late. I believe your son is waiting to take you home."

"Just outside, sir," said Ross cheerfully. "If you'd kindly step this way." Stooping slightly, the long-legged constable ushered Bentworth out with a helpful hand at his elbow.

"You were right, Miss Dalrymple," observed Tring, rising to his feet as she stood up and handed him the vast overcoat he had used to blanket her. "The poor old bird wouldn't have noticed if a herd of dinosaurs had trampled through that library, let alone what time they passed. I'll have Ross call a taxicab for you—the Met's expense."

"Thanks, but I'd rather walk," Daisy said. "It's not far, and I'd quite like a bit of fresh air and exercise after . . . Mr. Tring, do you know how Pettigrew was killed?"

"Stabbed, looks like, but it's a bit of a mystery how and what with. And I'm not telling you more than that," he said firmly, "because Sir Sidney'd be bound to notice if any more of his whisky disappeared. Good job he's gone off for a few days to some symposium or other. Time he gets back he won't remember the exact level, but I don't want you needing it."

"Oh. Oh well, I'll ask Alec tomorrow, when the whole business is a bit further away. At least . . . I suppose there's absolutely no hope of keeping my name out of it?"

Tring shook his head. "Afraid not, not a chance, when you were first on the scene. And with you in the thick of it, there's no way the Super'll give the case to anyone but the Chief!"

Six

"Miss Dalrymple, Crane? The Honourable Daisy Dalrymple?"

Sitting in Superintendent Crane's office, Alec heard the anguished yelp over the internal telephone, as clear as if the Assistant Commissioner (C.I.D.) were in the same room.

"First on the scene, sir," confirmed the Super gloomily. "Do you want to speak to Fletcher? I have him here."

Alec held his breath.

"No," said the A.C., after a pause which suggested he had counted to ten. "I suppose she doesn't do it on purpose. Does she?"

"Hardly, sir."

"No, and he couldn't stop her if she did. Yet. On second thoughts, give him to me."

Crane handed over the telephone.

"Fletcher here, sir."

"Fletcher, for God's sake and the sake of my sanity, marry the woman soon!"

"Yes, sir," said Alec, surprised but nothing loath.

"Then at least you'll have the right, if not the ability, to keep her out of trouble. You'll have to take this museum case. I can't ask anyone else to attempt to control her. I'm counting on you to keep her from getting any more deeply embroiled."

"I'll do my best, sir," Alec promised, sincerely though unhopefully.

His pessimism must have travelled along the wire, for the A.C. said something which sounded very like "Pshaw!" and hung up the 'phone.

The Super pushed a slim file across his desk. "All yours," he said. "Good luck, Chief Inspector."

"Tell me about it, Tom," Alec invited, dropping the file on his desk and himself in his chair.

Detective Sergeant Tring had on his most stolid expression, but Alec knew him too well to be deceived. Behind the moustache and the straight face, Tom was quivering with merriment. He had a soft spot for Daisy, if not the unquestioning adulation manifested by Detective Constable Piper.

"She wasn't just there, Chief," he said. He coughed a couple of times, though otherwise his cold seemed vanquished. Leaning back in his chair, at the desk at right angles to Alec's, he went on, "She knows all the suspects."

Alec clutched his head. "Great Scott! I might have guessed. She has been doing research at the museum for weeks, talking to the staff."

"But it's not only the staff. Miss Dalrymple knows the Grand Duke, too."

"Grand Duke?" Alec queried hollowly.

Tom Tring permitted his moustache to twitch in a grin. "Grand Duke Rudolf Maximilian of Transcarpathia. Miss Dalrymple put me on to him. I thought he was just a visitor."

"I'm going to have to talk to her about them, aren't I?"

"Oh yes, Chief. All I got last night was statements about people's movements, all there in that file. I didn't ask Miss Dalrymple about anything but what she actually witnessed, and not all of that. She was a bit shook up."

"*I'll* shake her," said Alec grimly, then discovered what he really wanted to do was take her in his arms and comfort her. "No, forget I said that, Tom. Was it very messy?"

"Not like you'd expect of a stabbing. Looked like he was stabbed several yards from where he fell. He left a trail of drops of blood staggering along, but the floor's made up of what they call mo-sake, little tiny bits in a pattern of white and black and red, so I don't expect Miss Dalrymple noticed the spots. She couldn't've missed the stain on his shirt and weskit, but there wasn't floods of blood, because the weapon was left in the wound."

"What was it? A dinosaur bone?"

"That's what we won't know, Chief, till Dr. Renfrew tells us. Whatever it was must've bust off, not enough left sticking out to identify. If it is a bit of bone, we'll never find the missing part. The place is full of 'em! For a start, the deceased crashed into a skeleton—not a dinosaur, some other kind of ruddy great monster—and smashed it half to pieces."

"I assume you bagged the remains."

"Got the lot, but if it was a bone he was stabbed with, I don't reckon it's among 'em. He was on his back, so the weapon didn't bust off when he fell, and by then the murderer had scarpered, if you ask me, while Pettigrew was staggering about. By the by, there's going to be trouble over them bones with the reptile man, Septimus Mummery by name."

"Mummery? I'd better get to know the *dramatis personae,* and where they claim they were." Alec pulled the file towards him. "Telephone Daisy—Miss Dalrymple—will you, Tom? Ask her if we can see her at home in an hour or so. Make sure she realizes this is an official visit. All we want is facts, her actual observations, not her opinions and theories."

"Ah," said Tring enigmatically, coughed twice, and reached for his telephone.

Opening the file, Alec sighed. Daisy's theories, though often misleading, were occasionally helpful. He couldn't afford to ignore them, any more than he could prevent her uttering them. As for her opinions, they tended to lead her to take one or more suspects under her wing, which created all sorts of difficulties for a detective striving to be

impartial. He could cope with that when her protégés
turned out to be innocent, but if not, it was decidedly
painful.

At least she was apparently not a suspect this time.

Alec read through the file, discussed the contents and
his plans with Tring, then sent for Detective Constables
Ross and Piper. With the sergeant beside him and the constables in the back, Piper reading the file, he drove his little
yellow Austin Seven to South Kensington. At the Natural
History Museum he dropped off Tring and Ross to talk to
the commissionaires and museum police. He and Ernie
Piper went on to Chelsea, stopping before Daisy's little
white house in Mulberry Place.

Mrs. Potter stood on the newly scrubbed doorstep, in-
dustriously polishing the front-door handle.

"Mornin', Mr. Fletcher," she said. "You're up and about
bright and early today."

"Good morning, Mrs. Potter. Miss Dalrymple is expecting us."

The daily noticed the detective constable behind him.
"Well, if it isn't Mr. Piper, too! Hello, ducks, how's
tricks?" Her eyes rounded. "Lawks, never say you're on official business, sir?"

"It's all right, I'm not going to arrest her," Alec assured
her, recalling the times he had been tempted to do just that,
for hindering the police in the course of their duties.

"As though I'd think such a thing! Miss got herself
mixed up in another p'leece case, has she?" Mrs. Potter
asked, folding plump arms across her substantial bosom
with an air of settling in to gossip. With discomforting per-
spicacity, she went on, "The Museum Murder what was in
the papers this morning, is it? Always popping round there,
she is."

"Now you know I can't talk about it, Mrs. Potter, and I
hope you won't either."

"Never fear, I'll keep it under me 'at," she sighed. Reluctantly she turned and pushed open the door for them. "There you go, sir. She's in her study. You 'ang on a minute, young feller-me-lad. Let's see you wipe your boots proper. I just done the hall."

Whether on purpose or not, the charwoman delayed Piper long enough for Alec to enter Daisy's study alone. It was just as well, since Daisy forestalled his carefully planned greeting—a judicious compromise between loving fiancé and interrogating officer—by flinging herself at him. She put her arms around his neck and kissed him, then laid her cheek against his chest and said, "Oh, Alec, I'm frightfully glad it's you."

"So am I," he said ruefully, hugging her cuddlesome curves and dropping a kiss on her feathery curls, "but I could wish it wasn't you."

She looked up at him with a half-guilty smile in her deceptively guileless blue eyes. "Not me in the case, I hope you mean, not not me in your arms."

So he kissed her again, properly.

"Er-hem."

Daisy broke away, blushing delightfully. Ernie's cheeks were equally pink, though Alec took no delight in them.

"Do come in, Mr. Piper," Daisy invited as she put the desk between herself and Alec. "The Chief didn't mention he'd brought you with him. How nice to see you. Oh, would you mind fetching yourself a chair from the dining room? Sit down, Alec, do, and stop towering over me."

However hard one tried, Alec thought, taking a statement from one's beloved was not quite the same as from a stranger.

"It's official business, love," he said.

"I know," she said mournfully. "I'm most frightfully sorry, darling. I would never have taken on the job, let alone taken Belinda there, if I'd known Pettigrew was going to get himself murdered."

"How could you guess?" said Alec, finding his plaint

preempted. And it really was not fair to blame her . . . only *how* did she manage it? "At least Bel wasn't with you when it happened this time."

"She rather liked Dr. Pettigrew, I'm afraid. He was quite good with the children, like Mr.—"

Alec held up his hand. "Please, darling! Let's stick to what you saw and heard yesterday."

"I'll try," she promised, as Ernie came in with a chair, "only you're always saying one never can tell what insignificant detail may be relevant."

Hoist by his own petard, Alec ignored the reminder and said, "Ready, Ernie?"

"Course, Chief," said the detective constable, his notebook and one of his everlasting supply of well-sharpened pencils already in his hands.

With a few nudges away from speculation, Daisy ran through the previous day's events, from leaving Dr. Smith Woodward's office to D. C. Ross fetching her to see Tom Tring.

"Who took a very incomplete statement from you," Alec observed.

"It wasn't his fault. I was telling him about finding the body and I suddenly felt awfully peculiar. I'm sure he would have gone on questioning me anyway if he hadn't already known I wasn't a suspect."

Piper snorted.

Recalling Tring's mention of Daisy's acquaintance with Rudolf Maximilian of Transcarpathia, Alec glanced again at the statement she had made last night. He frowned. No reference to the Grand Duke there, so at what point had they talked about him? After she turned "peculiar," had Tom let her stay on listening to the rest of the interviews?

If so, he was bloody well going to rap the sergeant's knuckles—except that Tom and Daisy would never give each other away, and Alec could not stoop to asking Ross. Especially as he himself had more than once been manoeuvred into the same misdemeanour.

"By the way, how is Mr. Tring's cold today?" Daisy asked, with the innocent expression which always made Alec suspicious.

"Much improved."

For some reason, she laughed. "Spiffing! Right-oh, Chief, that's all I have to tell you about yesterday, so now you can leave me to get on with my work."

"Not so fast," Alec said reluctantly. "Who was nice to Belinda and Derek may be irrelevant, but as Tom pointed out to me, you've been consulting these people for your article. You'd better tell me about them."

Daisy tried hard not to look smug. "Right-oh, Chief," she said again.

"Unofficial notes, Ernie. Let's go through them in the order in which Tom interviewed them." He reached for the file he had laid on her desk.

"Dr. Smith Woodward, Chief," said Piper, who had a phenomenal memory for anything to do with names or numbers, "Keeper of Geology. But he was with Miss Dalrymple when the incident occurred."

"Yes," said Daisy, "I can't see how he can have had anything to do with it. Besides, he's the epitome of the dedicated scientist, and though Pettigrew was pretty offensive to him, I don't believe he would waste precious time retaliating, even in words. He's twice broken limbs because he reads while he walks."

"Cor, honestly?" interjected Ernie Piper.

"Honestly. I heard it from more than one person. He wouldn't even go to hospital to—"

"Thank you, Daisy!" Alec cut her off. "Only evidence of some sort of incredibly complicated booby-trap could implicate Dr. Smith Woodward. Piper?"

"Mrs. Ditchley, Chief."

"Ah, yes, grandmother and ex-nurse. You're not telling me you knew her, Daisy."

"Not before. I talked to her quite a bit while we waited. But she's not a suspect?"

"She was very close to the scene. Tom didn't ask the children if she stayed with them the entire time, but as he says, we couldn't rely on their testimony where their grandmother is concerned. We'll have to investigate whether she had any link with the deceased."

"I suppose so. I'm pretty sure she didn't, and still surer that she wouldn't have killed him there and then, however good a motive she had, not with her grandchildren liable to run after her."

Daisy was going to argue that he should talk to the children anyway. It had dawned on her that she had really only asked the two eldest what they had seen. At least, only they answered, and she was not sure the younger ones were even attending to her questions. They might not have been attending to the toothy Megalosaurus either, so they could have noticed something Arthur and Jennifer missed.

But she doubted they would speak freely to a policeman, especially little Katy, whereas if Daisy just dropped in to ask after . . .

"Daisy?" Alec said in his patient voice, dark eyebrows raised. "Are you going to emerge from your trance? What about Miss Fellowes and Mr. Chardford?"

"I've never heard of . . . Oh, the young couple? I didn't exchange a single word with them. I'd say they were far too wrapped up in each other to care about anything else. Come in," she called as someone knocked on the door.

Mrs. Potter entered, panting, with cups and teaspoons rattling on a precariously balanced tray. Piper jumped up and took it from her to set it on the desk.

"Ta, ducks. I shoulda put the teapot in the middle. It's a mite early for elevenses, miss, but I thought you'd want a cuppa while the gentlemen are here. We're clean out of biscuits," she said reproachfully.

"Oh dear, I ate the last of them yesterday evening when I was waiting for my egg to boil. I'll buy some more today, promise."

"I could pop round the shops."

"That's all right," said Daisy, who had no intention of paying for the char's time while she "popped"—and gossiped. "We'll manage without, and you can have bread and jam with your elevenses. I'll buy something extra special to make up."

"Don't you go wasting your pennies on fancy biscuits, miss," Mrs. Potter advised. "Nothing but a boiled egg to your supper? Well I never!" She fixed Alec with an accusing glare and marched out.

"I'll take you out to dinner tonight, Daisy," said Alec, looking abashed.

"That will be spiffing, darling, but don't worry, I'm not starving. I was just too tired last night to cook. Lucy and I don't live entirely on eggs, cheese, and sardines since I started writing for the Americans."

"I don't want to keep you from your typewriter longer than I need. Let's get on with business."

"The Grand Duke Rudolf Maximilian of Transcarpathia," anounced Piper grandly, as Daisy poured tea.

Handing cups, she told them all about the gaudy but threadbare young exile and his grandfather's jewel. "He's pompous but rather pathetic, in a way. Pettigrew was really foul to him. I don't know if he (Rudolf) properly understands that he (Pettigrew) doesn't . . . didn't have the authority to turn over the ruby. He (Rudolf) honestly seems to believe he's entitled to it."

"So he could suppose a new Keeper of Mineralogy might be more accommodating," Alec mused. "Motive, opportunity . . . as yet we don't know enough about means. That's a big help, Daisy. We might easily not have tumbled to your Grand Duke's connection. Who's next, Ernie?"

"Sergeant Wilfred Atkins, Chief, the dinosaur gallery commissionaire."

"Is he a sergeant, too?" Daisy asked.

"D. C. Ross said lots of the commissionaires are ex-army, miss, and most of 'em sergeants. But all the

commissionaires in the east wing ground floor give each
other alibis, Chief."

"Any comment, Daisy?"

"The only one I talked to much was Sergeant Hamm, in
fossil mammals. In between quoting and misquoting the
Bible, he told me Pettigrew was perfectly beastly to Reg
Underwood, who lost a leg in the War."

"We don't know much about the means yet, but I
wouldn't say this was a one-legged man's crime. Pettigrew
was pretty hefty, Tom says."

"Yes, but all the commissionaires were sympathetic to
Underwood and loathed Ol' Stony, as they called Pettigrew.
Isn't it possible they might provide alibis for each other?"

"Possible," Alec agreed with a sigh. "We'll have to bear
it in mind, and also for the two assistants who claim to
have been together. Do you know them?"

"What are their names?"

Piper provided the names, and Daisy shook her head.

"I was introduced to them in passing, that's all. I don't
know of any particular motive, beyond the general one applying to all the fossil people, that is."

"Which is?" Alec asked, sitting up.

Daisy explained about the overwhelming scorn the Mineralogy Keeper poured on fusty old bones of no practical
or pecuniary value, and those who studied them. "It's hard
to see it as a reason for murder," she said, "though I know
it doesn't take much when tempers flare."

"I wish you had understood what Pettigrew said! If it
was extraordinarily insulting, it might have led to un-
premeditated murder. We don't know what he was doing
in the reptile gallery, whether he met his murderer by
chance, or had a rendezvous, which could mean premeditated murder. Great Scott, we don't even know what the
murder weapon was!"

"Dr. Renfrew'll know by now, Chief," Piper said.
"D'you want me to telephone?"

"No, Ernie, I'm just letting off steam. Let's get through

this list first. Did any of the museum staff have more particular reason to hate Pettigrew, Daisy?"

"Next on the list's not museum staff, Chief. Leastways, not that museum. A Mr. ffinch-Brown with two small *f*'s."

"The British Museum anthropologist," Alec recalled.

"He has quite a temper," said Daisy, "and he and Pettigrew were mixed up in a dispute over flint tools. Also, he feels that the Mineralogy Department's cut gems belong in his custody."

"Ah!"

Daisy and Piper looked at each other and grinned.

"What . . . ?"

"You sounded just like Mr. Tring, darling. The oracular 'ah.' I don't think I can tell you any more about ffinch-Brown. Who's next, Mr. Piper?"

"Mr. Mummery, Curator of Fossil Reptiles."

"He has an explosive temper, too. If he had a specific, personal reason to hate Pettigrew, I don't know of it. On the other hand, Pettigrew was killed in *his* gallery."

"Point noted. Ernie?"

"Mr. Witt, Chief, Curator of Fossil Mammals."

"Good-looking," said Daisy, "youngish, smart dresser, public-school, charming, helpful . . ."

Alec's brows met in a straight line above his grey eyes. "This is *not* helpful," he growled.

". . . ran a mile when I mentioned having Derek and Belinda with me," Daisy concluded her teasing list of Witt's attributes. "He was working with ffinch-Brown on the flint tool thing. Pettigrew bodily hauled him away to look at some flints when he was talking to me. He looked pretty fed up. It must have been rather humiliating."

"Aha!" said Alec.

Daisy chuckled. She nearly added that Tom Tring had got on very well with Witt, to the extent of joining him in a Latin music-hall turn. She remembered in time that she was not supposed to have been there.

"Mr. Steadman," said Piper, "Curator of Dinosaurs."

"He was very good with the children," Daisy recalled, "as well as helpful to me. He shared the general dislike of Pettigrew, but that's all, as far as I know. His disgruntlement was aimed at the museum's trustees, for not sponsoring a dinosaur-hunting expedition, and at the Americans for sending a model Diplodocus, not the real thing."

"So we'll know where to look when we find a dead trustee or a dead American on the premises," Alec said sardonically. "Do stick to the point, Daisy."

Daisy folded her hands and raised her eyes to the ceiling. "Any detail may prove significant," she quoted his oft-repeated maxim.

"Mr. Ruddlestone," Piper inserted hastily, "Curator of Inver . . . in-ver-tee-brates. What are they when they're at home, Chief?"

"Animals without backbones, Ernie, like so many petty criminals."

"Daisy darling?" The door swung open and Lucy appeared on the threshold. Alec politely stood up. "Oops, sorry, darling! What am I interrupting? Good morning, Alec. Or is it Chief Inspector today? You're looking rather official. How fortunate, Daisy, that you didn't fall for a uniformed policeman!"

"Good morning, Lucy," Alec said dryly. "I *am* official this morning, which is why I've brought D. C. Piper."

Lucy nodded to Piper, who had jumped to his feet when Alec rose, but she turned at once back to Daisy. "Good gracious, darling, what have you done now?"

"I suppose you don't know. You were out when I got home last night and up at some ungodly hour this morning."

"Yes, Lady Ashton wants her photos toot sweet and the tooter the sweeter, and they needed some delicate touching up. Darling, can you lend me half a crown for a taxi, or I shall be late."

"Not if I'm going to buy biscuits, and if I don't Mrs. Potter may quit."

"Horrors! And likewise blast and bebotheration!"

With a resigned air, Alec reached into his pocket. "Here you are, Lucy."

"Gosh, darling, thanks. I'll pay you back this evening—well, I'll give it to Daisy to give to you. Toodle-oo, I must run." Lucy *never* ran, but she had sauntered through the doorway and half closed the door when she stuck her head back in to say, "By the way, what is it I don't know?"

"A murder at the Natural History Museum," said Daisy bluntly.

"Darling, how too, too tiresome. You must tell me all about it later. Pip pip."

"Toodle-oo," Daisy responded as the door closed and the men sat down. "Don't worry, Alec, I shan't tell her more than I ought. Besides, she isn't really frightfully interested. Murder is vulgar. Where were we? Ruddlestone?"

"Yes. Do you know him, or did you skip the invertebrates?"

"For the first article I did, but they have to go into the *Dilettanti* article. Luckily Ruddlestone is enthusiastic enough about his field to make it sound interesting. Again, I don't know that he had anything more against Pettigrew than the general dislike. Pettigrew rubbed him the wrong way, but he didn't let it rankle."

"All right. That just leaves Dr. Bentworth, doesn't it, Ernie?"

"Right, Chief. Curator of Fossil Plants, retired."

"Blind as a bat," said Daisy. "If he tried to kill someone, ten to one he'd get the wrong man."

"You mean Pettigrew might not have been the intended victim?" Alec groaned.

"No, no, darling. Dr. Bentworth couldn't possibly have stabbed anyone, on purpose or by accident. You'll see as soon as you meet him, though, knowing you, you won't cross him off your list just because he's ninety."

"Certainly not," said Alec, grinning, "but he can sink to

the bottom. Mummery, ffinch-Brown, Witt, and the Grand Duke seem to have floated to the top. All right, Ernie, let's go and see them all."

"Right, Chief. 'Bye, Miss Dalrymple."

"Cheerio, Mr. Piper. I'm sorry you didn't get a biscuit with your tea."

"Never mind. Most places, we wouldn't even've got tea," said Piper philosophically. "Ta, miss, be seeing you." Tactfully he removed himself.

Alec leaned with both hands on the writing table. "Thanks, Daisy, you've given me some useful pointers."

"Loath though you are to admit it."

"Not at all! You won't go back to the museum, love, will you, till this is cleared up."

"I have to, Alec. I shan't go today—I've plenty to keep me busy at home—but I'm nowhere near finished with the Geology Department, and the deadline approaches."

"For heaven's sake, Daisy . . ."

"I've given my word," she said stubbornly. "They need the article. If I let them down, news will spread and no one will give me work. And don't tell me I shan't need to work when we're married!"

"I wouldn't dare! You know I don't expect you to drop your writing. But Daisy, if you really must go to the museum, please *try* not to talk about the case."

"I'll *try*," Daisy promised.

Seven

To her regret, Daisy had not been present when Grand Duke Rudolf gave his address to the police. He was not likely to turn up at the museum again, she thought. Not, of course, that if he did she would talk to him about the murder, having promised not to, but she might learn more about him.

One address Daisy had overheard, and it was an easy one to remember. Mrs. Ditchley lived in Balaclava Terrace, Battersea, just across the Thames from Chelsea.

Having stuck diligently to her typewriter till half past three, Daisy needed—no, *deserved*—a break. The sun had come out after what seemed like weeks of rain and overcast skies, so she decided to walk over the Battersea Bridge.

She stopped in the middle of the iron bridge to look at the sparkling river. A brightly painted narrow-boat hauled its train of barges downstream. From the shadows under the Albert Bridge appeared a pleasure steamer, puffing upstream, with few passengers on a weekday so late in the season, in spite of the warm sunshine. The trees of Battersea Park were already touched by autumn's hand, Daisy noticed, though lightly as yet. If she had had Bel's Nana with her, she would have been tempted aside from her errand to give the pup a run.

When she was married . . .

Walking on, she gave herself up to rosy daydreams, but without losing sight of her goal. She found Balaclava Terrace, a grim and grimy brick row backing onto one of the

railway lines which criss-crossed the industrial area.
Though outwardly grimy, the houses were respectably
dressed with white net curtains shrouding every window,
and front doors painted in vivid colours. They were larger
than most workmen's terrace houses, built for foremen and
factory clerks perhaps.

Mrs. Ditchley lived with her daughter and son-in-law at
Number 7. Daisy tapped on the vermilion front door with
the gleaming brass lion's-head knocker.

Katy opened the door, wearing a navy school uniform
gym slip. Her eyes opened wide at the sight of Daisy, then
she gave a shy grin and scampered away down a dark hall,
calling, "Granny, it's the museum lady. It's Miss Dimple."

Mrs. Ditchley emerged from the nether regions, swathed
in an apron bestrewn with large yellow flowers, Katy
hanging on her arm. With her came a smell of baking.

"Miss Dalrymple, how nice, come in. Katy gets out of
school at half past three, but the rest of the kiddies will be
home any moment, and I just put the kettle on."

"Oh, but I only dropped in to see if you've all recovered from yesterday's shock," Daisy protested, less than
sincerely.

"What a nasty business that was! Come in, dear, come
in, if you're not in a hurry, and we'll have a nice cup of tea.
There's jam tarts in the oven."

As Daisy stepped in, Mrs. Ditchley opened a door on
the left, through which was visible a glimpse of the front
parlour. Obviously rarely used, it was a stiff, chilly room,
wallpapered with roses in an unnatural shade of purple and
furnished with antimacassared Victorian horsehair furniture. An unhappy aspidistra in a brass pot lurked by the net
curtains. The only bright spot was a collection, on the
mantelpiece, of china figurines which looked from Daisy's
distance like Presents from Southend and Clacton-on-Sea.

The children were probably rigorously excluded from
the room. Daisy had no desire to be thus isolated.

"Mayn't I join you in the kitchen?" she asked.

Mrs. Ditchley beamed. "It'd be more convenient," she admitted, leading the way, "if you don't mind. The kiddies'll want their tea before they go out to play, and it's easier if I'm on the spot. My daughter works down the foundry, like her husband. They took women on during the War, when they were making munitions. It was a reserved occupation, but lots of the lads volunteered, and so many didn't come back, some of the girls stayed on after. She likes it, and the extra money comes in handy, and I'm here to mind the little ones."

The kitchen was quite large, taking up the entire back half of the ground floor, presumably designed for a servantless class for whom it was the main living room. Big windows with gay cotton-print curtains looked out on a small garden, full of washing hung to dry, and the railway. The centre of the room was largely taken up by a long, well-scrubbed table which showed signs of pastry-making at one end. On the gas stove, a kettle was beginning to steam.

"Nasty business yesterday," Mrs. Ditchley repeated as she poured water to heat the teapot. "But like I said, I was a nurse before I married and I went back when my daughter was grown, till the grandkiddies came along. I've seen worse in the hospital."

"I worked in a hospital during the War," said Daisy, "but in the office. What about the children? Has it upset them?"

"Not so's you'd notice. They're always seeing cowboys and Indians shooting each other dead at the pictures these days, aren't they? Except Katy here, she says she's never going back to that museum. Bustle about now, Katy, and lay the table for your brothers and sisters. First bring me one of the good cups and saucers for Miss Dalrymple."

Mrs. Ditchley somehow managed to make tea, take two trays of jam tarts from the oven, stir a pan, and turn toast under the grill all at the same time. Daisy was admiring; her attention tended to wander in the kitchen, so that disaster generally followed any attempt to do more than one thing at once.

Katy carefully brought her cup of tea.

"Not a drop spilled," Daisy congratulated her. "Were you afraid at the museum?"

"A bit," the child confessed. "Please, miss, was it the man with the loud voice which got killed?"

"He did have a loud voice," Daisy agreed. "There was no danger for little girls. You heard him, did you?"

"After he talked in a loud voice, he made a horrable noise and then there was a great big crash. Arthur says he fell in a skellington and it was all smashed to bits."

"Part of it was badly broken. Mrs. Ditchley, did you hear Dr. Pettigrew speak?"

"That I did not," Mrs. Ditchley said emphatically, "and there's nothing wrong with my hearing. But there, Katy was right by the archway. It was when I was going to fetch her back, not wanting to call out in the museum, I heard the crash and she came running back, naughty monkey."

"I didn't like them bones, Granny."

"Those bones."

"I didn't like those. I wanted to see the furry ephalunt again. It's nice."

"Times I've told you not to wander off alone!"

"Do you remember," Daisy started, when the front door slammed open. The three middle children rushed in like a herd of furry ephalunts, shedding coats, hats, and satchels en route.

"Gran, I'm hungry."

"Arthur went to the park to play football, Granny. Did you say he could?"

"I got all my sums right, Gran. What's for tea?"

"Now mind your manners! Here's Miss Dalrymple come to see us."

There was a momentary lull as they all said hello, and then the clamour began again, to be halted only by full mouths. Vast quantities of Heinz baked beans on toast disappeared, while Daisy nibbled a raspberry jam tart and debated whether it was worth trying to question Katy with the others present.

If she asked to see Katy alone, what should otherwise pass for common curiosity would begin to look rather odd. Mrs. Ditchley could well object, and the little girl might be frightened.

The children moved on to jam tarts. Mrs. Ditchley abandoned her post at the cooker, wiped clear a spot at the pastry end of the table, and with a sigh sat down with her cup of tea.

"What was it you were asking, Miss Dalrymple," she said, "when this noisy lot interrupted?"

"I wondered whether Katy heard what Dr. Pettigrew said just before the crash, and if she can remember."

"Bet she's forgotten," jeered her nine-year-old brother.

"She can too remember, Billy. Give her a chance. Go on, Kate," urged Jennifer, "what did he say?"

Katy swallowed a mouthful of sticky, flaky jam tart and announced importantly, "He said, 'You think you're so clever, but I know how it was done!'"

"That's right," Jennifer crowed. "That's what she told me before, just those exact words. Told you so. There was another bit first, though, Katy, remember?"

"Not 'xackly." A note of doubt entered Katy's voice.

"She told me, Miss Dalrymple," Jennifer persisted. "She told me when we were by the Megalosaurus waiting for Granny. She doesn't remember 'cause she didn't understand properly. Is it all right if I say it for her?"

Since Daisy was not bound by the rules of evidence regarding secondhand evidence, she eagerly assented, hoping the beginning would shed light on the cryptic end, perhaps even supply a name.

"'You fossil-eyed fool.' That's what he said, wasn't it, Katy?"

"Maybe." Katy was still dubious.

"Was it 'fossilized,' Katy?" Daisy asked. "'Fossilized

fool'?" That was the sort of cheap insult Pettigrew liked to
throw around.

"Maybe. I thought he said eyes. And fools." Her lips
trembled. "I don't know for sure. Granny, I don't know."

"Told you so!" Billy triumphed.

"William Albert, that's enough of that. Clear the table,
and you can help me wash up. I don't care if it's not your
turn. It doesn't matter, duckie, there's nothing to cry about.
Come to Gran, then."

"I'm sorry," said Daisy. "It's all right, Katy. Much better to say you don't know than pretend you do. Will you
tell me one more thing, if you know the answer?"

Katy raised her jammy face from Mrs. Ditchley's yel-
lowflowered bosom and nodded dolefully.

"You too, Billy, and Mary as well. Give me an honest
answer. Did any of you see anyone crossing the dinosaur
gallery while your granny was gone?"

Three heads shook in unison.

"I was looking at the dinosaur's teeth," said Billy re-
gretfully. "Was it the murderer, miss? Cor, I wish I'd seen
the murderer!"

"You get on with collecting up those plates sharpish,
young man," said his grandmother. "I've your mum and
dad's supper to cook yet."

"I must be going," said Daisy. "Thank you so much for
the tea and the delicious tarts."

Mrs. Ditchley set Katy on her feet, told Jennifer to wash
her sister's face, and accompanied Daisy to the front door.

"Are you working for the police?" she asked bluntly.

"Not exactly," Daisy temporized. "I thought it might
be easier for the children to talk to me rather than a police officer."

"Very likely," Mrs. Ditchley conceded.

"I can tell the police what they said, and maybe they
won't need to ask any more questions. You see, as a matter
of fact, it turns out that the detective in charge of the case
is my fiancé."

"Well now," said Mrs. Ditchley, her amused face lit by daylight as she opened the door, "what a coincidence!"

"Actually," Daisy confessed, "I believe he was put in charge because I'm mixed up in it."

"I wouldn't be a bit surprised, dear. You tell him from me, if he wants to talk to the kiddies, he'll do well to bring you with him."

"Thank you, Mrs. Ditchley. It doesn't sound to me, though, as if they saw or heard anything really useful."

"Thank heaven for small mercies," said Mrs. Ditchley.

Daisy was less grateful to heaven. Whatever her rationale, Alec was not going to be pleased by her meddling, but if she had had something significant to report he might have forgiven her more easily.

Sighing, she hoped tonight's dinner was not going to turn into an acrimonious argument.

Nonetheless, her heart sank when the telephone rang at half past five and Ernie Piper's voice replied to her recital of her number. "D. C. Piper, miss."

"Don't tell me," she groaned, "the Chief can't make it."

"He can, miss," Ernie anxiously reassured her, "but he says d'you mind going early and somewhere nearby. He'll pick you up at half six if that's all right. He hasn't got time to change. He's still got to see the an . . . an-thro-pologist and your Grand Duke this evening."

"*My* Grand Duke?"

"That's what Sarge calls him, miss." Piper's grin was audible. "I gotta run. What'll I tell the Chief?"

"Tell him right-oh, six-thirty."

Daisy was ready to go when Alec rang the doorbell at twenty-eight minutes past six.

He kissed her and said, "Thank heaven you're not one of those women who makes a man wait."

"If I were, I'd never see you. It's difficult enough already. If you're in a hurry, let's walk round to the Good Intent, in King's Road."

"I wouldn't mind stretching my legs, but isn't that an artists' haunt?" he asked with caution.

"Used to be. The Bohemians have abandoned it as old-fashioned, but it still serves good, cheap food, and quickly. A starving artist who's scraped together the price of a meal can't wait to be fed. How did it go at the museum?"

"I didn't learn much of significance," Alec said gloomily. "As Tom says, the place is a regular rabbit warren, connecting doors and back-stairs everywhere. Even with the plans, it took me an hour to sort it out. All the suspects could quite well have been where they claimed to be, but they also could have got to the reptile gallery and back without being seen."

"Does that mean you think Pettigrew had an appointment to meet someone there?"

"It's possible, but the murderer may have met him by chance."

"I can't see why Pettigrew should have been there by chance," Daisy objected. "He despised fossils."

"Witt suggested he might have been on his way to the General Library, perhaps to look up something about prehistoric flint implements. I gather he had recently developed an interest in the subject."

"Yes, that was what he was on about when he dragged Mr. Witt bodily from my side."

"Witt admitted to that incident. He claimed not to have taken offence. Pettigrew being such a mannerless boor, it would be a fruitless waste of energy."

"Fruitless to protest, I dare say," Daisy observed, "but he didn't exactly look as if he took being manhandled at all kindly."

Alec was equally sceptical. He neither trusted nor liked Calvin Witt, who appeared suspiciously eager to be of assistance. The Fossil Mammal Curator was too smooth, his manner suave, his hair sleekly pomaded. His face was too young for the years his curatorship suggested, especially as he was of an age to have fought in the War, which should have taken several years from his work experience. Or perhaps he had gained the position at an early age through family influence, which would not make Alec like him any the better.

It was *not* jealousy, Alec told himself. He must not succumb to the niggling worm which still now and then reminded him that he was ten years older than Daisy and not of her class. She had been joking when she described Witt as handsome and charming.

Alec looked down at her as they turned into King's Road. As if she felt his gaze, she glanced up, smiling happily, and slipped her hand through his arm. They might have been discussing sitting-room wallpaper, not a brutal murder.

He *ought* to be discussing wallpaper with her, not murder—but it was damnably difficult to avoid a topic in which they had a mutual interest.

He was about to change the subject when she said, "I suppose Ol' Stony could have been on his way to consult Witt about the flints. Or rather, to demand information. That was more his style."

"Yes, Witt actually proposed that possibility, too, though he seemed to think Pettigrew would be more likely to send for him. The route is the same as to the library. There are private stairs next to Pettigrew's office which go all the way down to the basement, but on the ground floor they debouche only into Smith Woodward's office. So Pettigrew would go either down the main stairs and through the mammal gallery . . ."

"In which case I would certainly have seen him."

". . . Or down the private stairs at the east end of the mineral gallery."

"And then through to the reptile gallery where he died," Daisy said. "Mummery's domain. How did your interview with him go?"

"You warned me he was explosive."

Alec made a funny story of Mummery's temper. The fossil reptile curator started out furious at having his work interrupted by police with nothing better to do than pursue the benefactor of humanity who rid the earth of Pettigrew. Especially as Pettigrew had ruined his Pareiasaurus, which, if repairable, would take months of hard work to restore.

Diverted to the question of what he was doing in the General rather than the Geological Library, he was provoked to another outburst: He was consulting an obscure German text comparing modern with ancient Crocodilia; it obviously ought to be in Geology but Zoology also claimed it, so it was relegated to General.

Asked to suggest why the mineralogist's corpse was found in his gallery, Mummery had snapped that he certainly did not belong there. He then embarked on an irate and very technical lecture on why—unlike Pettigrew—the dinosaurs did belong among the reptiles.

"So I gave up on him," Alec confessed ruefully, "for the present. Here we are."

He pushed open the door of the Good Intent. A pug puppy danced forward to welcome them to the small, quiet restaurant, its chequer-clothed tables mostly empty. While Daisy greeted the little dog, Alec glanced around at the once avant-garde paintings on the walls. One was a portrait of a smug pug with a violet ribbon round its neck, perhaps the present tutelary canine's predecessor.

Seated, Daisy gave her attention to the menu, which offered a solid rather than exciting choice. Selecting Scotch broth and shepherd's pie did not occupy her for long. Alec plumped for celery soup and Lancashire hot pot. By the time he had given the waitress their order, Daisy's thoughts had returned to the museum murder.

"Who else did you see? The commissionaires, I expect, and Dr. Smith Woodward, though he's out of it, and Dr. Bentworth, though he couldn't possibly have done it. What about Ruddlestone? He's far too cheerful to commit murder, isn't he?"

"Being under suspicion certainly didn't cow him," Alec said dryly. "Far from it. He presented us with his theory that detective work and palæontology have a great deal in common, in the painstaking following up of often insignificant-appearing clues. The notion amused him."

Daisy smiled. "He's easily amused, and quite amusing. You didn't winkle out any particular reason for him to hate Pettigrew?"

"No, nothing beyond the general dislike."

"And Steadman?"

"Again, nothing specific. He struck me as a nervy type, and the sort of chap to hold a grudge, but you were right, his animosity is directed at the museum trustees and at Americans who send plaster models instead of real fossils."

Their soup arrived. Daisy took a few spoonfuls in meditative silence, then said, "Perhaps Pettigrew jeered at Steadman about his biggest dinosaur being plaster, until it was beyond bearing. He was obnoxious enough about the uselessness of real fossils. I can't imagine what he might have had to say about a fake."

"I asked," said Alec. "According to Steadman, Pettigrew never said a word about the model because he didn't have a leg to stand on. The biggest diamond in the mineralogy collection is a fake."

Daisy laughed. "Oh yes, I'd forgotten. The Cullinan is paste. I have an appointment with one of Pettigrew's assistants tomorrow, Alec. Grange, his name is. You're not going to make a fuss, are you, darling? I really must get on with my research."

"That's all right, Grange and Randell are in the clear. They left on time and went together to the Crooked Elm in Old Brompton Road. They claim always to need a drink after a day with Pettigrew."

"Oh dear, no one mourns him, do they? At least, did he have any family?"

"He was a widower, with two grown sons. One's in the army, stationed in Ireland at present. The other's a solicitor in Truro."

"So you didn't have to break the news to them."

"No, thank heaven." Alec found informing bereaved relatives of a murder far more distressing than dealing with a corpse no longer capable of feeling pain. "The Truro police and the soldier's C.O. had to cope with that. Both sons are on their way, and I'll have to see them, but parricide isn't on the cards."

"Two fewer suspects to worry about," Daisy said blithely. "How was your soup?"

"Soup?" Alec looked down at his empty bowl, and confessed sheepishly, "I didn't even notice eating it. Or drinking it, if you prefer."

"Well, it can't have been too dreadful, at least. Eat or drink rather depends on whether it's thick soup or thin, I suppose. Supping is really the best word: to sup one's soup. A pity it's dropped out of use."

Over the second course they talked about language. Alec entertained Daisy with examples of eighteenth-century slang, picked up while studying the Georgian period at Manchester University. She blushed adorably when he reminded her that the little mole by her mouth was placed just where Georgian ladies used to stick the face-patch known as the "Kissing."

Had the A.C. meant it when he ordered Alec to marry Daisy with all possible speed? Would he really expedite leave, the difficulty of obtaining which being the main obstacle in setting a date?

Pondering, Alec fell silent over his Double Gloucester and biscuits. Daisy, engaged in demolishing a dish of Queen of Puddings, was too stickily occupied to talk.

He had got away without telling her much about the case, he congratulated himself. Then it dawned on him that she had not actually asked much, not even the claimed whereabouts of the suspects at the time of the murder. His uneasy suspicion of collusion between Daisy and Tom Tring reawoke. He nearly taxed her with it, but decided on the whole it was best to let sleeping dogs lie.

She remained quiet as he paid the bill and helped her on with her coat. Leaving the Good Intent, they turned down King's Road, past illuminated shop windows—many displaying artists' supplies, one or two showing artists' works—and an extraordinary number of pubs. They were passing a milliner's, filled with amazingly diverse variations on the basic cloche all women seemed to wear nowadays, when Daisy spoke.

"Alec, how was he killed? I've been putting off asking, because part of me doesn't really want to know."

"Then I shan't tell you."

"Do. Please do, darling. It can't be worse than the frightful things one imagines."

"No, maybe not. In effect, it was no different from any stabbing, but it's quite extraordinary, nonetheless. The pathologist found a sharpened flint in Pettigrew's chest."

Eight

A flint! Daisy's first thought was that she should have guessed. The second was, "But how did it get there? I mean, if he was stabbed with it, surely the whole thing couldn't have disappeared inside him—ugh! But you know what I mean. Enough should have stuck out to hold on to. Could it have been bunged with a sling or something?"

"Unlikely," Alec said. "Even if it hit hard enough to penetrate, according to our ballistics man, the odds against its striking the right spot point first are astronomical. Well, palæontological, anyway."

"Biblical, rather. Doubtless David could have done it," Daisy commented. "So you don't have to worry about delivery from a distance. Then how . . . ?"

"There's a dab of glue at the rounded end of the flint. We think it was stuck onto some sort of shaft to make a spear, or perhaps a dagger. The museum uses every glue known to mankind, but none makes a strong bond between wood and stone, apparently. When the shaft hit the skin—there's a suggestive bruise—the bond broke. The shaft came away, while the head stuck in the wound and impeded leakage of blood."

"Ugh!" Daisy said again.

"Sorry, love, but you did ask."

"Yes, I know. Does it mean Witt and ffinch-Brown are at the top of your list?"

"Not necessarily. Witt was messing about with flints in the work room behind the General Library. Anyone could have picked one up. But Pettigrew himself was experimenting with them, too. He might have brought it with him, perhaps to show Witt."

"Gosh," said Daisy, "I wonder if that's what he was talking about?"

"Talking about?" Alec said sharply. The lamppost at the corner of Mulberry Place illuminated lowered brows over glinting ice-grey eyes. "When?"

Daisy sighed. The moment of truth was upon her. Confession could no longer be postponed. Besides, Alec would probably go to see Mrs. Ditchley tomorrow, and she was bound to mention Daisy's visit.

"To start at the beginning, I called on Mrs. Ditchley this afternoon," she admitted, and crossed her fingers in her coat pocket before fibbing, "just to make sure she and the children had recovered from the shock."

"I trust they had?" His politeness had a dangerous edge.

"Oh yes," she said airily. "The children came home from school while I was there, and of course they wanted to talk about it."

"Of course. Without a single question from you."

"Do you want to know what they told me or not?"

"If you please." But leaning back against his Austin Chummy, Alec regarded her with unmistakable grimness. "Go on."

"It came out that Katy, the littlest, had wandered off from the others towards the arch to the reptiles. She didn't see anything, but she heard a man say, 'You fossilized fool, you think you're so clever, but I know how it was done!' He might have been referring to a flint he'd chipped himself, don't you think?"

"Possibly," Alec conceded. "It hardly seems so inflammatory a claim as to lead to murder, even prefaced by an insult. Are you sure of his words? Is the child?"

"Not exactly," Daisy conceded in her turn. She explained Jennifer's part in the reconstruction, and the uncertainty over the precise terms of the insult. "And of course there's no way to know for absolute certain whether it was in fact Pettigrew Katy heard. But, Alec, ffinch-Brown told me Pettigrew meant to challenge him to distinguish between genuine ancient flints and one he'd chipped himself."

"He did? Great Scott, Daisy, what else haven't you revealed yet?"

"'I tell thee everything I can. I've little to relate,'" Daisy misquoted the White Knight's song.

"I hope you're not going to produce another 'aged aged man,'" Alec said somewhat sourly. "Bentworth's as much as I can cope with. He fell asleep in the middle of our interview."

"I don't know of any more. But honestly, darling, you did rather rush me along, with Piper popping up with a new name every thirty seconds. At a more leisurely pace, bits and pieces have a chance to come to mind."

"Sorry!" He leaned forward and dropped a kiss on her nose, then checked his wrist-watch. "But I haven't time for leisure just now. I still have ffinch-Brown and your Grand Duke to see. Incidentally, Grange confirmed that the Grand Duke visits the Mineralogy Gallery several times a week, to stare at the ruby. Now what's this about ffinch-Brown?"

"Ffinch-Brown claimed to be confident of picking out a new-made flint tool, but what if he actually had doubts?"

"Then Pettigrew waving a flint he claimed to have shaped himself might well upset him. 'I know how it was done,' he said?"

"Yes, that part Katy was sure of."

"I'll have to tackle ffinch-Brown about Pettigrew's challenge. Thank you, love. If any more nuggets come to the surface, do write them down, will you? I must run."

He glanced up and down the street, pulled Daisy into his arms, and gave her a kiss which left her breathless despite its brevity. Before she could pull herself together, he had hopped into the Austin, pressed the self-starter, and tootled off.

"Whew!" said Daisy.

* * *

It was either kiss her or shake her, Alec thought ruefully as he drove towards the café where he had left Tring and Piper. He did not for a moment believe she had gone to Mrs. Ditchley's with nothing but sympathy in mind.

On the other hand, she might well have got more out of the children than any policeman could. Only last year the force had admitted it needed women officers, not just the grim guardians known as police matrons. In April, twenty female constables had been sworn in, but they were still inexperienced and whether they would ever be allowed to join the detective branch was doubtful. Still, someone must see Mrs. Ditchley and her flock tomorrow. He wondered whether he should go, or whether Tom would manage it better.

Picking up his troops, he drove on into Hyde Park and across the bridge over the Serpentine.

"My apologies to Mrs. Tring for keeping you out another evening, Tom," he said as Tom coughed cavernously. "That cold still doesn't sound quite vanquished."

"Seems to be worse evenings. I can't say I'm feeling up to par, but I'll manage."

"I'd let you go, but a certain retinue may help to gain the respect of a Middle-European grandee."

"Might help," Tring agreed sourly, "though what we really need is fancy-dress uniforms. Just wait till you see this laddie, Chief. Enough gold braid for half a regiment, though a bit moth-eaten."

"And he's living in lodgings in Bayswater," Alec reminded him.

"Poor bloke," said Piper unexpectedly, from the back seat. "Paddington Terrace, Bayswater, is no great shakes after a swish castle in a country where he was the top dog, even if it was a little tiny country no one's ever heard of."

"True, laddie," Tring rumbled, "too true."

"I just hope the Special Branch isn't interested in him,"

said Alec, stopping at the Victoria Gate before crossing the Bayswater Road. "Tangling with them once was enough. Paddington Terrace, Ernie?"

"Nineteen B, Chief."

Piper had an amazing memory for numbers, names, addresses, maps, and things of that sort. He provided directions through the maze of streets. Respectable late Georgian and early Victorian terraces had come down in the world, like the Grand Duke. Now divided into maisonettes or even odd rooms, by daylight they would reveal peeling paint and missing railings. Daisy and Lucy had shared a flat in Bayswater, Alec recalled, before moving to Chelsea, before he met her.

Number 19, Paddington Terrace, was not too badly run down. A half-barrel of bedraggled Michaelmas daisies attempted to bloom beside the front door. If the brass letterbox and knocker were tarnished, at least the door's dark blue paint was in good shape, as was what stucco was visible by the lamppost across the way.

There were two bell-pushes. The lower had a card drawing-pinned below it. Protected by cellophane, it said FERRIS in blunt block capitals. Above the upper bell, an unprotected card rather the worse for damp announced grandiosely:

TRANSCARPATHIA
Regierung in Exil.

"Government in Exile," Piper guessed as Alec rang the bell. "D'you reckon, Chief?"

"I do. Let's hope he hasn't got some kind of diplomatic immunity!" Alec held up his hand as he heard a door close somewhere inside. Heavy, halting footsteps descended stairs.

The door opened. Instead of a slim, fair young man, a grizzled veteran faced them. Within his ill-fitting uniform tunic, his large frame was gaunt, slightly stooped. Half-hidden by a grey, white-flecked cavalry moustache, a scar slashed across his hollow cheek.

Souvenir of a sword duel, Alec guessed. Dashing young Germans still went in for such proofs of manhood and bore the marks proudly.

But was this man the real Grand Duke? Had the young fellow led Daisy—and Tring—up the garden path?

"Detective Chief Inspector Fletcher of Scotland Yard, to see Grand Duke Rudolf Maximilian," he said noncommittally, presenting his warrant card.

A flame leapt in the other's eye, but he bowed slightly, stiffly, and said, "His Excellence expects you. Come."

The shared hall was cluttered with two bicycles and a pram. The shared staircase was dingy, its maroon flocked wallpaper unchanged in decades. Alec followed the limping Transcarpathian, and behind him came Tom, lightfooted, and Ernie, clumping a bit in his police boots but no longer thumping along like a copper on the beat.

In one of the ground-floor rooms, a baby began to wail.

The electric light went off as their guide reached the landing. It must be on a timer: another humiliation. Piper stumbled, muttered something fortunately indistinguishable.

The old man did not bother to press the switch. By the faint light from outside, coming through a high window, Alec saw him cross to a door. As he opened it, light spilled from an entrance hall scarcely bigger than a cupboard. The Transcarpathian opened an inner door to the right.

"Exzellenz, die Polizei," he announced in tones of ineffable disdain.

With no idea what to expect, Alec moved past him into the room.

The young man who stood on the hearth was a peacock in a world of sepia and grey. Every surface in the room, every spare inch of wall, was covered with photographs. Alec's gaze flickered over them, picking out Queen Victoria and the Kaiser, noting the cheap deal frames, before his attention returned to the peacock.

And the crow sitting near him in a shabby armchair, a sallow woman in black with a back as straight as a ramrod. Her regal carriage somehow transformed the old-fashioned wisp of black net covering her fading fair hair into a crown.

Did Grand Dukes/Duchesses wear crowns? How the dickens did one address them? Alec, a free Englishman though a commoner, was damned if he'd stoop as far as the subservient "Excellency."

Inclining his head in a courteous acknowledgment of the woman's presence, to which she failed to respond, Alec turned to the Grand Duke and said, "Good evening, sir. I'm Detective Chief Inspector Fletcher. I hope I shan't need to keep you long, but I have one or two questions to put to you."

"I told dis man everysing," the Grand Duke said petulantly, pointing at Tring. "Dis sergeant, he has not reported mine answers?"

"Detective Sergeant Tring has presented a full report, sir. It's a matter of routine for the officer in charge of a case to hear a possible witness's evidence for himself." Especially when new information had come to light—information which the young man might prefer not to have broadcast to his family and old retainers. "No need to disturb anyone else. Is there somewhere private we can go?"

The woman said something sharply in German. Rudolf Maximilian answered in the same language, his tone sulkily argumentative. The old soldier moved forward and interjected a few pacifying words.

The Grand Duke explained to Alec. "Mine muzzer, de Grand Duchess Elizaveta Alexandrovna, she wish to hear, but is not women's business, I say. Instead comes viz us mine Chancellor, General Graf Otto von Czernoberg."

Count Otto clicked his heels with a minuscule nod.

The Grand Duchess rose. *"Komm', Gertrud!"* she snapped, and swept from the room, followed by a pale girl in grey who rose from a table by the window, a book in her hand. Alec had not even noticed her, colourless but live, amongst all the photos.

"She believes not I am not longer child," said Rudolf Maximilian, glaring after them with a sullen, distinctly childish pout.

However, with the ladies out of the way, they quickly got down to business. On Alec's suggesting that they would be more comfortable seated, Grand Duke Rudolf ungraciously waved them to threadbare chairs, while he himself took a nervous perch on the arm of his mother's seat. Piper, in a corner by the door, unobtrusively took out his notebook and ever-ready pencil. Alec glanced at Tring.

"Now, sir," said the sergeant in an officious voice, "please describe for the Chief Inspector your whereabouts from five o'clock yesterday until the constable discovered you lurking behind—"

"I vas in de museum visiting! It is no crime, *nicht wahr, Herr* Inspector? You are a reasonable man." He cast a resentful look at Tring. "I was not *lurking.*"

"I expect the constable exaggerated," Alec soothed. "It's an interesting place, isn't it? You go often?"

The Grand Duke visibly dithered, and decided a lie would be too easily exposed. "Not often. Sometime. Here have I no affairs of state mine time to occupy."

"None, sir?"

"Little. I try mine contrymen to help, but vhat can I do vhen I have nozzing?" His gesture took in the room and the flat beyond, the chancellor who answered the door, perhaps the chancellor's wife in the kitchen, for all Alec knew. "Nozzing—only pictures to remind of past life."

"It's an unhappy situation," Alec sympathized. "I expect you would do anything for a chance to regain lost glories."

"Any—"

"*Vorsicht, Exzellenz!*" Count Otto warned. Alec silently damned him.

"I vish to fight," Rudolf said hotly, "to drive de Bolsheviks from Transcarpathia. But vizzout soldiers can I nozzing, and vizzout money, no soldiers."

"I wonder whether you could raise enough money to hire an army if you regained your grandfather's gift to Queen Victoria. How valuable is that ruby?"

"Ru—ruby?" faltered the Grand Duke.

Tom Tring's dry cough, intentional or not, was a masterpiece of skepticism. Clearing his throat, he proceeded in a toneless voice as if reading a report: "A number of witnesses attest to your frequent visits to the Mineralogy Gallery under the direction of the late Ralph Pettigrew, where you were observed to spend what several describe as an inordinate length of time studying the gem commonly known as the Transcarpathia ruby." He coughed again. "Sir."

"Oh, *dat* ruby," said the Grand Duke unconvincingly. "Vhat is 'inordanot'? I know not this vord."

"A purely subjective judgment," Alec put in, "a matter of opinion. It means longer than might be expected of anyone with no special interest in the object."

"Of course His Excellence has a special interest!" Count Otto barked. "As you know, this jewel was his grandfather's gift to your Queen, a magnificent gift, which Her Majesty choosed to discard to be gaped at by peasants. It is worth more than all that we were able to bring from Transcarpathia."

"And most of zat is sold by now," the Grand Duke bemoaned.

"If King George for the ruby no use has," the Chancellor continued, his hitherto excellent English deteriorating in his agitation, "why not give back where it is needed? Has not the Bolsheviks murdered his cousin, the Czarina? But is for the King to decide. How it helps us a museum fellow to murder? To imagine this is foolishness!"

True, Alec thought, but the question remained whether the Grand Duke was foolish enough to believe Pettigrew's death might help his cause. It was interesting that Count Otto, apparently more intelligent than young Rudolf as well as more experienced, had jumped to the conclusion that the police suspected his ducal master of murder.

"Greed isn't the only motive for murder," said Tring offensively. "The young gentleman had words with Dr. Pettigrew, that's common knowledge."

"Vords, vords!" cried the Grand Duke, à la Hamlet. "I talk viz him vun time, two time, yes, is true. But is no greed for vanting money for to save mine contry!"

"A bad choice of words, Sergeant," Alec reproved. He went on courteously to Rudolf, "To have words with someone, sir, means to quarrel. You and the late Keeper had a bit of an argument, I dare say."

"Dis man not like dat I look at de ruby, but he cannot stop. He is very rude, he shout, but I have not argumented. Vhy argument when he cannot stop me?" said Rudolf reasonably.

"But even if you didn't argue, I'm sure you must have been angry at his rudeness."

Rudolf flushed, but shrugged. "In England is many peeople rude to foreigners. Dis is vhy I not rush out when de police come in de museum."

Back to square one. "Ah yes," said Alec, "you were in the fossil mammal gallery. You went down from the mineral gallery?"

"Yes."

"Did you see Dr. Pettigrew there yesterday?"

"No! He vas not dere."

Pettigrew had been busy in his private office most of the afternoon, according to his assistants. He had not yet emerged when Grange and Randell left at five-thirty.

"So you did not leave the mineral gallery because Dr. Pettigrew chased you out."

"Nein! He cannot." The indignation was followed by a shamefaced glance at his Chancellor. "I am sometimes bored viz looking alvays at mine ruby. I decided to look at ozzer sings."

"Very understandable, sir. What time did you go downstairs?"

The Grand Duke thought he had reached the fossil mammals at about five-twenty, which agreed with Sergeant Hamm's recollection. He swore he had not left the gallery until the constable discovered him *not* lurking behind the Irish elk and sent him to the cafeteria.

Of course Hamm could not confirm that, having deserted his post to go and chat with the one-legged Underwood.

Count Otto escorted the three detectives downstairs, and closed the front door behind them with a firm click which said "Good riddance" as eloquently as a slam.

"Without the General's intervention, we might have got something out of him," Alec sighed as they climbed back into the Austin.

"Least we know they haven't got diplomatic immunity, Chief," said Piper, " 'cause the General would have said so straight out."

"Very true, laddie," Tring said approvingly. "Living in cloud-cuckoo land, aren't they, Chief, thinking they could throw the Reds out of their country if they had the ruby to sell?"

"I don't know what it's worth, but it doesn't seem likely," Alec agreed. "I'm not sure even the Crown Jewels would do it, but that doesn't make getting hold of the ruby less of a motive. I'm just not sure Rudolf Maximilian is naive enough to believe killing Pettigrew would help. I need to get hold of him without his watchdog—or his mother, who struck me as a formidable lady."

"Did you see that picture of her with the Czar, Chief?" Tring asked.

"No, but it doesn't surprise me. Her name is Russian, and I did see Queen Victoria and the Kaiser."

"They had King Edward and the Emperor Franz Josef up on the walls, too, and some others who looked sort of familiar."

"Hmm," said Alec, turning right on the Bayswater Road.

"Bearing in mind that the whole thing could be an elaborate hoax, a con-game to wangle possession of the ruby, I'm inclined to believe he really is . . . or was . . . the Grand Duke. If so, it may not be easy to get him on his own."

"I bet he goes back to the museum," said Piper, "now he knows we know about the ruby. He can't keep away from it, even if he sometimes gets bored hanging over it. And like as not he wouldn't take his mum or the old man with him."

"A good point, Ernie."

"Two in a row!" said Tring in a marvelling voice. "Now don't go getting above yourself, laddie. We can have the commissionaire keep an eye out for Rudolf, Chief, and let us know if he turns up. Pavett may be deaf as a post but he's not dumb."

"We'll do that. Now, ffinch-Brown. He was talking to Witt, the mammal man, in Witt's office, right, Tom?"

"Right, Chief. He left about five forty, went through the cephalopod gallery, then, he claims, on through the reptile gallery, without seeing Pettigrew nor anyone else, to the east pavilion. He stayed there, studying a giant sloth—would you believe it?—till one of the Chelsea constables found him. Very excitable gentleman."

"Like Mummery, I gather. Bad luck to have two of them in one case."

But when they called at Mr. ffinch-Brown's modern villa on the golf links in Perivale, they found a quite different character from the one Daisy and Tom had described. At home, the anthropologist was a subdued little man.

For this, Alec guessed his wife to be responsible. That ffinch-Brown had married above his station was obvious, the ffinch likely being added to plain Brown on his marriage. His smartly marcelled wife had what Ernie later referred to as a posh accent. Though not openly imperious, she evidently expected to be deferred to, and to be present at the interview. At this stage in the investigation, Alec did not even attempt to exclude her.

Under her eye, ffinch-Brown repeated unchanged his

description of his movements the previous evening. He admitted to a scholarly difference of opinion with Pettigrew.

"But scholars are always prone to differences of opinion," he said mildly, pushing his spectacles up on his nose. "That is how knowledge increases, Chief Inspector. I had not the least doubt of my ability to pick out any flint Dr. Pettigrew shaped with his own hands from any number of genuine ancient artifacts. The case is not at all similar to the dispute over bone harpoons in which Dr. Smith Woodward is unhappily enmeshed, far less the Piltdown controversy."

Fearing a technical lecture on the difference, and unable to see how bone harpoons could possibly figure in his enquiry, Alec hurriedly moved on. "I believe you also differed with Dr. Pettigrew over the gems in his collection, sir?" he said.

Ffinch-Brown flushed, opened his mouth, glanced at his wife, and gave a nervous titter. "That was a matter for the museum trustees," he explained, as much to her as to Alec. "Neither Pettigrew nor I have . . . had any say as to which department should hold the finished jewels, so though we disagreed, there was no cause for ill feelings."

"I should hope not," Mrs. ffinch-Brown pronounced decisively. "Ill feelings have no place in academic circles, which ought to be dedicated to the pursuit of knowledge."

"They are, my dear. We are."

"You will undoubtedly find, Chief Inspector, that Dr. Pettigrew's assailant was an outsider."

The words were a dismissal. The detectives left.

"We can always catch him at the British Museum," said Alec. "In the meantime, we'll have to get the murder weapon to a disinterested expert and find out if it's ancient or modern."

"What I don't see," said Piper as they drove east, "is why a lady like that'd marry a man like that. Anyone can tell she's a nob and he isn't. He's not even good-looking. Looks like a farmer with them scrappy whiskers."

"P'raps that's the best he can do in the way of an academic beard," Tring suggested. He paused to cough hollowly, then went on, "I dare say, when she was a girl, she got bored with all the young nobs without two thoughts to rub together. Can't you just see him, young and eager, 'dedicated to the pursuit of knowledge,' like she said, sweeping her off her fashionable feet?"

"She's got him under her thumb now, all right," said Piper.

Alec could not avoid comparing the ffinch-Browns to himself and Daisy. Would Daisy grow disillusioned with her middle-class husband and try to remake him to suit? The doubts he was never quite able to banish raised their heads. Together with the difficulty of getting leave, they had made him delay even discussing a date for the wedding.

The leave question was no longer a valid excuse.

He dropped Tom and Piper at a tube station and drove home to St. John's Wood. His mother had already gone to bed, leaving hall and landing lights on for him. Shoes in hand, he crept up the stairs.

"Daddy?" came a sleepy voice from Belinda's room.

"Did I wake you, sweetheart?" He went in and sat on the edge of her bed.

"No, I woke up anyway, then I heard the car and the door. Daddy, is it true someone was murdered at the Natural History Museum? One of the girls at school said."

"Yes, I'm afraid so. One of the staff, not a visitor."

"Oh." She sounded relieved. "Who was it? Aunt Daisy knows lots of them."

"Dr. Pettigrew."

"Isn't he the stone man? I'm sorry it was him. He was nice to me and Derek . . . Derek and me, though he was perfectly horrid to the Grand Duke. Poor man! Will you find who did it?"

"Of course, pet," Alec assured her, though so far he felt he was floundering in mud to the waist, without solid ground in sight. He bent to kiss her. "Nighty-night, sleep tight."

"Mind the bugs don't bite," Bel responded drowsily.

He turned at the door to look at her. She was already fast asleep. She had no doubts of his competence. Nor, he reminded himself, of the rightness of his marrying Daisy.

Sam Johnson described a second marriage as the triumph of hope over experience. He was talking about a bad first marriage, though, and Alec had been very happy with Joan. Yet to be lucky twice seemed too much to hope for.

All life was a gamble, he reminded himself. If Daisy was prepared to take a gamble on him, then how could he not reciprocate?

Besides, he couldn't live without her, even when her interference in a case was driving him round the bend.

She was not interfering, Daisy assured herself. She could hardly interview the victim's senior assistant in the victim's private office without making some reference to the deceased. And it would be rude to cut him off in the middle of his account of Pettigrew's determination to master flint-flaking and his malicious triumph in his growing success.

At last Grange exhausted the subject. Daisy embarked on her questions about the work of the Mineralogy Department, and Grange suggested they should go along to the gallery to look at specimens.

For the first time in ages, the sun was shining. Brilliant light flooded through the tall windows on the south side of the gallery, lighting dancing dust-motes and gleaming on polished wood and glass. The fishy mouldings on the rectangular pillars stood out in sharp relief.

With measured steps, Pavett patrolled the gallery. There were few visitors, several school parties having cancelled trips because of the murder, Daisy gathered. But over by the windows, the sun picked out a pale blue uniform garnished with a surfeit of gold. The Grand Duke was leaning over the display case that held the ruby.

"Dash it!" Grange exclaimed. "He's back. I'd better go and see what he's up to. Excuse me a minute, Miss Dalrymple."

Naturally Daisy followed. At the sound of their approaching footsteps, Rudolf Maximilian looked up with a frown. He beckoned imperiously and Grange hurried.

"You work here, *nein?* Come, see mine ruby."

"Not yours," Grange muttered half-heartedly, bending over the case.

Catching up, Daisy saw that the Transcarpathia ruby was in full sunlight. The stone cast a pool of red light, all too reminiscent of blood.

Grange straightened, his face pale. "That's not beryllium aluminium silicate," he gasped, with an accusing glare at the Grand Duke. "That's paste. Strass glass. What have you done with the ruby?"

Nine

"Don't touch!" Alec commanded.

Much to Daisy's relief, he had miraculously appeared in the mineral gallery just as Grange made his accusation and pulled his bunch of keys from his pocket. A uniformed constable now stood by the iron-grated entrance. Tom Tring had gone first to the commissionaire, notebook in hand, then joined Ernie Piper in approaching each visitor and asking them to leave.

"Are you certain it's not the real thing?" Alec continued.

"Fairly certain," Grange said grimly. "It's not easy to tell with the naked eye, but with the sun full on it, I ought to be able to see the 'silk.' I can't."

"Silk?"

"Rutile inclusions." The explanation left his listeners none the wiser. "A closer look will settle the matter."

"To me appears it not right," put in the Grand Duke. "Mine muzzer and mine sister had once many gems. I know how should look, how should sparkle."

"I bet you do," snapped Grange, "since you pinched it."

The Grand Duke drew himself up stiffly to his full height. "If you was nobleman," he declared, "I meet you at dawn. In Transcarpathia, I take the horsewhip."

Alec shook his head. "Here in England, you could sue for slander, but I don't advise it. I suggest you watch what you say, Mr. Grange. I came up here to speak to the Grand Duke, but now I shall want a word with you, too."

"So do I," said Daisy. "We were just getting going. Can I have him first?"

"Sorry, I want a definitive answer on the ruby right away. At least, as soon as Sergeant Tring has checked it for fingerprints. The case too, Sergeant, before it's opened, though I imagine the cleaners have wiped off any evidence. By the way, Mr. Grange, just how valuable is the real Transcarpathia ruby?"

"I couldn't put a current retail value on it, Chief Inspector. We don't deal in such matters. I can tell you this: It is considerably larger than most gem-quality rubies, but not of the most favoured Burmese pigeon-blood colour, and with rather more silk than is generally thought desirable."

"It is very fine, of first quality," shouted the Grand Duke.

"I dare say, sir," said Alec pacifically. "Now, I'd like you to come down to the Director's office with me."

"Do you want to use the Keeper's office, Chief Inspector?" Grange asked. "No one's there now. Here's the key."

Accepting the key, Alec went off with Rudolf Maximilian, looking tempestuous and Middle-European, and Piper. He left the uniformed officer guarding the entrance, Daisy noted. He had not gone so far as to make her leave, though.

"Would you mind answering a few questions, Mr. Grange, while Sergeant Tring works his magic?" she said, as Tom blew powder over the display case.

Grange obliged, though rather distractedly. They moved away from the ruby case to look at some other displays, but both kept half an eye on the sergeant's actions. When he straightened after peering closely at the results of his powdering, they were both ready to dash back.

"What have you found?" Daisy asked.

Tom threw her a quizzical glance, but answered. "A few dabs on the glass and this front edge of wood, probably just visitors, including the Grand Duke. Nothing on or near the lock. Can you open it up, sir, without touching this area here? I haven't got my camera with me so we don't want 'em messed up."

"We wear gloves to handle polished stones." Grange took a white cotton pair from a pocket, put them on, and delved again for his keys. As he unlocked the case and cautiously raised the glass top, he said, "It *must* be that foreigner who made the substitution—after all, he claims the ruby is his. But supposing it wasn't, I can't help wondering if it's the only stone missing."

"I'm sure the Chief Inspector is considering the possibility, sir, but we'll just make quite sure you're not mistaken about the ruby first, shall we, before we look any further. Just a moment while I check it for dabs."

The red gem, real or fake, was as immaculate as its sheen proclaimed, with no sign of a fingerprint on any surface. Grange polished off the powder with a soft cloth, stuck a glass in his eye, and held up the stone to the sunlight, turning it this way and that. Daisy held her breath.

"Paste," he said flatly. "No dichroism, no rutile or other characteristic inclusions, only the round bubbles typical of glass."

There was a moment's silence. Then Tring said, "Have a look at the rest of 'em, sir."

"I will, and at the other gemstones. But lots of them I can't be sure of without the refractometer. I'll fetch it up from the work room."

Daisy saw her article disappearing into limbo. A glimpse of the work room would be something to go on with. "I'll go with you," she proposed.

"You do that, Miss Dalrymple," said Sergeant Tring. "I'll just have a word with the constable there."

He headed for the entrance while Grange led the way to the east end of the gallery and unlocked a door on the left. Behind the wooden door was another of solid steel, now folded back against the wall.

"That's locked and barred at night," said Grange, "and only our museum police sergeant has the key."

He continued down a narrow staircase. On the landing at the bottom of the first flight, halfway between the first and ground floors, a room opened off to the right. There, amid bookcases, shelves of rocks and pebbles, maps and diagrams of geological formations, and battered work-tables laden with gadgets, they found the second mineralogy assistant.

Grange explained what was going on, then picked up a smallish instrument and a reference book, and turned to go. His junior moved to join him.

"I'll stay for a bit, if you don't mind," Daisy said quickly. Work before pleasure, alas. "Perhaps Mr. Randell wouldn't mind explaining some of this stuff to me?"

"Yes, do help Miss Dalrymple, there's a good chap," said Grange, departing.

Obviously wishing himself upstairs sharing the excitement, Randell hurriedly answered Daisy's questions, showed her specimens and demonstrated equipment. Daisy, just as eager to know what was going on in the mineral gallery, was soon satisfied.

"Sergeant Tring hasn't got his camera with him," she said. "I'm sure he'd appreciate the loan of yours, to photograph fingerprints."

"Of course," Randell agreed eagerly, glad of an excuse to go with her. Bearing camera, tripod, plates, and one of the ubiquitous bunches of keys, he ushered her back up the stairs.

During her absence, Alec had returned to the gallery, with Piper but without the Grand Duke. The constable still guarded the entrance, and Sergeant Jameson was just arriving. Half a dozen display cases were open. Near one of them, the detectives stood around a bench where Grange slumped, his head in his hands. Pavett, unheeded, continued his fruitless patrol, casting frequent anxious glances at the knot of men. Daisy came to a halt slightly to Alec's rear.

Sergeant Jameson strode in, crying, "What's this, sir? That foreigner's pinched the big ruby?"

"It's gone," said Alec, "but I have absolutely no evidence on which to hold the Grand Duke, especially as most of the rest of the unset precious stones are missing."

"Oh lor'!" groaned Jameson. "On my watch, too!"

"Mine," Grange wailed.

"Now that's what I'm trying to find out." Alec's patience appeared to be wearing thin. "How soon would the substitution of paste gems be noticed? It seems Mr. Grange needs a machine to tell the good from the bad."

Grange was beyond lucidity. Randell spoke for him.

"Ages, to be frank. We can go for weeks without any reason to examine the stuff on display in the gallery. It's for the public, and not many of them know anything. Occasionally, we get accredited experts coming to take a look. We open up the cases for them, of course."

"How long since you did that?"

"Weeks. A couple of months, at least."

"Would you know if Dr. Pettigrew had shown anyone the jewels more recently?"

"Not necessarily," said Randell, shaking his head.

Daisy put in her twopenn'orth. "Dr. Pettigrew opened one case and let Belinda and Derek hold a couple of opals."

Alec had not hitherto noticed her presence. His mouth tightened in exasperation. "The opals have not been stolen," he said irritably. "It seems they are virtually impossible to imitate. What you are saying, Mr. Randell, is that weeks can pass without any of the mineralogy staff so much as glancing at the contents of the cases?"

"Glancing, yes, especially when lecturing to parties of visitors. Examining, no. What's on display has already been thoroughly investigated. Besides, as you've seen, for the most part it's practically impossible to tell good strass glass from the real thing without instruments. A large ruby in bright sunshine . . ." He shrugged. "What are the chances of someone knowledgeable happening to look when the sun happened to strike it?"

"So the theft could have occurred weeks ago," Alec sighed. "I must telephone my superintendent."

"The Director will have to be told," said Grange unhappily. "He's at a symposium in Cambridge."

"I'll have someone at the Yard try to get hold of him," Alec offered, and he went off to the Keeper's office.

Tring gratefully accepted the loan of the camera and started photographing fingerprints. Ernie Piper, intercepting the worried commissionaire, tried to explain with gesture, paper, and pencil what had happened. Grange and Randell muttered together.

"It was that Grand Duke done it," Sergeant Jameson said to Daisy.

"I doubt it. Actually, he drew Mr. Grange's attention to the ruby in the first place."

"That'd be a ruse, miss, so's people'd think like you. Knowing it'd be found gorn in the end, see, and everyone'd suspect him right away, because of him claiming it's his."

"Well, if I'd stolen a ruby, I wouldn't keep going back and laying claim to the substitute. Besides, lots of other jewels are missing, too."

"So we don't notice the ruby special, miss," Jameson explained earnestly. "It's another ruse. They're cunning, these foreigners. Specially the Huns."

As an example of muddled reasoning, that took the biscuit. Jameson would never make it into the plainclothes branch, Daisy decided. Nevertheless, she persevered.

"It seems to me it must have been a museum employee," she said. "None of the cases was broken open, and only they had access to the keys."

"Skellingtons," said the sergeant darkly.

Daisy's mind flew momentarily to the fossils down below, especially the Pareiasaurus Pettigrew had wrecked in dying. Was there a connection? Then she realized, "Oh, skeleton keys. I suppose it's possible. But surely the theft couldn't have taken place during opening hours, and the

Grand Duke couldn't have got in when the museum was shut."

"Could've hid, couldn't he? I mean, the night shift patrols the whole building, but it's a big place, you can't look everywhere with just a sergeant and two constables on duty, and the lighting in the basement's something chronic. So I reckon the Grand Duke hid hisself at closing time—not in here, prob'ly, 'cause we check in here pretty thorough before we lock up—but if he's got skellington keys for the cases he could have one for the big gate, too. See?"

He beamed when Daisy conceded he had made a persuasive case for the Grand Duke obtaining access. She did not bother to tell him she still failed to believe Rudolf Maximilian would have drawn attention to the false ruby if he were the thief.

Alec returned, looking harried, and went to confer with Tring. Piper joined them, then Alec and Piper haled Grange and Randell off to the interrogation chamber. Tring came over to Daisy and the sergeant.

"Here's a pretty how-d' ye-do!" he said. "Mr. Jameson, the Chief Inspector'd take it kindly if you'd get him a list of all the coppers seconded to the museum, and he'd like a word with you when he's finished with them two in there."

"Right you are, Mr. Tring. Only thing is, with one of my men posted at the entrance here . . ."

"Don't worry about that. Detective Constable Ross is on his way and he'll take over there. Oh, and Mr. Fletcher wants the keys to the doors to this gallery. It'll have to be locked up till further notice, I'm afraid."

"No skin off my nose. Er, Mr. Tring, the Chief Inspector doesn't blame *us,* does he?"

"You do the best you can with what you've got, don't you?" Tom Tring said, a trifle evasively to Daisy's ears. "He might have a suggestion or two about safety measures after he's talked to you and seen what's what."

Looking as unhappy as Grange, Jameson trailed off.

"Does the Chief blame the museum police?" Daisy asked. "For not preventing the robbery, that is. I don't see how he can for the murder."

"Not to say blame. Time enough for recriminations when we know how it was done. Now, Miss Dalrymple, the Chief says he hopes you're done here for today and he won't keep you, but seeing when the discovery was made you were on the spot . . ."

"As usual," put in Daisy with a sigh. "I bet he said 'as usual.'"

Tring twinkled at her. "That'd be telling. He wants to talk to you about just what was said between the Grand Duke and Mr. Grange before we arrived. He'll ring up when he's done here—no knowing when that'll be, I'm afraid—and he'll come round to your house."

"Tell him 'right-oh,' please, Mr. Tring. I'll be there."

"Cheer up. He could have told me to take a statement from you."

"Thus depriving himself of a chance to tick me off," said Daisy gloomily.

Walking homeward, she started to wonder again about a possible connection between the theft and the murder. It seemed altogether too much of a coincidence that the burglary in the Mineralogy Gallery should be uncovered within a couple of days of its Keeper being bumped off. The obvious answer was that Pettigrew died because he had noticed the substitution of false for real gems.

Yet if so, why had he not reported the theft to the police? He could have rung up on the telephone in his office. Or supposing he wanted to go in person to the museum police post, the direct way was through the fossil mammal gallery, not the reptile gallery.

Had he somehow worked out who the thief was? Had he arranged to meet him among the reptiles (an unlikely spot, Daisy thought, unless Mummery was the villain), or had he been on his way to confront the culprit and happened to encounter him?

Either would point to someone in the Geology Department being the cause of his sudden death.

What exactly had his last words . . .

"Watch out, miss!" A helpful hand jerked Daisy back from sudden death beneath the wheels of an omnibus.

She decided to postpone further pondering until she reached the quiet streets nearer home, but Pettigrew's words, as reported by Katy and Jennifer popped into her head: "You think you're so clever, but I know how it was done." They had assumed he was referring to the flint-chipping business, but he might equally well have meant the theft of a fortune in jewels.

Or the thief, labouring under a guilty conscience, might have thought so.

Daisy wished she knew whether the flint which killed Pettigrew had been shaped by his own hand or that of some Neolithic hunter. Had the weapon which killed him been wrested from him in a panic or brought to the meeting with malice aforethought? Or had the murderer happened to have it on him when he met the mineralogist, which would point inexorably to Witt or ffinch-Brown?

Not ffinch-Brown. His involvement with fossils was peripheral, and Pettigrew had addressed his assailant as a fossilized fool—or something similar. The murderer was surely someone in the Geology Department.

And the thief?

With this question as unanswered as the rest, Daisy somehow reached home unsquashed. She found Lucy down in the kitchen, heating up tinned oxtail soup for lunch.

"Mmm, that smells good. I'll make some toast."

"Not for me, darling. Mrs. Potter brought me a biscuit with my elevenses tea and I actually ate it. I shan't be able to get into any of my clothes."

"That's the trouble with being fashionable." Daisy took out a loaf and cut a couple of slices, saying defensively, "I shan't butter them. Darling, what do you know about Queen Vic and rubies?"

Lucy, though she had defied her family to take up a career in photography, remained much more interested than Daisy in the customs and quirks of the upper echelons of society. "Queen Victoria and rubies?" she said. "What on earth . . . ? Oh, is it something to do with your dashing Grand Duke? Daisy, he isn't mixed up in the museum murder, is he? Too, too frightful!"

"Sort of." The newspapers would undoubtedly report the jewel theft tomorrow, if not this afternoon, but she didn't want Alec to be able to blame her for breaking the news. "I'd just like to know a bit more about the subject."

"There speaks the dedicated writer—all is grist to her mill. I know she was given a couple of famous rubies. One once belonged to the wife of the Indian rajah who built the Taj Mahal. An emperor, I think, not a mere rajah, but it wasn't he who gave it to the Queen."

"Hardly. The Taj Mahal was built centuries ago."

Lucy sniffed. And sniffed again. "Your toast's burning."

"Oh blast! It's rescuable if I scrape it. Is the soup ready?"

Stirring, Lucy said, "Not quite. The other ruby I've heard of was given by a maharani who was presented at Court. My grandmother still fulminates about the impropriety of presenting natives at the Court of St. James."

"I dare say. What happened to the rubies?"

"The Queen left that one to the Duchess of Albany, who left it to Princess Alice. She often wears it, as you'd know if you read the right magazines. As far as I know, Queen Mary has the other one."

"Victoria didn't give any away during her lifetime, though?"

"Not that I know of. It is odd that she disposed of the Transcarpathia ruby to a museum, especially as it was given to her by a European ruler undoubtedly distantly related."

"They all are," Daisy agreed, sitting down at the kitchen table as Lucy ladled soup into bowls. "It's hardly surprising Rudolf Maximilian resents the rebuff and wants it back, quite apart from his need for money."

"I'll see if I can find out any more," Lucy offered. "Gosh, darling, don't let me forget I owe your Alec half a crown. Lady Bitherby wants a portrait in a new gown this afternoon and she's usually pretty good about paying on the spot."

After lunch, Daisy went to her study, with the noble intention of typing up the latest lot of shorthand notes for her article. Fingers poised over the keys, she stared blankly at her notebook for several minutes.

It wasn't that she could no longer read her own shorthand, though she sometimes wondered if that moment would come. Her mind was not on the doings of the Mineralogy Department, but on what had been done to it, to its keeper and its collection. She decided to write down the chain of reasoning she had followed on her way home. Putting it into black and white ought to clarify her thoughts, and it just might be of some use to Alec.

The exercise failed to provide any brilliant insight or inspiration. She set it aside and got on with her work.

Just when Daisy was beginning to long for a cup of tea and to wonder if Mrs. Potter had left any biscuits, the doorbell rang. Rushing to finish the sentence she was in the middle of, she heard Lucy go to answer the door.

"Ah, the debt collector," Lucy drawled. "Daisy told you I expected to be paid today?"

"I raced round at once," Alec responded lightly.

"Daisy's typing away, judging by the rattle. I'm on my way to put on the kettle for tea. Will you have a cup?"

"Yes, please. I didn't manage any lunch today."

"I can take a hint. Scrambled eggs? Come on down to the kitchen, if it's not too infra dig for a Chief Inspector. Daisy will come as soon as the kettle whistles."

Daisy was glad to hear them on such friendly terms. When she took up with a middle-class policeman, Lucy had been almost as sticky as the Dowager Viscountess, and there had been a memorable row or two.

Reaching the end of the paragraph, she went to join

them. The kettle was burbling happily to itself, butter sizzled in a frying pan, and Lucy was whisking eggs in a bowl while Alec kept an eye on the bread toasting under the grill. He looked tired, Daisy thought. Perhaps a meal would restore his energy.

As the burble rose to a screech, she took charge of the tea-making.

"Darling, I was just going to tell your pet copper about the Transcarpathia ruby," said Lucy. Pouring the eggs into the pan, she did not notice Alec's dismay, or his positively inquisitorial look at Daisy. "I popped in to see Aunt Eva. She knows absolutely all there is to know about royalty."

"I just wondered why the Queen gave it away," Daisy said defensively.

"It seems your Grand Duke's grandfather was a boon companion of Bertie's—King Edward's. He thought it very funny that the ruby once belonged to a famous courtesan, and when he presented it to Queen Victoria, he was so unwise as to make a little joke about it. Needless to say, our good Queen was Not Amused. She gave it to the museum even before he left the country, which I must say I think was a bit thick. Do you like them runny or set, Alec?"

Alec opted for set. When he had eaten, he and Daisy took their second cups of tea up to the sitting room. This was furnished with an eclectic mixture of furniture from Daisy's and Lucy's family homes. It was all good, but as Daisy had chosen with an eye to comfort and Lucy to elegance, and the upholstery had been intended for different houses, the overall effect was a bit of a hodgepodge. The bookcase and its contents were Daisy's, the Beardsley prints Lucy's.

"I didn't tell Lucy about the robbery," Daisy said as Alec sank into a deep, leather-covered wing chair abstracted from the library at Fairacres. "The Grand Duke is mixed up in the murder, too, remember."

"How can I forget?" Alec said wearily.

"Do you think they're connected? By more than Pettigrew being Keeper of Mineralogy, I mean."

"Unlike Superintendent Crane, I'm not convinced. If not, it would be quite a coincidence admittedly, but coincidences do happen. The flint Pettigrew was killed with has been identified by an independent expert as a modern copy. He laughed like a hyena, by the way, over its having been glued to a shaft. Primitive man used to bind them together, apparently."

"Mr. Ruddlestone would doubtless call that an educated deduction not much advanced from guesswork. I'm sure there is an expert somewhere prepared to swear they were always stuck together with sap, or pitch, or something. Still, whatever Pettigrew did with it, he made it, so he was probably taking it to show to Witt."

"Probably. I haven't had a chance to consider the implications thoroughly." He rubbed his eyes. "Only in the disjointed way one does during a wakeful night. And now there's this blasted jewel theft to be dealt with, too. Though I appreciate your discretion about that, incidentally, it'll be in the later editions of the evening papers. You might as well tell Lucy."

"What are you doing about it?" Daisy asked.

"Setting up the usual routine. That is, we get a descriptive inventory of what's missing, notify jewellers, pawnshops, and customs, and put pressure on known fences; we interview all the security staff to find out whether they've noticed anything out of the ordinary; and we investigate whether any of the suspects have a particular need for money, or have suddenly improved their standard of living."

"Gosh, all that must take an army!"

"Crane's given me every man he can spare, in and out of uniform, because of the probable connection with the murder. It takes a lot of organizing. And of course, I have to interview the suspects. I must get moving, Daisy." He drained his cup. "Tell me what happened this morning before I reached the scene."

"You're not cross because I was there when the theft was discovered?"

With a rueful grin, Alec reached for her hand. "I've decided it's Fate, with a big *F*. You can't help being on the spot. I can't stop you. And Tom—blast his cheek!—reminded me that I'd never have met you if it wasn't for your propensity for falling over bodies."

"Bless him!" said Daisy, but added indignantly, "When we met, that was the first crime I'd ever been even remotely mixed up in. The 'propensity' developed afterwards. Darling, I wrote down what happened this morning while I remembered the exact words. Shall I get my notes?"

"Yes, do."

The two sheets she was looking for were buried under a subsequent blizzard of paper. It took a couple of minutes to dig them out. When Daisy returned to the sitting room, Alec was fast asleep.

Ten

Should she wake him? Alec had lots to do, but he would be much more efficient after a nap.

Daisy sat down opposite, her feet on a petit-point footstool embroidered by her great-grandmother. Things would be just the same when they were married, she knew. She'd never be sure when he was coming home, and often he'd arrive too tired to be sociable. Sometimes he would share his cases with her, and sometimes shut her out. If she was ever involved in a crime again, a highly unlikely circumstance whatever he and Tom said about propensities, he'd be angry, Fate or no Fate.

Belinda and Mrs. Fletcher would go on sharing his time and attention. Daisy would not have it any other way—at least as far as Bel was concerned, she admitted to herself. Not that she had any intention of displacing Mrs. Fletcher. Alec's mother might disapprove of her working, as well as of her noble birth, but her mother-in-law's presence would allow her to go on writing.

Alec had no intention of trying to stop her. That was one of the reasons she loved him. Few men recognized a woman's right to a career.

She contemplated the sleeping man, recalling their first meeting. From the first, even while she was still surprised to find a policeman so gentlemanly, he had impressed her as forceful and determined. From the first she had been attracted by the way his dark hair sprang crisply from his temples, and by the way his smile warmed his grey eyes.

The dark, heavy eyebrows between, skeptically raised or wrathfully lowered, had not intimidated her. Not for more than a moment, anyway.

Knowing him had healed the raw wound of Michael's death in the War, blown up by a landmine with his Friends' Ambulance Unit. Daisy would always have a place in her heart for the memory of her first love, but she wanted to marry Alec. She wanted to marry him soon.

Ay, there's the rub, she thought. How were they to escape the combined toils of her mother and Scotland Yard?

Alec yawned, settled more comfortably, then stiffened and opened his eyes. "Great Scott, have I been asleep?"

"Only for a few minutes. I hoped a nap would do you good, but it's barely been a catnap."

"I think it's helped, all the same." He sat up straight. "Your notes?"

She handed them over. "The first bit's what you asked for. The rest is just trying to sort out my thoughts."

To her gratification, he read the whole thing before, returning to the beginning, he said, "So the Grand Duke did draw Grange's attention to the ruby. I agree it's unlikely he'd have done so if he was responsible for the substitution."

"I can't believe he'd have gone on visiting the museum, let alone fussing over that blasted jewel. I don't think he'd have pinched the rest, either, whatever Sergeant Jameson says about ruses and wily foreigners. What about Grange? He need not have taken any notice of Rudolf Maximilian's concern, let alone have insisted on examining the rest of the collection."

"They're both low on my list at present, though Grange was in a good position to manage the theft, as was Randell. The Grand Duke is still near the top of the murder list."

"If murder and theft are unconnected. Alec," Daisy cried, as inspiration struck, "has it dawned on you that the person who could most easily have stolen the gems was Pettigrew himself?"

"It had crossed my mind," Alec said, with a grimace.

"That would be the very dickens of a complication, which I haven't time to think through just now. I must be on my way, love." He heaved himself to his feet, waving the papers. "May I take these?"

"Yes, I have a fairly readable carbon copy."

"Then will you type out the first couple of paragraphs alone—the facts, not the speculation—and sign and date them, for an official statement?" Folding the two sheets, he slipped them into his jacket pocket. "By the by, it had *not* dawned on me that Pettigrew's last words might have referred to the jewel theft, or have been misunderstood by the thief to do so. That would tie everything together very neatly, which would please the super no end."

"Really, darling?" Daisy flung her arms around his neck and kissed him. When he reluctantly let her go, some minutes later, she said, "I'm frightfully glad my idea helps. Are you going to tell Superintendent Crane it was mine?"

"Credit where credit is due. But Daisy, don't take it as encouragement to put your oar in. You've finished at the museum, haven't you?" he asked hopefully.

"Gosh, nowhere near. I got a bit on Mineralogy today, despite the disturbance, but I'll need more. I haven't even started on Entomology, and I was just getting my teeth into Geology when the fossils started crashing about my ears."

"Great Scott, I thought you were done with Geology at least! All right, if you must go back you must, but for heaven's sake limit your questions to scientific matters. There's a murderer on the loose, remember."

"I'll remember," Daisy promised.

"If I were you, if you don't absolutely have to be there tomorrow, I'd wait a day or two. We're searching the place from towers to basement tonight, and it's going to be chaos for a while."

"You think the jewels may still be there?" she asked, surprised.

Alec shrugged. "Who knows? They may have been taken away two or three months ago, but we have to look.

There's always a chance, too, of finding whatever it was Pettigrew used as a shaft for his spear or dagger. We have to look, however hopeless it may be in that labyrinth."

"But you don't really need to search everywhere, do you, darling? I mean, most places there'd be a risk of someone other than the thief coming across the jewels by accident."

"Yes." Alec stared at her bemusedly. "Of course. Yes, of course! I must be tireder than I thought not to realize that. Tired enough to be grumpy enough for none of my men to point it out to me! But there is still a dickens of a lot to do. I really must go, love. I'll 'phone when I can."

Daisy saw him out. The sun had sunk below the houses in the cross street, casting Mulberry Place into shadow. A chill in the air felt more like autumn than summer. Shivering, Daisy closed the front door and went upstairs to fetch a cardigan before going back to work.

Now that Alec was gone, she thought of all sorts of questions she wished she had asked while he was in a communicative mood—or too tired to resist. Who, for instance, were his suspects?

As far as the murder was concerned, it seemed to boil down to the four curators, Mummery, Ruddlestone, Steadman, and Witt, plus ffinch-Brown and the Grand Duke. Daisy wrote down their names. The theft was much more complicated. Without knowing when it took place, no one could be eliminated for lack of opportunity.

Pettigrew, Grange, and Randell had the most opportunity, assuming theft and murder were not connected. If they *were* connected, the curators had more opportunity than ffinch-Brown and the Grand Duke. Daisy was prepared to eliminate Rudolf Maximilian—from the theft, not the murder—but Sergeant Jameson's notions about skeleton keys and hiding when the museum closed could apply to ffinch-Brown.

And to any jewel-thief in the kingdom, habitual or one-time, assuming the murder was unconnected.

Daisy felt her mind going cross-eyed. No wonder Alec was tired! If she was going to get anywhere, she had to concentrate on two entangled crimes and leave other possibilities to the police. Of course, she really ought to leave the whole lot to the police and get on with her article, as Alec would heartily agree. But it was jolly hard to come up with interesting questions about insects when a double mystery waited to be solved.

She wished she had asked Alec how he imagined the theft had been accomplished. It was not a simple burglary. Somehow the thief had substituted false gems which looked sufficiently like the real ones to deceive a casual glance from people who knew them well.

Good quality strass glass jewelry, though vastly less valuable than genuine stones, was not cheap. Daisy's mother had muttered ominously about having her jewelry copied when she was first reduced to the penury of the charming Georgian Dower House, with its mere five bedrooms (excluding servants' quarters) and delightful garden. Discovery of the cost had allowed the Dowager Viscountess to back down gracefully.

The thief had had to pay for the paste gems. If he had not yet sold them, Alec should look for someone who was suddenly poorer, not suddenly richer.

The Grand Duke?

Alec also needed to look for the jeweller who copied the gems, not only for possible purchasers. Daisy wondered whether he had realized. Should she drop a hint?

Surely the police would not miss anything so obvious.

What was less obvious was how on earth the thief had accomplished the substitution. It *must* have taken more than one visit, and even then it could not have been easy. More difficult of course for ffinch-Brown and the Grand Duke than for the four curators, who at least had good reason to be in the museum after closing hours.

Oh blast, she was going round in circles again. The sound of the telephone bell ringing out in the hall came as a relief.

She gave her number.

"Aunt Daisy?"

"Belinda! Hello, darling."

"Aunt Daisy, is Daddy there?" Belinda sounded on the verge of tears.

Only a dire emergency would make the well-trained child telephone in search of her father, Daisy thought in alarm. "No, darling, he left quarter of an hour ago. What's the trouble? Can I help?"

"Oh, Aunt Daisy!" A sob broke through, then the story poured out. "It's Nana. She chewed up one of Granny's slippers and Gran's *awfully* angry and she says . . . she says Nana has to *go!*"

"Oh dear!"

"And I know this isn't your house yet and you're not my mummy yet but could you please, *please* talk to Granny and tell her Nana didn't mean to be naughty?"

Daisy quailed at the prospect of trying to persuade an irate woman who disapproved of her that the puppy should be forgiven for destroying a slipper because she did not mean to be naughty. And over the 'phone, too.

"Darling, I think I'd better come round. I'll hop on a bus and be there in no time. Hang on, I'm sure your grandmother won't throw Nana out without speaking to your father first. I'll be there in two ticks."

Two ticks was overoptimistic. Possessed by a feeling of urgency, Daisy hurried to the Fulham Road and soon caught a Number 74. The rush hour was in full swing, but at first she was going into town, so the worst of the traffic was heading the other way. Hyde Park Corner was the first check. At last the bus escaped from the jam and rumbled up Park Lane, only to be thoroughly entangled at Marble Arch. The right turn into Oxford Street took forever. From there on it was standing room only, up Baker Street and Park Road, till Daisy thankfully disembarked just beyond St. John's Church.

The bus rolled on towards Camden Town. Daisy left

behind the busy Prince Albert Road and plunged into the quiet residential streets of St. John's Wood.

Gardenia Grove was a dead-end street lined with early Victorian semi-detached houses. Any pair would have fitted easily inside one wing of Daisy's childhood home, and their gardens, set down in a corner of Fairacres' park, might easily go unnoticed. On the other hand, compared with the tiny Chelsea house, they were spacious.

To Daisy, the Fletchers' house sometimes seemed spacious, sometimes cramped. It was always very clean and tidy, almost excessively so, or had been until Nana's irruption into the quiet household.

Mrs. Fletcher blamed Daisy for the puppy's arrival. Daisy was, in fact, to blame. She was not at all sorry—Belinda's devotion to Nana precluded that—but she acknowledged that perhaps her future mother-in-law deserved a bit of sympathy for the inevitable disturbance.

Walking up the garden path, past the silver birch and beds of Michaelmas daisies and honey-sweet alyssum, she decided to start on the right foot by expressing her sympathy with Mrs. Fletcher. Belinda surely already knew Daisy was fundamentally on her side.

Belinda answered the door, red-eyed. Daisy hugged her, saying, "Where's the culprit?"

"Granny made me tie her up in the back garden. She's awfully sad."

"I expect she knows she's in disgrace, though she doesn't understand why. Come along, let's see what I can do."

Hanging on Daisy's arm, Belinda took her to the sitting room, which faced south, overlooking the back garden. It was a pleasant room, for which Daisy credited Alec's first wife. The furniture was rather heavily Victorian, but chairs and sofa had been reupholstered in cheerful prints. The walls, doubtless once covered with murky wallpaper, were painted white. If the Stag had ever stood grimly at Bay over the mantelpiece, he had been replaced with a colorful view of Montmartre.

Mrs. Fletcher, an angular woman of about sixty with a set face, sat knitting by the fireplace, where a gleaming Benares brass tray hid the empty grate. Her hair, worn confined by a hairnet in the fringed style favoured by the Queen Mother was of that greyish blond which suggests a red-headed youth. Skinny, ginger-pigtailed Belinda might well grow up to look very like her grandmother. Daisy was determined, however, that the child should not develop the older woman's rigid, stifling attitude to life.

"Hello, Mrs. Fletcher," she said. "I'm so sorry to hear Nana's in hot water."

"It's kind of you to come," snapped Mrs. Fletcher, her tone making plain that "interfering" would be a more accurate reflection of her thoughts. "But the dog will have to go. It has completely ruined a perfectly good slipper."

"Too maddening!"

Taken aback by Daisy's commiseration, Mrs. Fletcher said, "It's not the slipper so much—one can always purchase another pair—as the possibility that next time it will chew up something more valuable."

"Yes, of course. Puppies can be a bit destructive, especially when they're teething. Like babies. I expect Alec chewed things like mad when his baby teeth were coming in."

"So did I," Belinda put in eagerly. "Daddy said I used to gnaw his finger."

"Neither you nor your father ever destroyed anything," Mrs. Fletcher pointed out, her mouth pursed. "Nor left hair all over the carpets."

"No," Daisy agreed, "and there's no reason why Nana should be allowed to. She shouldn't be left alone in a room where there are things she can damage, Bel. When no one can be with her, you should shut her in the kitchen or the scullery. Make sure she has sticks and hard rusks to chew. But mostly she will chew only when she's bored and hasn't had enough exercise. Did you play with her and walk her today?"

"No, Aunt Daisy," Belinda admitted, head hanging. She bit her lip. "I went to play with Annette after tea, and she's afraid of dogs."

"If you want to keep Nana, you're going to have to take responsibility for her, you know."

"I know. I'm frightfully sorry, Granny. I'll save up my pocket money and buy you some new slippers. And I'll absolutely walk Nana after school every single day and play with her lots and make sure she's shut up somewhere safe, *and* brush her oftener, so please, *please* can she stay?"

"Sooner or later, you'll forget," said Mrs. Fletcher, "or the dog will get out."

All too likely, Daisy thought, but she said, "It won't be forever. Puppies grow out of chewing. It just takes patience."

"Derek's dog, Tinker Bell, doesn't chew things up," Belinda earnestly informed her grandmother. "When she's not going for walks or playing, she mostly just sleeps, doesn't she, Aunt Daisy? So *please* can I keep Nana?"

Mrs. Fletcher sighed. "We'll see what your father says when he comes home."

Belinda, knowing perfectly well what her father would say, correctly interpreted this as grudging surrender and beamed. "Thank you, Gran, most frightfully," she said, and went to give her grandmother's cheek a decorous kiss. Then she ran to Daisy and hugged her, whispering, "Thank you most even more frightfully, Aunt Daisy, for coming to the rescue."

At that moment, the Fletchers' cook-maid came in and announced supper.

Daisy knew that when Alec was not expected, his mother and daughter ate together early. "I must be on my way," she said, gathering up her handbag.

"If you have no other plans, do join us," said Mrs. Fletcher, if not exactly gracious then at least not altogether hostile.

Daisy had, after all, given her a way out of an untenable

position. She probably had not realized how fearfully upset her granddaughter would be. She did, one presumed, love Belinda in her way.

"Yes, do stay, Aunt Daisy!" cried Belinda with enthusiasm.

"Thank you, I'd like to."

"Belinda, go and wash your hands and face while Dobson sets another place at table. And the dog is to stay outside until after we have eaten," commanded Mrs. Fletcher.

Whatever her usual expectations of a child's table manners in the presence of her elders, over the Brown Windsor soup Mrs. Fletcher encouraged Belinda to talk, perhaps as a buffer. Bel chattered about Derek and Tinker Bell, then moved on to Derek's inexplicable keenness on dinosaurs.

"He liked the one with the big teeth best," she said.

"The Megalosaurus," said Daisy.

"That's right. Can you imagine what it'd be like to have a baby Megalosaurus instead of a puppy?" Belinda giggled, then glanced at her grandmother and stifled the giggle. "I thought its teeth were horrid. I'm glad the other dinosaurs were so tall you couldn't see their teeth properly, aren't you, Aunt Daisy? They're gigantic, Gran, bigger than a house, some of them."

"And who dusts them, I'd like to know?" said Mrs. Fletcher. "A gigantic waste of time and money, if you ask me." Thus having put herself firmly on the late Dr. Pettigrew's side, she changed the subject back to Daisy's nephew. "I must say Derek is a polite child, if rather rumbustious. But then, boys will be boys," she added tolerantly.

And girls must be young ladies, Daisy completed the hated maxim, one of her mother's favourites. Really, if Mrs. Fletcher and the Dowager Viscountess ever got to know each other well, they would get on like a house on fire.

* * *

While Daisy meddled in his home as a change from meddling in his work, Alec was supervising a search of all the museum staff as they departed for the day.

Fortunately, almost all were men, who could be checked, even asked to remove their jackets, by uniformed constables under the watchful eyes of Tring or D.C.s Piper or Ross. But there were the ladies' room attendant and the switchboard girl, as well as two saleswomen (what they sold he did not enquire) and four artists under contract to draw or paint botany and entomology specimens.

Alec did not see these as serious suspects in the burglary, but the thief might have inveigled one into carrying his spoils out of the museum. To search them, Alec requested one of the new woman constables. He was sent a police matron.

These matrons were more like prison wardresses than police officers. They took charge of arrested females, often drunk and disorderly, and rarely had anything to do with the innocent public. As a result, they tended to be hefty viragos, and to take a jaundiced view of all women they dealt with in their work, automatically regarding them—and inclined to treat them—as criminals. Tom Tring, who was not afraid of anything in trousers, claimed to be terrified of police matrons.

Mrs. Morble, sent round by Chelsea Division, was no exception. Tall and robust, with a red face and very pale eyes, she had a harsh voice and a bovine expression.

Bulls, as Alec reminded himself, are stubborn and belligerent as well as not exceptionally bright. What he needed was a women who was an ordinary officer, accustomed to frequent contact with law-abiding people, but the search could not wait.

He explained to Mrs. Morble what he wanted her to do. "I consider it highly unlikely that any of these women are involved," he stressed.

"There's a bad apple in every barrel," said Mrs. Morble.

"Somewhere in the museum, yes. But I doubt it's any of the women."

"The female of the species is more deadlier than the male," said Mrs. Morble.

"Er, possibly, though it's quite impossible that any of them murdered Pettigrew. It's the jewel theft we are concerned with here."

"Set a thief to catch a thief," said Mrs. Morble obscurely.

"It's more a matter of catching the thief and hoping he'll turn out to be, or at least lead us to, the murderer."

"You can lead a horse to water, but you can't make him drink," said Mrs. Morble. She elaborated. "If you was to ask me, there's a lot to be said for what the Yankees call the Third Degree."

Trying not to quail visibly, Alec stringently reminded her, "However, such methods are against the law in Britain. What is more, these women are not under any particular suspicion. They are to be searched as a general precaution, and they are to be treated with proper courtesy. Understood?"

"Yes, sir. What can't be cured must be endured. But you can be sure, sir, if any of 'em's got so much as a jet bead on 'em, I'll find it, and let the devil take the hindmost," said Mrs. Morble.

"No jet has been stolen. Here's the list." With deep misgivings, Alec repeated his instructions and let the matron loose on her prey.

Either none of those unfortunates was deeply disturbed by her notion of proper courtesy, or none was brave enough to complain.

Obviously disappointed, she reported back to Alec: "All clean as a whistle. Leastways, far as I can tell without making 'em peel. The which you said not to do, sir," added Mrs. Morble reproachfully.

Relieved that she had not tried, Alec thanked her and thankfully dismissed her.

Searching the men proved equally unproductive. Alec

had not really expected the thief to attempt to walk out with his booty when the museum was under siege by the police, but it was a possibility which had to be covered. Though the museum had yet to be searched, the odds were that the jewels were long gone, either already sold or concealed at home.

Alec had applied for warrants to search his chief suspects' homes. The only way to bring them down to a manageable number was to assume the thief and the murderer were one, which was Superintendent Crane's view, fortunately. As Daisy had pointed out in her notes, the assumption simplified matters no end, even if one included the Grand Duke and ffinch-Brown.

Alec did, since the two were high on the murder list, though like Daisy he considered them unlikely thieves. The magistrate agreed, and refused to grant search warrants. He also refused in the case of Grange, who had raised the alarm, but allowed Randell, both added to the list by Alec on the grounds of opportunity.

That left the four curators and the junior mineralogy assistant, too many to cope with in one evening. As Randell was not a murder suspect, Alec sent a detective sergeant and constable from the Yard to his lodgings.

Leaving Detective Inspector Wotherspoon in charge of the cohorts of constables who were to start searching the museum, Alec departed with his own little troop. Little in numbers, not in size: with Tom Tring beside him in the front and both Piper and Ross in the back, the Austin Chummy was heavily laden. He hoped the springs would stand up to the load.

"I'll leave most of the searching to the three of you," he said. "I shan't do any formal questioning this evening, but I want to get a feel for the way they live. Tom, try to manage a word with any servants, just to break the ice. You can go back later to pump them, if necessary. Ernie, you've worked out the best route?"

"Mr. Mummery first, Chief, in Wimbledon. Start out

across Vauxhall Bridge. I can give you directions when you need 'em. After him, Mr. Ruddlestone in Twickenham, Mr. Steadman in Ealing, then back to Mr. Witt in Mayfair."

"You know how to find all their houses?"

"Course, Chief."

"Y'ought to be a taxi-driver," Ross said admiringly.

"Very efficient, but I'm afraid it's going to be a long evening anyway," said Alec, glad that he seemed to have got his second wind. "We'll stop for a quick bite later. How's the cold, Tom?"

"None so bad, Chief. Just a bit of a cough now and then. I'll leave tearing up floorboards and crawling through attics to the young uns."

"You wouldn't fit in an attic anyways, Sarge," said Piper.

"You watch your lip, young fella-me-lad, or I'll have you climbing chimneys," Tom threatened mildly. "And don't neither of you go tearing up any floorboards till I've had a dekko and said they look suspicious, or the repairs'll come out of your pay. Nor I don't want anyone to be able to see that we've been through their things."

Though addressed to both constables, the words were directed at Ross. Young Piper had worked with Tom Tring often enough to know what the sergeant expected. Tom had picked Ross to help tonight, saying he seemed a quick learner.

Alec was sure one of the things Ross had learnt quickly was to keep quiet about Daisy's presence at several interviews. Her notes made it plain she knew exactly who the murder suspects were, and Alec had not told her. He only wished he could believe for a moment that the knowledge would make her steer clear of them.

Eleven

In the dusk, Alec drew up in the street outside Septimus Mummery's abode. It was not one of the mansions with acres of gardens backing onto Wimbledon Common, once a favourite haunt of highwaymen. Nonetheless it was sizable, built of red brick, with an air of solid worth. Judging from the extent of the front garden, separated from the street by a neat beech hedge, the house probably stood on a good half acre.

"Cor," said Ross in dismay, disengaging long legs from the Austin Seven's less than spacious back seat, "a house that big's going to take forever to search."

"Not too bad," Piper disagreed from the vantage point of experience. "There'll be servants, and where there's servants there's not many places they don't stick their noses in. Right, Sarge?"

"Right, laddie. Doesn't look as if Mr. Mummery's short of a penny, Chief."

Though Alec had not yet seen the numbers, he doubted a Natural History Museum curator earned much more than a Met Detective Chief Inspector. He himself had inherited his house from his father, a bank manager. It looked as if Mummery had money in the family, which meant there was a chance he was living beyond his income in an effort to keep up appearances.

The garden appeared well kept, the visible part all trees and shrubs rather than labour-exacting flowerbeds. The house was in good condition too, with no sign of peeling or flaking paint on window frames or doors.

At one of the ground-floor windows, a light shone behind drawn curtains. A cheerful-looking middle-aged parlourmaid answered the door—just the sort Tom Tring got on with best. While remaining devoted to his wife, Tom had a way with female servants that often provided useful information.

The maid's eyes widened when Alec showed his warrant card. "You've not come to arrest the master?" she gasped.

"No, I'd like to speak to him."

Leaving the others in the hall, he followed close on her heels as she headed towards a door at the rear. He wanted to see Mummery's reaction to his arrival.

Unfortunately, the Curator of Fossil Reptiles was facing the other way, only his untamable mop of hair visible above his chair's back. He was seated by a cheerful fire, with a chess board on a small table in front of him. His opponent was a young man in a wheelchair.

In spite of the scars, the black patch over one eye, and the pallor of ill-health, the round facial bone structure and mismatched hook nose revealed the relationship. Mummery's son had no right arm. When he turned the wheelchair to look towards the door, Alec saw his legs ended above the knee. He had to pivot the wheelchair to see, because his head was immovably tilted towards his right shoulder.

Unfortunately, young Mummery's condition did not alter Alec's duty to search the house. It just made him feel like an absolute rotter.

He hoped he had at least succeeded in hiding his shock.

Mummery jumped up. He looked anxious, but no more so than any householder unexpectedly called upon by the police. He still had on the dark suit with sagging pockets which he wore at work when he was not in a laboratory coat. No money for evening clothes? Alec wondered. Or did he not change for dinner in deference to his son's difficulty in doing likewise?

"How can I help you, Chief Inspector?" he asked, surprisingly civilly.

"May I have a private word with you, sir?"

"Oh, no secrets here! This is my son, Andrew. Andy, Detective Chief Inspector Fletcher of Scotland Yard."

"How do you do, Mr. Fletcher." His voice was a hoarse, breathless gasp. Mustard gas, Alec guessed—a bad hit, attacking the tissues and followed by gangrene, but he must have managed not to breathe too deeply or he would be dead.

Not that he was likely to live long anyway, when a simple cold would inevitably lead to deadly pneumonia in those corroded lungs. Five years since the War ended—he must have very good care. Expensive care.

He gave Alec a crooked grin and wheezed, "My father may not look it, but he's delighted at the interruption. I have him in check."

Alec crossed to the board and studied it. He didn't have time to play often or seriously, though he had taught Bel the moves, but he could see Mummery was in trouble. "So you do, sir," he said.

"Andy had a good teacher," Mummery observed affectionately, "though I say it as shouldn't."

"I shan't keep you from your game, sir. I'm afraid I have a search warrant and I must ask you not to hinder my men in the execution of their duty."

Mummery's lips tightened, but instead of the expected outburst he said mildly, "Go ahead. My daughter's upstairs but she's not likely to take fright."

Tom was at the hall door. Alec nodded to him, and turned back to the sitting room as Mummery asked the obvious question: "Looking for those damned gemstones, eh?—Sorry, dear. My wife, Chief Inspector."

A woman stood in the doorway connecting with the front room. Tall—nearly a head taller than her husband, Alec estimated—and fine-drawn, she wore a well-cut but plain navy wool dress and pearls, a circlet at her throat, not

a fashionable knee-length rope. She gave Alec a rather re-
mote nod, her gaze going past him to her son.

Her tense shoulders relaxed a little as Andrew produced
that heartbreaking, lopsided grin and said, "Excitement
upon excitement, Mother. I'm beating Dad hollow, and
now, to top it, a police raid!"

"Excitement upon excitement," she echoed dryly. "Darling, perhaps the Chief Inspector would like a sherry. I
know I should."

Mummery cocked his dishevelled head at Alec, who
said, "Not for me, thank you."

"No booze in the course of duty," said Andrew. "I don't
know that you ought, Mother. Goodness knows what effect
it will have on those lectures you're working on. Mother's
preparing for the Michaelmas term, Mr. Fletcher. She's a
prof at Bedford College, if you haven't ferreted out that
tidbit for yourself."

"I hadn't," Alec admitted. Two incomes, then. "Have you
a desk in there, sir?" he asked as Mummery took his wife a
glass of sherry. They deliberately touched hands, Alec noticed, inferring a close relationship. "Do you mind . . . ?"

Mummery's shaggy eyebrows twitched in exasperation.
"Do I have a choice? Here's the key." He turned away.
"Just you wait, Andy, I'll escape and checkmate you yet."

"Nothing, Chief," Tom Tring reported when they all returned to the car. "Leastways, if he split 'em up and hid
them all separately, we could've missed them, but I'd've
thought we'd find at least one, and there'd be a big risk of
someone else finding them."

"You looked at the daughter's room?"

"Yes. There wasn't any place she or the maids wouldn't
get into. Nice young lady, dolling herself up to go out with
college friends, she being a student. She was worried her
brother'd be upset about us. I told her he didn't seem like
it to me."

"Turn left here, Chief," said Ernie Piper from the back seat.

It was dark now, and out here in the suburbs lampposts were few and far between. For a few minutes, until Piper had extricated them from the winding streets around the common, Alec concentrated on driving. Then his mind returned to the Mummerys.

The curator's desk was covered with books and journals on fossil reptiles, and a monograph in progress. Papers in the drawers, however, revealed an adequate income, from earnings and a few minor investments, with no evidence of debts. The house was freehold, unmortgaged. The latest quarterly bank statement had no extraordinary payments in or out.

The only unusual expenditures were for Miss Mummery's college fees and a nurse to care for Andrew part-time during the university terms. Neither apparently strained the family budget.

But Alec had found a file of brochures and letters describing a cure for gas-injured lungs. They came from America, land of medical miracles and quacks, and the price quoted was enormous. At the bottom of the file was a letter from a Harley Street doctor and professor at Guy's medical school, which mercilessly unmasked the "cure" as sheer fraud. The sheet had been screwed up, and then smoothed out again. Alec could not begin to guess at the emotions consequent on its receipt.

Yet Mummery had kept the papers. Did hope linger? If so, the jewels lying in their cases in the Mineralogy Gallery might have presented an irresistible temptation, and one difficult to condemn.

The last thing Alec had expected was to come away from Wimbledon full of sympathy for the choleric reptile curator. Now he saw the man's bad temper at work as a respite from the tight hold he must keep on his emotions at home. And his focus on the complex details of his profession could be seen as a temporary refuge from the inescapable horror of his son's condition.

"D'you reckon," said Tom Tring, who had been meditating in silence while the two in the back talked quietly, "they could all be in it together, Chief? The family, that is, if it was for the young chap's sake." He pitched his voice too low for the constables to hear.

"It's possible. Would you have searched differently if you had thought of that before?"

"Mebbe," Tom admitted reluctantly.

"Forget it," said Alec, "unless we find evidence tying Mummery to the murder."

He drove over Richmond Bridge, and Piper directed him to Ruddlestone's house.

Ruddlestone lived at the end of a narrow street leading down to the river. The houses were also narrow but tall, quite substantial though joined in terrace rows of five or six. The last three, at the lower end of the street, had low, gateless walls in front which had to be surmounted by steps—a reminder that after centuries of effort, the Thames was only partly tamed. The coincidence of spring tides with heavy rains upstream still brought flooding.

One by one, the detectives tramped up the steps and down the other side, crowding the small paved forecourt already occupied by a tub of scarlet geraniums as yet untouched by frost. Alec rapped with the shell-shaped iron knocker.

No one answered, but lights glowed in windows and the sound of voices came to them. He banged again, more vigorously.

A boy in grey flannels and a Fair Isle jersey opened the door. There was no question of his welcome—he was thrilled to death to have four Scotland Yard 'tecs requesting admittance. As he invited them in, a small girl peered at them from behind him, then dashed off crying, "Daddy, it's the police. There's *lots* of them. Come and see."

Through an open door on the right, Alec saw a dining table with school books spread across it. The mantelpiece beyond was crammed with shells and bits of coral—the tools of Ruddlestone's trade, so to speak—varied by a doll and two toy motor-cars.

The boy said dismissively, "I'll finish my homework later. Have you come to talk to my father about the museum murder?"

Alec left Tom to answer or evade the lad's questions. As Ruddlestone did not appear, he went after the girl, towards the rear of the hall.

She popped back into sight. "Daddy says he can't leave the jam just now or Mummy will have his guts for garters, so will you please come in here."

The fossil invertebrate curator was in his shirtsleeves, standing at the stove in a large kitchen. Face and bald dome red from the heat, wooden spoon in massive hand, he stirred a huge pan from which rose steam scented with cooking blackberries. Empty jam jars waited on the nearby table. A girl of twelve or so was washing up at the sink, with a younger boy drying.

Ruddlestone grinned at Alec. "Good evening, Fletcher. Sorry, but if I take my eyes off this for more than ten seconds, it will infallibly boil over."

"Undoubtedly," Alec agreed.

"It's a sort of corollary to Boyle's Second Law. You know the one? Watt's pots never Boyle." He laughed. "My wife's upstairs putting the little ones to bed, and this stuff gets too hot for children to handle safely. What can I do for you?"

Ruddlestone kept stirring, his eyes on the bubbling, deep red contents of his pan, as Alec explained about the search warrant. The small girl, busy cutting lengths of string and squares of waxed paper to top the pots, interrupted.

"Daddy, you're s'posed to keep checking if it's ready to set, or it'll cook too much and waste all the berries we picked."

"Quite right," Ruddlestone said cheerfully, and dropped a splodge of jam onto a saucer. "No, still runny. All right,

Fletcher, you'd better get on with it, but please try not to upset the children upstairs. James, run up and warn your mother that they're coming, please."

"How many more?" Alec asked.

"Let's see, three in here; Roger doing his homework, I hope; that leaves three, if I'm not mistaken."

"You know you're not, Daddy," said the dish-drying boy severely, departing with the damp tea-towel slung rakishly around his neck.

Seven children, Alec thought, as he went out to the hall to set his waiting men to work. Jovial as Ruddlestone appeared, providing decently for so large a family was no joke. A small fortune in gems would come in very handy.

When Alec returned to the kitchen, the jam had reached setting point. He was pressed into service to help fill and cover the pots.

"You must take some with you," said Ruddlestone, "unless it would get you into trouble."

"Bribery and corruption? I think a jar of jam would pass."

"You might find a ruby in the bottom."

"Fortunately, I've seen these filled. But since you mention it, if you have any more home-made jam in the larder, perhaps I'd better have a look."

Ruddlestone chortled. Alec felt an utter idiot holding jars of jam up to the electric light and stirring up the contents of one or two. He found no jewels.

Nor did the others. Tom Tring had been through the curator's papers, the few deemed worthy of keeping, chucked in an unlocked drawer along with more fossil shells and corals, because there was no room in the house for a desk. "Nothing suspicious there, Chief," he reported, steadying the jar of hot jam on the car's floor, between his feet. "Frankly, I can't see how he'd ever have saved enough to pay for the copies.

"Nor can I," Alec gladly admitted. Another suspect he didn't want to have to arrest. "But he could have borrowed it." Ruddlestone was still on his list.

They headed north to Ealing.

Steadman lived in a newish semi-detached, in a feature-
less street full of indistinguishable newish semi-detacheds.
The front garden was too small for any trees. The patch
of lawn was shaved to near baldness, but by the nearby
lamppost Alec, who always wished he had more time for
gardening, picked out the leaf-rosettes of dandelions and
daisies. In the strip of flowerbed along the shared path, a
few straggling pansies struggled through the smothering
yellowed foliage of long dormant daffodils.

The front door was heliotrope, as (very much) opposed
to its neighbour's canary. No knocker. Alec pressed the
electric doorbell and heard it shrilling inside.

The man who came to the door looked like Steadman
gone to seed. He was as tall and narrow-shouldered, his
faded hair similarly thinning, but his face was jowled, his
eyeballs red-tinged, his belly straining at the braces beneath his royal blue blazer.

"Mr. Steadman?" Alec said.

"That's me. What can I do you for, gentlemen?" Taking
a closer look at Alec's companions, he exclaimed, "Uh-oh,
it's the rozzers, right? It's my brother you want, I expect—
I hope, ha ha! He's not here."

"Mr. James Steadman *does* reside at this address?" Usually Alec would have said "live here," but the officialese
sprang to his lips in reaction to the other's loud heartiness.

"Oh yes, Jim-boy lives here all right, when he's at home.
The old man left the house to both of us, see, and I wasn't
going to sell a nice place like this, nice bit of freehold
property, not with house prices—"

"Who is it, Teddy?"

A buxom blonde came up behind him. Her hair was
marcelled and all too clearly peroxided. Her fringed, heavily beaded dress was in the height of fashion, yet somehow
missed elegance, at least to Alec's inexpert eye. He knew
only as much of women's clothes as any observant detective experienced in judging their wearers. In this case it

was as much the wearer as the lime-green cloth that made him suspect artificial silk rather than the real thing.

"It's the busies, sweetie."

"Well, don't leave them on the doorstep for all the neighbours to see! Oh, plain clothes. All right, then. Are you after Jimmy, over that museum business? He's out, so you can just go away again."

"I'm afraid not, ma'am." Alec introduced himself and explained about the search warrant.

Mrs. Steadman protested shrilly.

"Oh, shut up, Mavis," said her husband, waving her out of the way and the detectives into the house. "They're the law, aren't they? It's not like we've got anything to hide. Nor has Jim-boy, I'll bet. The poor weed hasn't got the gumption to pinch those sparklers."

Tom and the D.C.s went about their business.

"I suppose you'd better come into the lounge," Mrs. Steadman ungraciously invited Alec.

He followed the Steadmans into a sitting room furnished with a modern couch and easy chairs wildly patterned in jazz colours—mostly magenta, sulphur-yellow, and black—and matching curtains. One corner was occupied by an expensive wireless set, another by a gramophone, playing a tango. A low table held two glasses, a large glass ashtray, a fashion magazine, the pink *Sporting Times,* and the *Evening Standard* with its banner headline: MUSEUM MURDERER STRIKES AGAIN? There were no books, and no pictures on the walls. In spite of the bright hues, the room had a stark feeling.

Mrs. Steadman dropped sulkily into a chair. Picking up a lit, lipsticked cigarette between two crimson-nailed fingers she puffed it back to life, then reached for a tumbler holding a liquid much the same sickly color as her dress.

"Cigar, old chap?" Teddy Steadman offered Alec, taking his own, still burning, from the ashtray. "B-and-s? Or are you a whisky man?"

"Not for me, thanks."

"Not on duty, eh? Never could see why anyone'd want to be a copper, no offence. I'm in insurance myself, and doing very nicely, thank you. I keep telling Jimmy he could triple his income if he joined me, but he hasn't got the gumption to switch."

"Now that's not fair, Teddybear. If Jimmy gets into the pictures he'll make a packet, and all because he knows about those stupid bones."

Alec blinked, but managed not to let his jaw drop. "The pictures?" he said weakly.

"That's where he's gone tonight," said Mrs. Steadman. "Not the cinema, but to the Dorchester to talk to Harry Hoyt, from Hollywood! Mr. Hoyt's going to make a film of that book by Sherlock Homes, *The Lost World,* that's all about dinosaurs, and he came to London to talk to our Jimmy. He's got Lewis Stone, who's in *The Prisoner of Zenda* with Ramon Novarro, and Wallace Beery that was in *The Last of the Mohicans,* and Bessie Love, and—"

"And our Jimmy won't make a penny out of it, mark my words," said his cynical brother. "I told him he shouldn't even talk to this bloke without a contract in black and white, but does he listen to me? He does not!"

As the pair wrangled, Alec decided that if James Steadman took it into his head to commit murder, he would start with his brother and go on to his sister-in-law. On the other hand, he might commit theft so as to be able to escape them.

"He wouldn't know what to do with a lot of money if he had it," Mrs. Steadman proclaimed. "What's he do with what he's got, I ask you, after he's paid his share of expenses? He hasn't got a lady-friend, and you never see him go out for a bit of fun, not even down the local."

With a glance at the Pink 'Un, her husband shook his head. "Not even a bob each way on the Derby," he confirmed.

Tom knocked on the door and came into the sitting room, electric torch in hand. "There's a padlocked shed out the back, sir," he told Alec.

"Jim-boy keeps some old bones there," said Teddy. "Works on 'em out there evenings and weekends, if you call it work."

"I won't have them in the house, disgusting things," Mrs. Steadman said self-righteously. "There's a spare key in a drawer in the kitchen."

"One of these, madam?" Tom held out his large hand, full of keys of every shape and size and degree of rustiness.

"I think it's that one. Or maybe that. I never go out there."

"We didn't used to lock it," Teddy said, "not keeping anything valuable there, but some kids got in once and messed about with the bones. I thought Jimmy'd have a stroke."

He guffawed and his wife tittered at the memory.

"Treat the bones with care, Sergeant," said Alec.

"With great care, sir," Tom said emphatically. Departing, he murmured to Alec as he passed, "No bank papers visible, Chief."

Alec nodded. With a word of apology, he poked around the sitting room. Bare as it was, there were few hiding places. No stolen gems in the gramophone's or wireless's innards, none behind the ugly modern clock on the mantelpiece, none down the sides of the chairs or sofa. As he searched he continued to encourage the Steadmans to talk about James. Not that they needed much encouragement.

Tom returned, shaking his head, and the detectives took their leave.

"No jewels," said Tom. "Like I told you, Chief, I didn't get a look at any financial papers. There's a locked box—one of those metal cash boxes—in his bedroom. No key. I shook it, and nothing shifted about like the jewels would, just papers rustling."

"But why'd he lock it, Chief," said Ernie Piper, "if there's nothing in there to give him away?"

"Because his sister-in-law is a snooper, I dare say."

"There's a key to his room in the kitchen drawer," Tom said, "and it's not one of the rusty ones. It's not that big a room, but he's got it all fitted up nice like a bed-sitter and study combined. Bookcase full of dinosaur books and desk covered with dinosaur drawings. I don't reckon he spends much time downstairs, Chief."

"Hardly congenial company for a gentleman of intellectual pursuits," Alec commented, "and nosy with it. Mrs. Steadman says her brother-in-law banks at the South Ken Lloyd's. Tomorrow, as soon as the banks open, I want appointments made for me to talk as soon as possible to all the suspects' bank managers, Tom. Unless we strike lucky with Witt."

Calvin Witt's residence was a service flat in a luxury block in South Audley Street, Mayfair.

"Blimey, must cost him a pretty penny!" observed D. C. Ross as the red-carpeted lift bore them smoothly upwards.

"Fishy, on museum pay," said Piper hopefully.

"I had a word with the porter who let us in," Tom rumbled. "Mr. Witt's lived here twelve years, since the building went up. Must have private means besides his salary."

The young constables' disappointment was reflected in the gilt mirror hanging on the back wall.

Private means could be squandered, Alec reflected, leaving their erstwhile possessor accustomed to a style of living he could no longer afford. Or fine living might lead to a desire for finer. Perhaps Witt yearned to give up his job and retire to a place of his own in the country.

The Curator of Fossil Mammals answered his own doorbell. He was as sleekly self-assured as ever, in a superbly tailored dinner jacket and Old Wykehamist tie.

"Good evening, Chief Inspector," he said resignedly. "I was half expecting you. You're looking for gemstones, I expect?"

"That's right, sir." Once again Alec explained the search warrant. Hearing voices from an inner room, he added, "We'll disturb you as little as possible. My men will go through the rest of the flat, but I'm afraid I shall have to take a look at the—" He hesitated: not lounge;

sitting room? drawing room? He chose the last. "The drawing room."

As if reading his mind, Witt smiled a trifle sardonically and said, "I'm not so high-falutin'. Sitting room will do. Come in."

The spacious sitting room was as modern as the Steadmans' lounge, but of a different kind entirely. The predominant colours were ivory and lavender, with russet accents but a minimum of pattern. Chairs and sofas were leather-covered, as sleek as their owner. In contrast, a cabinet and occasional tables of probably-genuine Chippendale somehow humanized the whole.

Alec recognized at once the woman seated in one of the chairs. Maggie Weston was a well-known actress, the sort who plays Juliet or Rosalind, not the ingenue in drawing-room comedy. The couple on the sofa looked familiar, more as a type, Alec thought, than because he knew them. They reminded him of Daisy's sister and her husband, Lord John Frobisher.

"Detective Chief Inspector Fletcher, from Scotland Yard," Witt introduced him dryly. "My sister-in-law Lady Genevieve, Chief Inspector; Miss Weston; and my stepbrother Lord Meredith."

While Alec appreciated the courtesy of the introductions, it added to the doubts aroused by Witt's previous improbable helpfulness. A policeman, even of his comparatively superior rank, was not normally considered worthy to be presented to such company. Lord Meredith, in fact, looked surprised and made no move to rise and shake hands.

"Darling, too thrilling," said Miss Weston in her famous throaty voice. "Has Mr. Fletcher come to arrest you?"

Witt cocked an eyebrow at Alec, who said, "Not tonight, Miss Weston."

"Pity! One ought to see how it's properly done, and I'm sure Mr. Fletcher would have done it properly. Well, darling, if you don't need my support through this ordeal, I'm off. I've a rehearsal at an ungodly hour tomorrow."

"We'll give you a lift, darling," Lady Genevieve said languidly, rising. "It's time we made a move. Do let us know, Joker dear, if you have to be bailed out."

Witt kissed the cheek she offered, and then Miss Weston's—rather more warmly. Lord Meredith, who had stood up when the ladies rose, put his hand on his step-brother's shoulder and said in a low voice, which just reached Alec's ears, "Don't want to desert you, Joker. Gen can drive Maggie home and come back."

"That's all right, old man. Fletcher's a gentleman, and I've nothing to hide." Witt raised his voice. "I'll be with you in a moment, Chief Inspector." He went out to see off his guests.

Alec used his absence to peek behind the half dozen framed drawings hanging on the walls. Contraband had been stuck to the backs of pictures before. He found nothing, and when Witt returned, he was contemplating a drawing of a bison. It was crude and misshapen, yet there was something oddly satisfying, even graceful, about its sweeping lines.

"Prehistoric art," said Witt, coming up behind him. "They're copies of wall paintings found in caves in France and Spain: Altamira, Pair-non-Pair, Font-de-Gaume."

"I've heard of them, but not seen any before. Interest-ing. It's an attractive room."

"So I'm told. I can claim no merit, at least not for the colour scheme. It was designed for me by a friend who does that sort of thing. I'm colour-blind."

"Ah," said Alec, in the best tradition of Tring in-scrutability, but he warmed slightly towards Witt. At least his suspected lack of war service was explained. "Mind if I poke around a bit?"

"Not at all." He grinned. "As if I had any choice in the matter. There's just one favour I must beg, Chief Inspector."

"Which is?" Alec asked, peering into a beautifully shaped vase with a lavender glaze.

"Please refrain from mentioning at the museum that I'm

known to friends and family as Joker! A schoolboy play on my name, of course. I am not given to jokes, verbal or practical. But it wouldn't go down well with my colleagues."

"And you care what they think?"

"Naturally. I see them and work with them daily."

"You'd be sorry to give up your position, then."

Witt gave him a sharp look, then laughed, with a mocking edge to his tone. "Ah, I see, you think I might have purloined the jewels so as to be able to quit work."

"It's a possibility I have to consider, sir."

"Yes," Witt mused, "it is a possibility. I do need a job. You see, Chief Inspector, the comforts of my life are provided by my father. He's an American—my mother divorced him and brought me back to England as a baby, then married Meredith's father."

"A wealthy American," Alec assumed.

"Oh, very. The fly in the ointment, so to speak, is that Poppa came up the hard way and believes idleness is bad for the soul. He requires his offspring to hold down a job of work in order to profit from his millions. I refused to go into his ironmongery business—hardware they call it over there. Fortunately I had an alternative to offer, though it was not easy to persuade my father it qualified as a career."

"Palæontology?"

"Yes, I was already hopelessly addicted to fossils. It is a sort of addiction, Chief Inspector. We may not all be quite as single-mindedly obsessed as Dr. Smith Woodward, but it's not the sort of job one falls into by chance. You will have realized by now that we're all dedicated, even passionate about our subject."

Alec recalled Witt's words as Tom described the man's study:

"Full of bones and books about bones, Chief, and drawings of bones, and drawings and models of mammoths and such."

"I reckon they're all a bit dotty," said Piper.

Even Ruddlestone, his house crammed full of children and associated paraphernalia, had found space for a few fossils. Yes, they were all dedicated, passionate, perhaps a bit dotty!

Twelve

Ascending the steps far enough to be sheltered by the great rounded arch, Daisy paused to shake out and close her umbrella. It was drizzling again, yesterday's sunshine forgotten.

At the top of the steps stood a familiar figure, shifting impatiently from foot to foot. Rudolf Maximilian had arrived early at the museum. His long nose touched the glass as he peered through the door into the interior.

Daisy glanced at her watch. *She* was dead on time. A shadowy shape unlocked the central doors as she reached them.

"Good morning, Grand Duke," she said.

He started, turning. "Ach, it is Miss Dalrymple. Goot morning, *gnädiges Fräulein.*" He bowed, and rather reluctantly let her enter first.

Sergeant Jameson had unlocked the doors and stayed to hold one open for Daisy. His greeting to her was friendly enough, but his harried gaze was on the Grand Duke behind her. "What's he want?" he muttered. "His blasted ruby's gorn, innit."

"Mine ruby, he is finded?" the Grand Duke demanded.

"Not it, mate. Sir. You sure you haven't got it at home in a teapot?"

"Teapot? Vhy you talk about teapot? Vhy you not busy mine ruby to find?"

"Not my job, sir, is it? There's been dozens of men

searching all night, and a new lot come on this morning. Just the second floor and the towers to go."

"I help," said Rudolf eagerly.

"Not on your nelly you don't," exclaimed Sergeant Jameson, but he made no great effort to stop the Grand Duke when he pushed past. "D. I. Wotherspoon'll put a spoke in his wheel soon enough, or someone else will if he's dropped off. Poor ole Spoony's been up all night, but he's set on seeing it through. And I'll take it kindly, miss, if you won't mention what I just called him."

"I shouldn't dream of it," Daisy assured him, hoping that Alec had managed a good sleep last night. She stuck with Jameson as he went to unlock the other doors. "Have they not found anything at all?"

"They think they found the handle the flint was stuck to. Leastways they found a spare handle for a ge'logical hammer with a splodge of the right kind of glue on it in the right place, and what might be bloodstains. It was in the basement, but they're all over the place in fossils and minerals both, any road. They all use 'em, so it don't mean much."

"And anyway it was probably Dr. Pettigrew's. No fingerprints on it, I suppose."

"Nary a one, miss."

"They haven't found any skeleton keys?"

"Nor reckon to," said Jameson, strolling back towards the police post. "The thief's had plenty of time to get rid of 'em, seeing it could be weeks since the jewels was pinched. Me, I think it was done at night when Dr. Pettigrew was on holiday. He'd be the most likely to notice some little thing not quite right, but after a few days away he might not. Makes sense, don't it?"

"It certainly does," Daisy said warmly, leaning on the L-shaped counter as the sergeant opened the flap and stepped inside his sanctum. About fifteen feet square, it backed onto the front wall of the museum, with a partition filling the fourth side. "When was that?"

"First two weeks in July. I looked it up." Jameson flipped back through the pages of a large date-book, then swivelled it for Daisy to see, and pointed. "See?"

"A couple of months ago. That's about how long Mr. Grange said since the cases were opened, isn't it? Just right. I bet you're right. Were you on duty nights then?"

"No, miss, I was not," said Jameson emphatically. "Not neither week, though some chaps' shifts changed in the middle of that fortnight, and I done my share of night duty since. The fakes was discovered on my watch, but no one can't say the real jools was swiped on my watch."

"Mr. Fletcher asked for a list of all you museum police, I remember. Has he seen everyone yet?"

"Every last man Jack, or rather Sergeant Tring did, and no one saw nothing odd. Course, some of 'em wouldn't notice a stuffed mammoth waving its trunk, 'less you pointed it out to 'em special. Ole Westcott—he's retired, mind, so I tell no tales—he—"

"Retired? When?"

Sergeant Jameson consulted his tome again. "Well, now, miss, the end of July it was. What d'you know?"

"What do *you* know?" Daisy riposted.

He opened a drawer and took out a pile of past duty rosters. "Lessee, here we are, July, second week Westcott was on evenings—closing time till two in the morning. And I happen to know the sergeant in charge used to send him upstairs and not expect to see him again till the end of the shift. But like I was saying, miss, he wouldn't've noticed nothing in front of his nose 'less his nose was shoved in it."

"Did anyone mention him to Mr. Tring? Has anyone told Mr. Fletcher that Dr. Pettigrew took a holiday in July?"

"I wouldn't know about that, miss," Jameson said cautiously. "'Spect so."

"Is Mr. Fletcher in the museum now?" Daisy asked.

"Don't think so, miss. Sergeant Wilby that I just took over from would've said."

"Do you know if—" Daisy started.

"Yes, miss," Jameson said loudly, straightening, "you can go anywhere below the second floor, 'cepting the Mineral Gallery which is closed."

"Thank you, Sergeant."

Turning, she saw a constable approaching. Jameson did not want to be caught gossiping by his subordinate. He had been helpful, but obviously he was not deeply involved in the case. Daisy doubted whether the unknown Detective Inspector Wotherspoon would be equally receptive to her questions, especially as he'd been up all night.

She had come to the museum to finish her research, she reminded herself, and she headed for the east wing.

A few visitors had straggled in, but in the fossil mammal gallery she found the one-armed commissionaire alone. "Good morning, Sergeant Hamm," she greeted him.

"Morning, miss. Tomorrow will I bring the locusts, and they shall fill thy houses and shall eat every tree."

"Really?"

"Yes, miss. They've bin told they're not to be let into the Mineral Gallery till tomorrow. Not but what there's bound to be a few wandering around today, taking pictures of the gallery gate and barging through here to the pariosaurus again."

"Oh, the Press," said Daisy, enlightened.

"And the rubbernecks," Hamm added, descending from Biblical misquotation to American slang. "But the mighty strong west wind shall cast them into the Red Sea."

Daisy had no answer for this dire pronouncement, so she asked, "Is Mr. Witt available, do you know?"

"Far as I know he's in his office, miss. You go and ask Wilf Atkins in dinosaurs to knock him up for you. Tell Wilf I said."

Thanking him, Daisy proceeded through the hall where she had been with Dr. Smith Woodward when Pettigrew was killed. When she reached the reptile gallery, she was relieved to see the remains of the Pareiasaurus swathed in dust-sheets. Mummery was just lifting a corner to peer underneath. He dropped it and swung round as Daisy's footsteps approached.

"Oh, it's you, Miss Dalrymple," he said gloomily. "I have no idea yet whether he can be repaired. It's iniquitous, they won't even tell me when they'll give me back the broken bones. I wish you would have a word with your Chief Inspector—."

"*My* Chief Inspector?"

"Are you not engaged to Fletcher? I understood—"

"Actually, yes," said Daisy, a bit cross, "though I can't imagine how you know."

"Someone told me," Mummery said with a vague wave, then went on irritably, "Does he really grasp that fossils must be handled with extreme delicacy, and as little as possible?"

"I'm sure he does, and has given the proper instructions."

"I hope so, but I have little faith in his understanding since he had his men search my house last night. Jewels! What do I care about jewels after this terrible occurrence?" He gently smoothed the cloth over the reptile's massive shoulder.

That he was referring to the fate of the Pareiasaurus, not Pettigrew, was all too obvious. Losing patience with him, Daisy excused herself and went on into the dinosaur gallery.

Near the far end of the 150-foot chamber, a space had been roped off. Atkins, in his bottle-green uniform, stood nearby looking on. Several men were inside the rope, gazing down at something on the floor. Daisy's heart jumped and her breath caught in her throat—another body?

No, they were talking calmly. She recognized Steadman's lanky height, in a white coat today, while three of the men were in their shirtsleeves, the fifth in a blue suit. Drawing near, she saw behind them a wooden box some five feet high. Shavings on the floor and a hammer in the hand of one of the men suggested the box was newly constructed. On the floor between the men, the object of their interest, was an oddly shaped piece of metal about two feet long.

The commissionaire moved to meet Daisy. "Morning, miss. Can I help you?"

"I was going to ask you to find Mr. Witt for me, but what is going on here?"

At the sound of their voices, Steadman looked round. His thin cheeks were flushed, and a glitter of nervous excitement brightened his eyes. "Miss Dalrymple," he greeted her, "you might find this interesting. I'm about to start mounting a skeleton."

"I'd love to watch," Daisy assured him.

"May I introduce Mr. Willis O'Brien? Mr. O'Brien is visiting from Hollywood. He's going to be in charge of creating dinosaurs for a film of *The Lost World*. You know the Conan Doyle story? It will be an American film, but set partly in London. Mr. O'Brien came over here with Mr. Hoyt, the director."

Judging by Steadman's excitement, he was as keen to be "in films" as any teenage girl.

"I've done dinosaurs before," the American informed Daisy. "You maybe saw *The Ghost of Spirit Mountain*, ma'am? But Mr. Hoyt wants them realistic as can be, so I guess I can't beat seeing how the real thing's put together, before I turn Delgado, my modeller, loose."

"It sounds like a good idea." Daisy took out her notebook. "I'm writing an article about the scientific work of the museum. What is this dinosaur called, Mr. Steadman?"

"Saltopus. It's small, just about two feet in length. It was found in Scotland, but it was a German, von Huene, who studied it and named it, in 1910. It rather got shuffled aside during the War. I've been working on it recently. The skull is missing, but the rest is similar to Scleromochlus, so I've modelled a similar head. I haven't quite finished the rest of the missing bones. However, it's the nearest to being ready to mount of any I have, so when Mr. O'Brien asked . . ."

As they talked, the other men had retrieved two tall stepladders from the floor behind the pedestal and set them up. Two climbed the first few steps. The third handed the metal frame up to them. They set it on the box and balanced it in the centre.

"Like this, Mr. Steadman?" asked one. "This all right, sir?"

Steadman turned back, drawing a sheaf of papers from the deep pocket of his lab coat.

Daisy rather lost interest in the exact placement of the stand. She was wondering whether it would be rude to go and see Witt and return later, when Dr. Smith Woodward came up. He greeted her in his rather absent-minded way and started to talk to Steadman about Saltopus and Scleromochlus, which latter he himself had named.

After a very few minutes the talk grew too technical for Daisy. "Excuse me," she said tentatively, reluctant to interrupt but not wanting either to stay or to sneak off without a word, "I think I'd better go and see Mr. Witt. I'll come back when you start putting the bones together, Mr. Steadman."

"My dear young lady," said Smith Woodward, "allow me to unlock the door for you." Setting off towards the end of the gallery, he felt in his pocket. "Dear me, I seem to have mislaid my keys again. I wonder where I left them this time?" He turned back, looking around vaguely.

"Never you mind, sir," said Sergeant Atkins kindly, "they'll turn up right as rain. I'll let the young lady through."

"Does he often lose his keys?" Daisy asked in a low voice.

"Lor' bless you, all the time. They're gen'rally found on his desk or sticking in a lock somewhere." He took out his own jangling bunch.

"You all have to carry such a lot around."

"Not as many as it might be. Lots of the doors are keyed the same, see. This here I'm using now wouldn't open Dr.

Smith Woodward's office, but it's good for the liberries, f'rinstance. And his'll open any of the other Keepers' office doors. We each of us has just the ones we need, too. Elsewise we'd all be too weighed down to move. There you go, miss."

Daisy went on into the private studies, which were not much more than a wide passage cluttered with desks, bookcases, cabinets, and chairs. Along one side, doors at intervals led into the General Library, the various galleries, and the work room which connected with the Geological Library. Most of the light came from skylights, but opposite each door was a window, looking out on the Spirit Building and the Imperial College of Science.

The Fossil Mammal Curator boasted a window to himself in a private cubicle of sorts, walled with bookshelves. He was seated at his desk, studying a large-scale drawing of a quadrupedal skeleton, with the animal's outline sketched in, and enlarged views of individual bones.

"I don't want to interrupt, Mr. Witt," said Daisy untruthfully.

He looked up and smiled. "That's all right, Miss Dalrymple. Just yet another early horse."

"Tell me about it. I expect motor vehicles will entirely supersede horses one day, but meanwhile, people are interested in them."

Witt was good at tailoring his exposition to his audience. He gave Daisy just the sort of detail she wanted, and she took reams of notes.

"I can let you have a series of drawings, from Eohippus to the modern horse," he offered. "I'd appreciate it if you would trace them and return them, but it's not the end of the world if your editor should lose them. Do you ride?"

"I used to. I grew up in Gloucestershire."

"Fairacres," said Witt, to her surprise. "I knew your brother slightly. I . . . ah . . . Fletcher seems a good sort of chap."

Resignedly, Daisy realized that if Mummery knew of

her engagement, doubtless so did everyone else. "He is," she said firmly, "and a good detective as well."

"He came round to my flat last night, looking for the stolen jewels. I imagine he sees some connection between the theft and Pettigrew's murder?"

"He doesn't discuss all his reasoning with me," Daisy hedged.

Witt's sardonic look told her he recognized prevarication when he heard it. "He didn't find the loot, of course, though I'm aware that won't have convinced him of my innocence. I can't quite work out how the jewels were stolen, but I know I'm one of just half a dozen people who could have killed Pettigrew. Only why should I?"

"The police don't have to prove motive, though it's helpful in court."

"They don't?" Witt shrugged. "Well, the man was a pain in the neck, but I didn't have to see much of him."

"Even over the flints?"

"Ah, is that where Fletcher's looking? Pettigrew was making a pest of himself about the flints, admittedly. However, I claim no expertise on the subject. I always referred Pettigrew to ffinch-Brown. He bore the brunt. And he was around when Pettigrew died."

"Do you think he was worried about Pettigrew's challenge? That business of detecting a newly chipped flint?"

Witt grinned. "Much as I'd like to divert suspicion by throwing it on ffinch-Brown, who is also a pain in the neck, I have to say I believe him perfectly competent to distinguish anything Pettigrew could produce."

Which was as prevaricating as anything Daisy had said. Witt was quite clever enough to realize his encomium did not rule out ffinch-Brown's worrying, however competent he was. So was he actually attempting in an oblique way to throw suspicion on the anthropologist?

Spotting an invitation to circular reasoning before she was entangled, Daisy decided Witt's statement was really pretty useless.

"The stuff you've been doing for Mr. ffinch-Brown must have given you a lot of extra work," she said, poising her pencil above her notebook as if returning to business. "Do you and your colleagues often work late?"

"Only when we're planning a murder," Witt quipped. Daisy frowned at him. "Sorry! It depends—which is not a useful answer but true. One doesn't get into palæontology unless one is keen. One doesn't get on in the museum hierarchy unless one is keen enough to put in extra hours. Many are not, so there are Assistants and Attendants who will never rise above those Civil Service grades."

"Thus Curators are by definition extra keen and ready to stay late?"

"More or less. Sometimes one finds oneself at the end of the day deeply involved in something particularly fascinating which one does not care to leave. Occasionally there is work which simply must be completed on time. Human time, that is, as opposed to geological time."

Daisy laughed. "I'm glad we don't have to live by geological time. Imagine saying, 'I think I'll just wait for the ice age to finish before I take the dog for his walk.' So the dedicated scientists of the Geology Department frequently stay after hours." She wrote it down in her notebook.

"I shan't quarrel if you put that in your article," Witt said with a smile. "Dr. Smith Woodward expects a great deal of his people. Individual circumstances vary, of course. For instance, I quite often have evening engagements. Steadman has a rotten home life, so he frequently works late—there's always something interesting to do here, but also he accepts quite a few invitations to give outside talks. The public like dinosaurs. On the other hand, Ruddlestone has a family clamouring for his presence, so he rarely does overtime."

"Mr. Ruddlestone has a large family?"

"Lord, yes. I couldn't tell you how many children. He hardly ever stays. It was rotten luck he happened to be here on the very evening that Pettigrew . . . Unless . . . No, it couldn't have been Ruddlestone! Forget I said that. It wasn't so late when it happened, anyway, was it?"

"No," Daisy agreed.

"Just late enough for most people to have left, so as to make Fletcher's task easier," Witt said wryly. "Oh dear, we don't seem to be able to stay away from the subject, do we? What else can I tell you about my work?"

Glancing through her notes, Daisy said, "The information about the horses will do, I think, thanks."

"Right-ho. Let me just get you those drawings. Here we are."

"Spiffing. Thanks!"

"I'll be happy to answer any further questions, Miss Dalrymple, and if you have none, no doubt your fiancé will have plenty!"

He unlocked the nearest door for her, and she stepped into the cephalopod gallery. Passing through, she made one or two notes, rather half-heartedly. She still could not work up any enthusiasm for primitive squids and octopi.

Halfway down was the arch to the dinosaur gallery. If Mummery was the murderer, he must have gone that way to the General Library.

Daisy went through. The Megalosaurus skull was to her left. She pictured the children gathered around it, with little Katy heading for the far entrance and Mrs. Ditchley suddenly noticing her departure. The children would surely have glanced towards their sister, momentarily distracted from the monster. But that moment had coincided with the murder, so the murderer could not have taken advantage of it, unless he was a sprinter, and Mummery hadn't got the figure of a sprinter.

At best it would have been risky to cross the gallery with a family there, at worst downright foolhardy. Or would it? Mummery might well have reached the side arch when Mrs. Ditchley was joining Daisy and the children were clustered just inside the far arch, their attention fixed by the unseen drama beyond.

Alec had undoubtedly worked it out ages ago, Daisy thought with a sigh. Mummery was still on the list, or his house would not have been searched last night.

She turned right. Several spectators had gathered at the rope barrier around Mr. Steadman's new exhibit. Within the barrier, a trestle table had been set up and the workmen had been replaced by a white-coated technical assistant. Steadman and O'Brien leant over the table. Behind them, framed by the towering ladders, the pedestal topped by its iron frame rose like an incomprehensible modern sculpture. Sergeant Atkins was keeping an eye on the spectators.

"The pedestal is rather high, isn't it?" Daisy said to him.

"Kids," he responded succinctly. "Give 'em half a chance and they pinch the tail bones off them little ones. I can't be everywhere. There you go, miss." He moved aside one of the posts holding the rope. Stopping someone who made to follow her, he uttered one word in an impressive tone: "Press!"

On the table Daisy saw several sheets of paper with drawings of bones, spread out around a large, shallow, wooden tray. The tray held the bones themselves, neatly arranged to depict a creature which looked rather like a wallaby. Daisy couldn't help wondering how many people would ever know the difference if it really was a wallaby skeleton. Like the plaster of Paris Diplodocus with the wrong feet, beauty was in the eye of the beholder.

Steadman was telling O'Brien how a jumble of bones was transformed into a diagram of a plausible skeleton of a hitherto unknown animal. Daisy started taking notes, glad that he was talking to a layman.

He explained how ribs and vertebrae formed logical patterns. "Once we have a good notion of how the parts join, we have to work by comparison and analogy," he went on. "The Saltopus is in some ways similar to a kangaroo in form. We assume it sat on its haunches, with its forefeet in the air, and leapt along using both feet together to propel it. Hence the name."

"Huh?" said O'Brien.

"Sorry! From the Latin for 'jumping foot.'"

"Like octopus," said Daisy.

"Say, that's right!"

"And platypus?" said Daisy less certainly.

"Flat foot," Steadman kindly confirmed.

"Oh yes, *plat* is the French for flat." However ignorant of Latin and science, she did know her French. "And *sauter* is to jump."

"Jumping foot." Steadman returned to business. "That's why we chose this particular mounting position. However, we can't be sure. Actually, it might have run on the tips of its toes, for all we know."

He was painfully honest about his beloved dinosaurs. Whether his honesty applied equally to the collections of the other museum departments—Mineralogy, to be specific—was another matter.

Daisy listened for a while longer, as Steadman moved on to mounting techniques. With a delicate touch, he started to hook two bits of spine together, but it was obviously going to be a very long process, even for so comparatively small an animal. She decided she had all the material she could use, though she would come back later to inspect his progress.

What she really wanted was to chat with him, to find out what he had to say about murder and theft. No hope of that while the Saltopus was under construction before a fascinated audience.

Not counting ffinch-Brown, who was beyond her reach, the only murder suspect she had not spoken to this morning was Ruddlestone. Not that she had had any more conversation with Rudolf Maximilian than with Steadman, and he had probably left the museum by now. Blast! She should have sought him out earlier.

Finding an excuse to approach Ruddlestone was not easy, as Daisy had already interviewed him for her second article. Then she recalled what she had overheard him telling Tom Tring about the Special Palæontological Collections. She had not asked him about them before, and the historical aspect might make an interesting digression. No need to give away how she had learnt about them.

She went to the Special Collections gallery first, to refine her questions. To get there she had to go out into the reptile gallery. By the Pareiasaurus, two men with cameras were arguing with Harry Boston, the reptile commissionaire, about removing the cover to take pictures.

The real Press, Daisy concluded, forerunners of tomorrow's plague of locusts. She turned the other way.

In the end gallery she found one of Ruddlestone's assistants, whom she had met before. Harbottle, a weedy, bespectacled young man, was going through the displays and drawers of specimens and checking them off against a list in faded ink bound in a large volume.

"Making sure the jewel thief hasn't helped himself?" Daisy queried.

Harbottle grinned. "Not likely! No, Mr. Ruddlestone found some discrepancies and decided it was time to revise the catalogue."

Surely if Ruddlestone was a thief and murderer, he wouldn't be worrying about the inaccuracy of an ancient catalogue at this moment! "Do you know where he is? I have a couple questions."

"I'm afraid he's busy in the work room, Miss Dalrymple, with a gentleman who brought some fossils he wants to sell us. Can I help?"

"I don't want to tear you away from your work."

"I'll be glad of a change. This is going to be a long job at best, and the police searchers moved things about rather, which doesn't make it any easier. I say, you found Pettigrew's body, didn't you? *And* you were there when the jewels turned up missing. What luck!"

"Luck!" Daisy echoed quizzically, eyebrows raised.

"Nothing exciting ever happens to me," Harbottle mourned. "The nearest I've come to it was being searched

2

8585

before going home yesterday, but so was everyone else in the museum. I don't know why they bothered. The thief is too clever to try to smuggle the loot out yesterday, of all days, with police swarming around."

Daisy had not known about that search. It was logical, of course. Searching the museum was pointless if Alec had let the thief stroll out with the jewels in his pocket. "I presume nothing was found," she said, "or everyone would be talking about it. Do you have any ideas as to who did it?"

"Dr. Pettigrew," he said promptly. "It would have been easy for him. He was in league with the Grand Duke of Transcarpathia—their quarrelling was a blind. The Grand Duke killed him because he refused to hand over the ruby."

"It's a reasonable theory," Daisy acknowledged, annoyed with herself for not thinking through her own suggestion to Alec of Pettigrew as the thief.

"It's what most people here believe," Harbottle assured her with a touch of belligerence.

"Because it would mean none of the rest of the museum staff is implicated."

He sighed. "Yes. I suppose, really, we've had enough excitement already. There's just one thing I'm sure of, and that's that Mr. Ruddlestone is no murderer. Right-oh, I'd better answer your questions, if I can, and get back to work."

Harbottle knew quite as much as Daisy cared to know about the early collectors, and far more than she cared to know about their collections. Mind sated, body starved (she had missed elevenses), she left him finishing up a drawerful before lunch, and went off in search of sustenance.

Tomorrow morning, she would tackle Entomology—the Keeper of which, she had discovered, was known as the Creepy-Crawly man—and that should pretty much finish the research for her article. As far as criminal investigation was concerned, however, she did not feel as if she was the slightest bit forrarder.

Thirteen

Without going too far out of her way, Daisy could avoid the Pareiasaurus's corner of the museum, so she did. She was walking the length of the fossil mammal gallery, her mind on food, when she saw Rudolf Maximilian lurking—there was really no other word for it—by a fearsome cave bear. He managed to look both shifty and disconsolate.

"Hallo," said Daisy, "I thought you were long gone."

"Bitte?"

"I . . . Oh, never mind. Did they let you help to search?"

"No. Now to search is finish, and mine ruby dey have not finded. But it vas not a good search!"

"What do you mean?"

"See!" cried the Grand Duke, waving his arms. "See only dese aminals."

Daisy scrutinized the cave bear, which had an unfriendly look, and the sabre-toothed tiger beyond, with its positively hostile glare.

"And in de museum, how many aminals are!"

"Lots," she agreed blankly. "That is, after all, what it's for. Mostly."

"Inside dese aminals have dey not to searched. Comes de t'ief viz mine ruby, cuts in de aminal a hole—here under vhere is not easy seen, inputs mine ruby, and sews again togizzer. Like so." Parting the bear's thick fur (borrowed from a grizzly) in an unmentionable place, he prodded it indecently, pointing out a seam.

"I suppose it's possible," Daisy said doubtfully.

"Dis I tell to dem, but dey vill not de aminals open to cut." As he grew more and more excited, his uncertain grasp on the English language slipped still further. "Dey vill not me to let de aminals open to cut."

Daisy tried to envisage the blizzard of kapok disembowelling a cave bear would create, let alone a mammoth. "They really can't do that," she soothed him.

"If I mine sword had, I vould do!" Rudolf took up a fencing pose. "I go now mine sword to fetch."

"For heaven's sake, don't! Honestly, I can't believe the ruby is hidden in any of these animals. It wouldn't be easy to sew up a furry hide neatly enough, in a hurry, to pass muster."

He looked blank. *"Bitte?"*

"To be missed by the searchers," she elucidated. "It would take ages, and the police post is just around the corner, even if the counter doesn't face this way. The thief is too clever to take such a frightful risk. And think of trying to find the jewels again, in all that stuffing! Anyway, they were probably sold long ago."

By now, for all she knew, a jeweller might have turned up at Scotland Yard, ready to identify the miscreant. Hoping to tie him to the murder as well, Alec would not necessarily rush to arrest him, so Daisy would be left in the dark, her deductions based on false premises . . . unless she managed to extract the information from him, which in turn depended on her having a chance to talk to him. This was the first time she had been involved in an investigation so peripherally, and she was finding it absolutely maddening.

"Never more see I mine ruby," gloomed the Grand Duke. "Never more see I mine contry."

"Buck up," Daisy urged. "Have you had lunch yet? The world will look brighter after something to eat. Let's pop up to the refreshment room."

The Grand Duke heaved a sigh from the depths of his

much-tried Slavo-Teutonic soul. "De place to take a botiful yoonk lady is de Ritz," he said, "but dis I cannot. A sandvich for you I buy."

The botiful yoonk lady gladly accepted.

Over lunch, they talked about Transcarpathia. Its history had been turbulent, to say the least. At various times it had suffered the hegemonic attentions of Poland, Lithuania, Russia, Bulgaria, Hungary, Prussia, Turkey, Rumania, and Austria, always retaining shreds of independence because no one really wanted it much. Listening to a description, Daisy could see why.

What she could not see was why Rudolf Maximilian expected the downtrodden peasantry to rise up and restore their erstwhile masters to the throne (or whatever Grand Dukes sat on). Far from wishing to overthrow the Bolshevik invaders, they had probably welcomed them with open arms.

She tactfully refrained from saying so to the unhappy young man. He was not likely to gain possession of the ruby, but if he did, she could only hope he'd have the sense to use the proceeds to make a comfortable life in exile for his family.

It seemed less and less likely that he was the thief. On the other hand, given his eagerness to draw his sword on a defenceless cave bear, he still looked like a possible murderer. The two were not necessarily the same man, Daisy reminded herself. As Alec said, coincidences do happen.

After lunch, she went back to the dinosaur gallery to see how Saltopus was getting on. Not very fast, she discovered. A few inches of spine now held the absorbed attention of Steadman and his assistant. O'Brien was not present. A fair crowd was gathered around the barrier, its members coming and going.

"You won't miss much if you come back tomorrow, miss," said Sergeant Atkins. "They'll be at it for days."

Daisy went home to transcribe the day's notes.

* * *

Alec had had a frustrating morning. He had interviewed six bank managers, the four curators' plus the Grand Duke's and ffinch-Brown's. Five had refused to say more than that their clients were solvent and no unusual transactions had come to their attention.

Only Ruddlestone's had been more forthcoming, and he had reported nothing unexpected. Ruddlestone lived up to his income. He had not recently received a large legacy or won a large sum on the races, nor, as far as the manager knew, was he in debt.

As far as he knew—that was the problem. Any of the six could have had an account with another bank, or even in Post Office savings, which he had emptied to pay for the strass gems. Once the account was closed, the associated papers could be destroyed, leaving no trace except in the unknown bank itself.

To circularize every possible financial institution would be an enormous job, and very likely unproductive. The A.C. did not even feel justified in applying for warrants to compel the known bank managers to reveal their clients' secrets, if any.

"We have no reason to single these six out from any number of other possible suspects," he pointed out, "except an assumed connection with the murder. Sorry, Fletcher, but you need more evidence."

Stymied, Alec returned to his office, where Tom was sorting through piles of reports.

"All negative, Chief. What next?"

"Our best hope now is for a jeweller or fence to come forward. I'd better see Grange's and Randell's bank managers, I suppose, but I don't expect much there. We'll talk to everyone again, and I want to go over the ground in the museum more thoroughly."

"Search it ourselves, Chief?" asked Tom, appalled.

"Great Scott, no! Study the scenes of the crimes, how

to get here from there, what can be seen from where. The plans are useful but I need to take another look. Then, I'm afraid, we'll spend the evening reading every report through in case we've missed something. I swear, Tom, you shall have a few days off when this is over, even if half the population of London gets bumped off in the meantime."

"It'd make the missus happy," Tom admitted.

And maybe Alec could get married. Then at least he'd be able to go home to Daisy, even if he worked eighteen hours a day, seven days a week.

He rang her up from his office that evening.

"She's working," announced Lucy, who answered the 'phone. "No disturbances allowed . . . except you. Hang on a minute."

Daisy sounded preoccupied. "Hallo, darling. I'm glad you 'phoned, there's something I wanted to tell you. Now what was it?"

"If you can't remember, it can't be urgent, and I'm working too, love. We don't seem to be getting anywhere, just marking time. I just rang to hear your voice. Now I've heard it, I'd better go and see what Tom's waving at me. 'Night, sweetheart."

"'Night, darling. I hope Tom has found something useful."

But Tom hadn't. Sighing, Alec picked up the next report. He was glad that Daisy had her own work, and that she wanted to continue with it when they were married. It kept her from moping when he had to work late—and it reduced the amount of time she could spare to meddle in his work.

The next day, Friday, was equally busy and equally fruitless. Sir Sidney Harmer had returned to London, and he was not at all happy that the two crimes in his museum were still not solved. Nonetheless, Alec decided a rest would do them all as much good as poring over the same reports once more. He sent his men home at five.

On his own way home, he stopped at Queen's Hall and bought two concert tickets for that evening. Mendelssohn's *Hebrides* overture and Dvořák's *New World* symphony—those were safe—with between them a piano concerto by a young Russian, Prokofiev—risky, but with luck interesting. Anyway, he could be sure Daisy would not walk out.

He drove on home to 'phone her. Before he picked her up at seven-thirty, he'd have a couple of hours with Belinda.

She met him on the doorstep. "Daddy, there's an *urgent* message from work. They said to ring back *right away!*"

"Oh h . . . the dickens! Thanks, pet."

A young Hebrew had brought his grandfather to the Yard. The old man was a jeweller. He might have information about the museum jewel theft and he was willing to talk to the detective in charge, but he must be home in Whitechapel by sunset, when the Sabbath began. After that, he would not discuss anything to do with his work until after sunset on Saturday.

Alec suppressed a groan. However inconvenient, this was what he had been waiting for. A spark of excitement flared. "I'm on my way. Tell them I'll drive them home." Hanging up, he glanced at his wristwatch. "Bel, sweetheart, I must ring Aunt Daisy. Be an angel and find me an apple and a bit of cheese, or something I can eat with one hand while driving."

"Right-oh, Daddy." Another of Daisy's phrases Belinda had picked up, Alec thought fondly.

"Either I'll be making an arrest," he told Daisy, "or I'll pick you up for the concert even if we only make the second half."

"Right-oh. Good luck, darling."

Belinda was back with a tin pie-pan draped with a napkin. He kissed her and his mother, who came out of the sitting room, and dashed back out to the car. Setting the pie-pan on the passenger seat beside him, he drove off.

The two Jews were waiting in an interview room. Alec was pleased to see they had been brought cups of tea, though the old man had not touched his. With prejudice so prevalent in society, the battle to keep it from affecting the dealings, if not the opinions, of the supposedly impartial police force was never-ending.

"Detective Chief Inspector Fletcher," Alec introduced himself. "I'm in charge of the museum case."

The young man jumped to his feet. Short, wiry, wide-awake, he wore a beautifully fitted suit, light grey, in a cheap material and with something subtly foreign about the cut. His shirt was pale blue; in place of collar and tie, he had a blue silk foulard around his neck.

"Joe Goldman." His slight accent was pure East End with no hint of foreignness. Alec shook his hand. "This is my *Zeyde,* my grandfather, Solomon Abramowitz. He's got something to tell you."

The old man was dressed in the traditional gabardine and black hat. Apart from that, he could have been Dr. Bentworth's twin, another bent gnome with thick-lensed, gold-rimmed spectacles through which he peered uncertainly at Alec.

"I appreciate your coming in, sir. I gather you have information about the gems stolen from the Natural History Museum?"

"I t'ink so." Abramowitz's gnarled hands fumbled with a grubby sheet of paper on the table before him. Alec recognized the police circular. "Zis list—I have seen zese stones."

"You bought them?"

"No, no, I do not buy and sell. I make. For men who like to give nice present but not have much money. For peoples who need to pawn good stones and vant no one knows. For ladies nervous to wear real jewels to big public dance. All sorts reasons. Very good glass gems I make; very exact I copy."

"Zeyde's a real, old-fashioned craftsman," said Goldman, proud and affectionate.

"So the stones on the list were brought to you to be copied," said Alec.

"Yes, all them. I not know is stolen, is wrong," the old man said anxiously.

"I quite understand that, sir. There is no question of charges, I promise you."

Abramowitz looked bewildered. His grandson spoke briefly in Yiddish and he nodded. "I am honest man," he reaffirmed. "I believe Mr. Brown when he say—"

"Brown?" Alec interrupted. "That was the name he gave?"

"Brown," the old man confirmed, shrugging. "Is not his name?"

"I wish I knew!" Alec wondered if it was ffinch-Brown, or a simple alias, or if he was altogether on the wrong track.

"Smith, Jones, Brown." Young Goldman laughed.

"Brown," his grandfather insisted. "I write in my book, so." He took a diary from a pocket and slowly turned the pages, holding it a couple of inches from his eyes. "Many people give not own name. He say he has bought gems for investment, but his wife vants to vear. She is careless woman, often loses t'ings, so he comes to me. Here, see, Mr. Policeman."

He handed over the notebook. The writing was large and shaky and—to Alec—totally incomprehensible, in an unknown alphabet.

Seeing Alec's blank face, Goldman took the notebook from him. "Brown, evening," he translated, "and the date is Monday the second of July."

"Thank you. It fits nicely." The first day of Pettigrew's holiday. "But I assume, sir, you can't have made the copies on the spot?"

"No, no, Mr. Brown stay with me for all night, tell wife he is avay for business. I make many measurements, drawings, photographs, notes of colours. Vas much hurry, but no fancy settings to vorry. Early, very early in morning, he take stones and go."

"He must have smuggled them back into the museum," said Goldman admiringly, "and put 'em back so nobody knew they'd been gone, then pinched them again later on."

"Vun veek and some days he give me to make."

Goldman found the next entry. "Brown, midday. Friday the thirteenth."

Not generally regarded as an auspicious date. It had worked for "Brown." Pettigrew had returned to the museum the following Monday and noticed nothing wrong.

"Brown" had gone on his lunch hour to pick up the fakes. He must have stayed at work late that evening, made the substitution . . . and done what with the real gems?

Abramowitz was getting restless, muttering something in Yiddish to his grandson.

"Sorry," said Alec, "you wanted to be home by sunset."

"The old people think it's wrong to travel or work on the Sabbath," Goldman said indulgently.

"I'll get you there." Thanks to Summer Time. Now for the all-important question: "What did Brown look like, sir?"

"Dark clo'es. Hat. Big man."

Looking at the bespectacled gnome, Alec's heart sank. "Big wide or big tall?"

Abramowitz gestured vaguely. "Big," he repeated.

Goldman confirmed Alec's fears. *"Zeyde* thinks I'm big. He does close work with a jeweller's glass, of course, but he's practically blind without it."

Alec swallowed an oath. Without much hope, he asked, "What about his voice. Did he have any kind of accent?"

"No, he speak good English."

At best it was another indication that the Grand Duke was not responsible for the theft. Neither Ruddlestone's

Lancashire nor Witt's public-school pronunciation would make any impression on an immigrant from Central Europe.

"I hope we haven't wasted your time, sir," said Goldman rather anxiously, as if he expected imminent arrest for obstructing the police in the course of their duties.

"Not at all," Alec reassured him. "The dates and times give us something to work on. It's always possible the name may prove useful, though it doesn't seem likely. Most of all, we now don't need to waste any further effort looking for the maker of the imitations. No, as I said before, we very much appreciate your coming forward, gentlemen. And now let me drive you home."

Rescuing his dinner just as Abramowitz was about to sit on it, Alec transferred it to the Austin's back seat, beside Goldman. He delivered them to Whitechapel just before the sun touched the horizon.

"I'll have a constable drop in on Sunday, sir," he said to the old man, "just in case you remember anything else. And we may have to take a formal statement at a later date."

Leaving Goldman explaining this to his grandfather, Alec hurried back towards Chelsea, eating on the way. Dobson and Bel had done him proud, with cold chicken and cheese cut to bite size, a raw carrot, an apple sliced and cored, a bread-and-butter sandwich, and two of Bel's rock buns. These last were much less rocklike than her first effort, made months ago in Daisy's honour.

In Mulberry Place, Daisy was watching at the sitting-room window. She dashed out to the car before Alec had time to do more than get out and go around to open the passenger-side door for her.

"No arrest," she commiserated, "but the concert sounds simply spiffing, darling. What happened?"

He told her about the strass glass maker and his grandson, and she reciprocated with Grand Duke Rudolf Maximilian's near attack on the cave bear. As she finished, they reached Langham Place. Though they had to leave the car some distance from Queen's Hall, they were not quite the last stragglers to arrive.

"Sorry I'm not in evening togs," Alec said as they hurried up the stairs to take their seats.

"Darling, it's such a wonder to have you to myself for half an evening, you could wear bathers and I wouldn't care."

Between holding his hand and the waves of music surging into Fingal's Cave, Daisy had no thoughts to spare for crime for a while. The unknown Prokofiev piano concerto, his third, proved so spectacularly brilliant as to be all-absorbing. Yet somewhere in the back of her mind she must have been mulling over the new information, for when the interval came, the questions on the tip of her tongue were all about theft and murder.

Alec got in first, as they went to stretch their legs in the lobby. "How is your article coming along?"

"Very well. I went to the Entomology department this morning. I've typed up those notes, and read through the whole lot, and actually started really planning the article. It's more complicated than anything I've done before."

"But you're finished at the museum? Good."

"Pretty much. There are bound to be a few odds and ends to clear up once I start writing. Do you think the jewels are still there, hidden somewhere frightfully clever?"

"It's possible. Not inside a cave bear, perhaps. Your objections to that seem valid. But finding something so small in a place so large is as good as impossible."

"And you can't search everyone every day, of course. So what can you do?"

"It's a waiting game. We've bolted and barred all but one staff exit and we have men watching that and the main entrance. All the chief suspects are discreetly followed from the moment they leave the museum until they return. If any of them goes near a jeweller, we've got him."

"What a pity your fake-making jeweller is blind as a bat! Still, ffinch-Brown—even if he was idiotic enough to give half his real name—is small, and Ruddlestone is surely large enough to qualify as more than merely big."

Alec laughed. "Yes, that's a point. The dates may help, too, though it's rather a long time ago for people to remember whether they noticed anything odd."

"I guessed the jewels must have been stolen while Pettigrew was on holiday," Daisy said smugly. "Oh, darling, that reminds me! I suppose you know that one of the constables who was on night duty then has retired since?"

"What!" He stared at her, shaking his head. "Great Scott, Daisy, how the deuce did you . . . ? No, never mind, in this case ignorance is bliss. Do you happen to know and recall his name?"

"Southey? North? Eastman? Westcott, that's it."

"And his address?"

"Darling, I haven't the foggiest. The Chelsea police will know, won't they?" Daisy grabbed Alec's arm. "You are *not* going now. By the time you found out and got there, the poor old chap would be in bed and fast asleep. There's the bell, let's go back."

At the end of the concert, Daisy and Alec, along with the greater part of the audience, hummed bits of the symphony as they emerged into the rain-gleaming night. Daisy's head was too full of music to think of anything else. Alec had to open the windscreen and concentrate on peering into the darkness between lampposts all the way to Chelsea.

Sheltering under his umbrella, they stopped on the front step for a good-night kiss, then Daisy felt in her handbag for her key.

"That reminds me," she said.

"Not again!"

"Oh well, I expect you already know," Daisy said airily, sticking the key in the lock.

"I didn't know about Westcott. Tell me."

"Right-oh, darling. The museum locks match—not all of them, but, for instance, Dr. Smith Woodward's key opens Dr. Pettigrew's office."

"Yes, typical of government institutions. What's more, apart from the museum police, Pettigrew had the only key to the iron gate, which he may well have left in his office while he was away."

"And Dr. Smith Woodward is constantly losing his keys."

"He is? Now that I didn't know," Alec said thoughtfully. "So much the more likely that it's a museum staff member who burgled the mineral gallery, and of course a constable who recognized him wouldn't report it."

"Not when no hue and cry was raised until after he left," Daisy agreed. "Still, there's not much chance Westcott did see him."

"Not much chance, but some. I'll run Westcott to earth first thing in the morning. Thank you, love. You have saved me from sitting around waiting for a purchasing jeweller to turn up, or for the thief to go looking for one."

Alec was pretty good at holding the umbrella with one hand while hugging with the other. Quite some time passed before Daisy made use of her key.

Lucy was down in the kitchen, making cocoa. "Half an hour on the doorstep in the rain," she observed dryly. "Why didn't you invite him in, darling? I wouldn't have interrupted the billing and cooing."

"He didn't mean to stay. He has to work tomorrow, and so do I."

"Cocoa?"

In spite of cocoa, Daisy was too keyed up to fall asleep easily. One of the tunes from the *New World* kept going round in her head like a ghostly gramophone record, and above it sailed Alec's words. Not, alas, the sweet nothings he had whispered in her ear, but the comment about the probability of the villain being a member of the museum staff.

Witt, Mummery, Steadman, Ruddlestone.

Harbottle said Ruddlestone could not possibly be a murderer. Though that jibed with Daisy's opinion of the invertebrate curator, it was not evidence, of course, only a testimonial to his popularity as a boss.

But could any man keep up Ruddlestone's obviously genuine joviality under the pressure of being hunted by the police? And, concerned for his own skin, would he have any thought to spare for recataloguing centuries-old collections of millennia-old fossils?

The last argument applied equally to Steadman, who was absolutely obsessed with Saltopus. Daisy had gone to look at progress on the little dinosaur after her appointment with the Creepy-Crawly man.

O'Brien had left for good, having learnt all he wanted, Atkins told her. The loss of the Hollywood incentive had not visibly dampened Steadman's enthusiasm. Saltopus's spine had grown by several inches. *Sotto voce,* Daisy observed to the commissionaire that the construction would go faster if the assistant was allowed to do more than merely stand ready to hand up the next vertebra.

"Not flippin' likely, miss," Atkins had whispered back. "Has to do it all himself, does our Mr. Steadman."

Steadman was too obsessed with dinosaurs to care two hoots for a fortune in gems.

What about Witt? Daisy thought, turning over in bed and shaking her pillow, which felt as if it was stuffed with stones, precious or otherwise.

When she last saw him, Witt had been studying a primitive horse, but he had not been too absorbed to spend quite some time talking with her about the crimes. He had introduced the subject, as far as Daisy could remember. She rather suspected he had tried to pump her about the progress of the police investigation, and he might have tried to divert suspicion to ffinch-Brown.

Though she quite liked Witt, she was not at all sure she

entirely trusted him. He was by far the least candid and straightforward of the four curators.

Where could he have hidden the jewels? Was the Grand Duke right, after all, about the cave bear and its fellow shaggy mammals? Did one or more of them have precious stones in their heads, like the toad in the old tale? Alec agreed that it was improbable, but there might be other places no one but Witt was likely to disturb.

He also had the most obvious motive for killing Pettigrew.

Motives, rather: his humiliating exit in the Keeper's grasp; the business of the flints; and, if he was the thief, the discovery of the theft.

Too much Witt makes the world rotten, Daisy thought, beginning to grow drowsy. Tennyson? If she had learnt nothing else at school, she had had English poetry drummed into her. Lines often roamed through her head, accurately or inaccurately, when she was falling asleep.

But she must not fall asleep yet. She had not considered the case against Mummery.

> *There was an old fellow called Mummery,*
> *Who fell into a basin of flummery.*
> *He swam to the side*
> *Where he hung on, and cried,*
> *"I'm a victim of jiggery-pokery!"*

It didn't quite rhyme, and anyway, Pettigrew was the victim. Mummery would never have killed him within reach of his fragile fossilized fools. Reptiles. Except that Mummery had a whale of a . . . a *Pareiasaurus* of a temper, and when he lost it he was not apt to consider consequences.

Daisy drifted off with an image of the smashed Pareiasaurus in her mind. It metamorphosed into a Megalosaurus, strolling along on the end of a dog-lead, its ribs rattling. Bits of bone kept dropping off, all over the carpet.

"You mustn't do that," Belinda scolded. "Gran will be frightfully cross."

"Who dusts the dinosaurs, I'd like to know?" Mrs. Fletcher demanded angrily. "Don't you realize they have jewels in their heads, like the toad in the fable?"

In her sleep, Daisy smiled.

Fourteen

Pangs of hunger began to distract Daisy from her work. She glanced at the clock on the mantelpiece. Nearly lunchtime.

Practically all the planning for the article was done: the headings arranged in logical order, vital and particularly interesting bits of her notes underlined in red ink. Another hour or so and she could begin the actual writing. She needed a break.

Standing up, she stretched and went out into the hall.

Mrs. Potter was straightening her hat in the looking-glass, preparatory to leaving for the day. Artificial cherries bobbed, silk violets nodded, and sequins glittered as she turned to Daisy.

"I 'asn't done your study out proper in a month o' Sundays, Miss Daisy," she said severely. "You'll be able to grow spuds on that desk soon if you don't let me dust."

"As soon as I finish this article," Daisy promised, "you can have a whole morning at it. Toodle-oo, then, see you Monday."

"You take termorrer off, miss. All work and no play, like they say."

The char departed and Daisy went thoughtfully down to the kitchen. Dust—she had dreamt about dust, and she had a feeling it was important to remember the dream.

She took a tin of sardines from the cupboard. As usual when she was absent-minded, she put the key on crooked, so the lid rolled back crooked and only half way, and she had to extract the fish with a fork. Fish? Dust and fish? What on earth was the connection?

Eyeing the fish on her plate, she decided she wasn't really awfully keen on sardines. For a start, someone ought to be able to invent an easier way to open the tins than those idiotic keys. And then, there were the bones . . . .

Keys, bones, and fish. Dr. Smith Woodward, who kept losing his keys, was a recognized expert on fossil fish. The fossil fish were in the dinosaur gallery. *Who dusts the dinosaurs?*

The dream flooded back.

Who dusted the dinosaurs, those fragile fossils with their heads in the air, out of reach from the floor? Who but their curator? "Has to do it all himself, does our Mr. Steadman," said Sergeant Wilfred Atkins.

Yet Steadman showed no apparent interest in the police investigation, being almost feverishly engrossed in his Saltopus. Too feverishly, perhaps, Daisy thought. He was a nervy type who, having stolen the jewels, might well lose his head and lash out if he understood Pettigrew to say all was discovered.

Still, why choose what must be a nerve-racking time to start on a new and complex project? There was the *Lost World* man, of course, with the lure of fame and fortune which always accompanied the word Hollywood.

It dawned on Daisy that the man from Hollywood might have arrived like manna from heaven. Steadman himself said he had not yet completed models of all the missing bones, but O'Brien's interest was the perfect excuse to start assembling a skeleton not really quite ready for display. And for the assembly he needed ladders—

Ladders ready and waiting in the gallery, so that when the right moment came, he could seize his chance to retrieve the stolen gems from the dinosaurs' heads.

Abandoning the sardines, Daisy ran upstairs to the telephone. On the way, doubts arose. She refused to tell Alec that her insight arose from a dream. Was her reasoning good enough to ring him at Scotland Yard, or was there a fatal flaw she had not spotted? He would not be pleased if she disturbed him at work for nothing.

Perhaps he was at home. It was worth trying, though she'd be a bit pipped if he had gone home after seeing Constable Westcott and not 'phoned her to tell her what he had found out. After all, he might never have heard of Westcott but for her.

She dialled the St. John's Wood number. After several rings, she heard Belinda's breathless voice giving the number.

"It's Aunt Daisy, darling."

"Oh, hello, Aunt Daisy. Sorry I was so slow to answer. I was brushing Nana."

"Good for you." Daisy enquired after the puppy and her relations with Mrs. Fletcher, which had improved slightly. Then she asked, "Is Daddy there?"

"No, he had to go to Devon."

"Devon!"

"It's quite a long way, isn't it? He said he won't be back today. He went to see a man this morning, and the neighbors said he'd gone to stay with his sister in Devon, only they weren't sure of her name or the village or anything, just the name of the farm, near Taviscott. I think."

"Tavistock?"

"That's it. Daddy decided he really needed to talk to the man, so he and Mr. Tring went right away, in the car."

"Bother!" said Daisy. She gave Alec the benefit of the doubt and assumed he had rung her when Lucy was on the 'phone, as she had been for some time before going out.

"I'm sorry, Aunt Daisy," Belinda said anxiously. "Are you awfully cross with Daddy?"

"No, darling, it's no use being cross when he's just doing his job."

"It isn't, is it? Aunt Daisy, please will you hold on for

just a minute?" The ear-piece clicked on the table, then Daisy heard a muffled voice: "Granny, may I please invite Aunt Daisy to tea, *please?*"

The invitation was proffered and accepted, and Daisy returned to her lunch. The sardines looked less appetizing than ever, especially as she was going out for tea. Putting them away in the larder, she vowed never to eat them again once she was married to Alec.

Too maddening that he had buzzed off! And taken Tom Tring with him, as well. She would willingly have told Tring her deduction, but she hesitated to approach whomever Alec had left in charge at this end, let alone— heaven forbid!—Superintendent Crane.

There was always Sergeant Jameson. Strictly speaking he was not involved in the investigation, but on the other hand, he was right on the spot.

Daisy decided to pop into the museum and have a word with Sergeant Jameson on her way to St. John's Wood for tea. She worked hard for a couple of hours, then walked to the Natural History Museum. Fate was against her. It was Jameson's day off.

"He'll be in tomorrow, miss," his substitute promised her. "Ten till six, same as usual, but the museum opens at ha' past two, Sundays."

Sighing, she thanked him and went out to catch a Number 74 'bus.

By the next day, Daisy had demoted her educated deduction to guesswork. She was in two minds whether to trouble Jameson with it, or wait till Alec came back, or simply abandon it.

It was a bleak day, autumn showing its teeth. Sitting at the typewriter, Daisy grew chilled, her feet frigid. She decided a brisk walk was what she needed, and once outside, her steps turned of their own volition towards the museum.

When she arrived, the constables on duty were just dispersing on their regular patrols about the halls and galleries. "And keep an eye on that Grand Duke," Jameson admonished them as they departed, leaving him alone in the police post.

"Be with you in a minute, miss," he grunted, and filled in some figures on a duty sheet. "There we are. Now, what's up? I heard you was asking for me yesterday."

"I expect you'll think I'm a fearful ass," said Daisy tentatively, "but I've had an idea, and I decided you were the best person to try it on."

"Go ahead, miss. Nothing venture, nothing gain."

Thus encouraged, Daisy explained her reasoning—omitting its dream source. The sergeant listened intently, whether from politeness or interest, she could not tell. "So, you see," she finished apologetically, "it's not much more than a guess."

"Blimey, miss, sounds good to me! It's true Mr. Steadman won't let the housemen go near his skellingtons. Course, I'm not a detective officer, and I'm bound to ask, have you told Detective Chief Inspector Fletcher?"

"He's gone out of town. Looking for Constable Westcott, actually. He hadn't heard of him till I mentioned him."

Jameson blenched. "Flippin' 'ell, if you'll excuse my language, miss. He already thinks we're blinkin' idiots, letting a murder and a burglary go on under our noses. And now no one told him about Westcott retiring!"

"I'm afraid not." Daisy saw her chance and seized it. "But if you were to find the jewels, when everyone else has missed them . . . Of course, if they're not there, no one need know we looked."

"We?"

"You'd let me go with you, wouldn't you?" she coaxed. Without her to egg him on, she thought, he might get cold feet. "It's only fair."

"That's as may be." He gave her a harassed glance. "In

the dinosaur skulls, you think they are. We couldn't go while the museum's open."

Careful not to show her triumph at his choice of pronouns, Daisy glanced around. She had not noticed that the museum was busier than usual. A stream of visitors was still pushing in through the doors, and through the arches she saw crowds around the African elephant and wandering from bay to bay of the Central Hall.

"No, not till closing time," she agreed. "I could come back just before six o'clock."

"That's the ticket," said Jameson, his relief suggesting he doubted that, when it came to the point, she would actually return. "I'll have to clear it with Sergeant Drummond, that takes over at six, but I don't s'pose he'll mind."

"Right-oh, then, Sergeant, I'll see you at ten to six," Daisy vowed.

She decided to go and have a quick look at the dinosaur gallery, just to make sure the ladders were still there, she told herself. As she rounded the police post, she came face to face with Rudolf Maximilian.

"Hello," she said, "are you still hoping they'll let you cut up the animals?"

"Mine ruby is somevhere," he said sulkily. "I try to see vhere might it be, so to tell police."

Daisy thought he looked rather shifty, and she wondered whether he had been giving the extinct mammals a rather closer examination than was permitted to the public. Going through into the gallery, she saw that Sergeant Hamm had his hands full—his one and only hand, anyway—with the multitudinous visitors. In the midst of those swarms of locusts, he might not have noticed what the Grand Duke was about. Contrariwise, swarms of visitors could hardly have helped observing him if he had indecently molested the sabre-tooth or a mammoth.

In the reptile gallery, a crowd had gathered around the

Pareiasaurus, though it was still hidden by dust-sheets. In the dinosaur gallery, a lesser crowd stared at the dust-sheets concealing the Saltopus stand and the bone table.

For a moment, Daisy thought the ladders were gone, but then she saw them, folded and laid on the floor against the wall. Steadman would not have to risk arousing suspicion by asking the Superintendent of House Staff to have a ladder brought up specially, perhaps with the excuse of dusting his dinosaurs. He must have done that, she supposed, when he hid the jewels, but no one knew then that they had been pinched. Now all he had to do was stay late after work tomorrow.

Assuming she was right, once he had retrieved the jewels, what then? Daisy pondered as she left the museum and walked briskly homeward through the dank afternoon.

Then all he needed was patience. If he realized he was being watched, he must also realize the police could not spare the men to follow him forever. The police circular describing the gems would disappear into the backs of files or piles of papers, and jewellers would forget the details.

If Steadman waited long enough, and failing other evidence, he might get away with his crimes.

Daisy was pleased with this conclusion, since it meant she and Jameson were justified in looking for the jewels tonight, before Steadman had a chance to get there first. Whether Alec would accept her argument was another matter, but in his absence, she had to do what she thought best.

As Daisy approached home, and thus neared the Thames, she noticed wisps of mist curling up the street and lurking Grand-Duke-like between the houses. Cold air over the warm river was the breeding ground for London's famous pea-soupers, but it was early in the season for a full-scale fog. Most people in the megalopolis cooked with gas nowadays, and as yet few would have lit the coal fires whose smoke and soot nourished the river mists.

Shutting the front door firmly on the ominous vapours, Daisy hoped a breeze would come up and blow them away. Anyway, she wasn't going to let a fog stop her going back to the museum. She might be wrong about Steadman and his dinosaurs, but if she was right, she did not want Sergeant Jameson hogging all the glory.

She might be wrong. As Daisy sat down at her desk, she frowned absently at the sheet she had left half-typed in the machine.

Whatever Steadman's place on Alec's list, she had not rated him highly as a suspect. A passion for dinosaurs need not exclude a passion for money, she supposed. If only she knew something of his private circumstances. Alec had kept to himself whatever he had discovered.

Witt said Steadman had a rotten home life. A nagging wife, perhaps? Did he want money to be able to leave her? How would desertion affect his position at the museum, and thus his work with his precious dinosaurs?

Unable to answer any of these questions, Daisy tried to concentrate on her own work, but she was writing a passage about dinosaurs, so her thoughts kept returning to Steadman.

Steadman and his precious dinosaurs. Precious stones stolen. What was the connection, if any? The Grand Duke's motive was far more understandable. He was as mad about his lost country as Steadman was about dinosaurs.

His lost country and his lost ruby, doubly lost—unless *he* had pinched it—now that only a fake gem remained. Rudolf Maximilian left with a fake gem, Daisy mused, and Steadman with his fake Diplodocus. She remembered his chagrin as he explained to Derek and Belinda that the pride of his collection was just plaster of Paris.

Daisy sat bolt upright. Suddenly she remembered so clearly she practically heard Steadman's voice: "The

Diplodocus was found in America. The American museums bag all the best. They have the *money* . . ."

. . . The money to send out their own expeditions. The trustees of the British Museum (Natural History) had been debating setting up an expedition for years, without a decision. Was *that* what Steadman wanted money for, pots of money—his own dinosaur-hunting expedition?

In Steadman's eyes, Daisy suspected, that would be motive enough for robbing the mineralogy gallery. After all, as his colleagues agreed, compared to once-living fossils, what importance had mere inanimate stones?

Of course, coming up with a credible motive still didn't mean she was right, but it made her more determined than ever to find out.

With that decided, she managed to write a few paragraphs before Lucy brought her a cup of tea.

"It's perfectly beastly out," Lucy said. "Mrs. Potter laid a fire in the sitting room. I thought I'd light it later. We could turn on the wireless and eat by the fire—tomato soup, fillet of sole, runner beans, potatoes in their jackets—and have a game of Parcheesi or something."

"It sounds lovely." Glancing at the window, Daisy shivered. The air had taken on a sickly yellowish tinge. A haze blurred the roof of Lucy's studio and the houses on the other side of the mews. "But I have to go out for a bit first."

"Darling, must you?"

If the fog set in for several days, Alec's watchers might easily lose Steadman. She *had* to go, to keep Jameson up to the mark. "Yes, I'd better," she sighed.

"Too, too maddening. I won't light the fire till you get back, so that we don't have to bring up more coal."

Warmed by the tea, Daisy went quickly to put on her winter coat, hat, and gloves before the warmth vanished. As soon as she set foot outside the front door, the fog grabbed her by the throat. She coughed.

Breathing through her nose, she set out. The lamppost

at the corner was already lit, murkily haloed. Visibility was not too bad as yet. Turning into Church Street, Daisy saw a 'bus and a motor-car crossing at the top, in the Fulham Road. The few pedestrians she met had hunched shoulders and drips on their noses. They were obviously hastening home. She envied them.

Reminding herself that the game was afoot, she stiffened her sinews and, imitating the action of a sabre-toothed tiger in a hurry, she sped museum-ward.

In the quarter of an hour it took Daisy to reach Cromwell Road, the fog thickened perceptibly. The museum's towers, which should have loomed above the plane trees, were invisible. The planes themselves were greenish blotches. A lone 'bus moved cautiously down the street, and Daisy crossed in its wake. Sundays were always quiet, but this was morguelike.

A uniformed constable stood at the museum gates. "The museum shuts in a few minutes, miss," he said. "I'd get on home, if I was you, 'fore it gets any worser."

"I'm meeting someone," Daisy told him.

A couple with two children came out of the museum, stopped to stare in dismay, and scurried away. At the top of the steps, Daisy glanced back. The buildings on the far side of the street were vague shapes, details obliterated.

Successful or not, she thought, she would beg Sergeant Jameson to see her home.

A swirl of fog entered with her. Ahead, in the Central Hall, a haze softened the outline of the great elephant, as if it tramped across the dusty plains of Africa. Daisy almost expected it to raise its head and trumpet its disgust in this raw, clammy northern clime.

The earlier crowds had departed. A few stragglers were just leaving, shepherded from the galleries by commissionaires anxious to take their own leave. Each reported to the police post, where Jameson ticked them off by the light of an electric lamp. Not anxious to be seen, Daisy went and lurked out of the way, behind the nearest pillar.

Jameson's men were in the post, waiting to sign out. The evening shift sergeant leant on the counter, chatting. From the rear of the hall came two constables together, one of them coughing with uninhibited ostentation.

"That don't sound too good," said the evening sergeant.

"I'm ever so ill, Sarge. Can I go home?"

"It's just the fog, Sarge," the other constable said with a grin. Daisy recognized Neddle.

"Nice try, Mason." He caught sight of Daisy. "'Scuse me, miss, the museum's about to close. Hey, don't I know . . . ?"

"That's Miss Dalrymple," said Jameson. "Here, you lot, clear out. I want a word with Sergeant Drummond, private."

The day constables were only too glad to get off five minutes early. The two latest-comers strolled to the main entrance and stood gazing out into the gloom. Daisy went to join the sergeants.

Jameson invited her to explain, which she did.

"Well now," Drummond said cautiously, "I can't see no harm in it, long as you're careful not to bust nothing. You'll have to wait till all the commissionaires have reported everyone out of their galleries, and the front doors are locked."

Consulting his papers, Jameson said, "Ground floor's all clear. Just upstairs to go. No staff in today, and who can blame 'em."

A few members of the public trickled down the main stairs, followed by the commissionaires from the non-fossil mammal galleries and botany. Last of all came Pavett, from mineralogy, ushering a larger group than the others. With the stolidity of the deaf, he ignored their comments on the jewel theft.

He came over to the police post. "Everyone out, lights off, inner doors locked," he reported laconically. Laying two keys on the counter, he took himself off.

"All yours, mate," said Jameson, coming out through the flap in the counter.

Drummond locked the main entrance doors behind the last visitors, and returned to the police post. "Right, I'm going up to bar and bolt the Mineral Gallery," he said, "after the horse has been stolen as you might say. The dinosaurs are all yours, miss. I'll look in to see how you're doing when I come down. Neddle, you stay here. Mason, go and report everyone out to the chap watching the back door, then come back."

Sergeant Drummond and Constable Mason tramped off through the Central Hall on their way to the stairs up and down respectively. Daisy and Sergeant Jameson went round to the fossil mammal gallery.

The electric lights, on for the last half hour because of the fog, had been turned off. In the dingy daylight coming through the windows, the mammoths loomed larger than ever. But the fog had not penetrated thus far.

"What a difference!" Daisy exclaimed. "I didn't realize so much fog had got in back there."

"Nasty stuff," said Jameson.

"Beastly. I was wondering if you'd very much mind seeing me home afterwards."

"Don't you worry, miss. We'll get you home right and tight."

Jameson's boots echoed hollowly on the mosaic floor as they went through the hall to the fossil reptiles. Empty of people, lit only by the dreary light from the opaque skylights, the gallery seemed a fitting place for murder. Crossing it, they entered the dinosaur gallery.

The far end was lost in gloom. Daisy had taken several steps at the sergeant's side before she saw that someone was there before them.

"Hey, you!" yelled Jameson.

The figure on the stepladder, just withdrawing his hand from the Iguanodon's head, turned an aghast face. The Grand Duke!

While Jameson, immobilized by surprise, fumbled for his whistle, Rudolf Maximilian slithered down the rocking ladder and dashed through the arch to the cephalopods. Jameson blew a short sharp blast, then took off after the Grand Duke, his whistle shrilling between his lips. The sound, designed to call help from streets away, rang on after the sergeant had disappeared.

Daisy was about to follow when she noticed a white blob at the foot of the ladder. It was a handkerchief, embroidered with an elaborate crest, holding several gems embedded in some sort of putty. She was reaching to pick it up when heavy footsteps raced towards her from behind.

"What's happened?" cried Constable Neddle. "Where's Sergeant Jameson?"

"They went thataway," said Daisy, pointing. The picture-shows her brother used to drag her to in Ludlow, before the War, had often included William S. Hart cowboy films.

Neddle galloped off in hot pursuit. Daisy realized that the Grand Duke's way was blocked by the work room and Geological Library. From invertebrates, he would have to go out into the reptile gallery. She hurried back to the dinosaurs' main entrance arch, and stepped out into reptiles just as Jameson—still whistling—emerged from invertebrates.

However, instead of doubling back, Rudolf Maximilian had turned left. He was a vague shadow at the far end of the reptile gallery. Jameson tore after him. Daisy followed, meeting Neddle at the invertebrate entrance and continuing at his side.

Rudolf led them through the hall at the end, back along the mammal gallery, and into the Central Hall, now a somber cavern. There he headed for the main staircase, but as he reached the foot, Sergeant Drummond appeared at the top, a hazy figure in the intruding fog. The Grand Duke raced on under the arches to the North Hall, where he disappeared into the eastern enclosed staircase. Jameson, Neddle, and Drummond streamed after him.

Constable Mason, scarcely recognizable in the all-pervading gloom, came out of the stairs on the west side of the hall, roared "What . . .?" and joined the hunt.

Daisy did not fancy running up stairs. She knew the North Hall stairs were closed to the public above the first floor, so she went back to stand at the foot of the main staircase, looking up.

A moment later, the Grand Duke arrived at the top of the main stairs, apparently intending to descend. He saw Daisy at the bottom, changed his mind, and sped on along the giraffe gallery, still going strong, intermittently visible between the pillars.

Drummond led the pursuers now, Mason at his heels, Jameson and Neddle beginning to flag. From below, Daisy watched them chase Rudolf to the upper stairs. He took the lower flight two at a time, but he was panting now. Mason leapt up after him, Drummond trotted, the other two policemen stumbled behind. No matter, Rudolf would be trapped on the second floor.

But he didn't go on up. Loping across the half landing, he went down the opposite flight, and turned right to return through the British Nesting Birds.

Where he was aiming for, Daisy could not guess. There was no way out of the museum for him. Yet as long as the idiotic police failed to spread out and head him off, they would never catch him—as long as any of them was capable of movement. Everyone's speed had slowed considerably.

However, the Grand Duke, unlike the policemen, was young, slim, and desperate. He just might get far enough ahead to lose them temporarily. In that case he might conceivably double back to pick up the jewels, in the surely vain hope of hiding and somehow eluding searchers. He had, after all, hidden well enough not to be ejected from the museum when it closed.

The hunt disappeared into the passage leading back past the Refreshment Room to the stairs down to the North Hall—or round and back to the giraffes. Daisy decided to return to the dinosaur gallery.

That she had been astonished to see Rudolf Maximilian retrieving the jewels from the dinosaurs was the understatement of the year. His credentials as murderer were excellent, but he failed dismally as a burglary candidate. Could he have been in league with someone? Randell the junior mineralogy assistant, perhaps?

The theft would have been comparatively easy for Randell, but Daisy could not see why he needed the Grand Duke's help. Still less likely was it that either of them should hide the loot among the dinosaurs. No, the dinosaur man had to be involved. For some inscrutable reason, Steadman was in league with Rudolf.

So which of them was the murderer?

Passing the Pareiasaurus in its ghostly white shroud, Daisy once again entered the dinosaur gallery. The Diplodocus loomed creepily, its tail scarcely visible in the shadows eighty-five feet away. She wished she knew where the light switch was.

The tick-tock of her footsteps was the only, eerie sound. Then, from close behind her, came a creaking *c-r-r-rack*.

She started to turn.

The blow caught her on the side of the head. In an explosion of pain, she had time for one astonished thought: *Attacked by a dinosaur?* before she sank into darkness.

Fifteen

Beneath a wide mackerel sky, Dartmoor was pink with heather spotted here and there with the gold of late-blooming gorse, the emerald of bog grass. On either side of the narrow, hedgeless road, hillsides rolled up to the tors. It was not difficult to imagine long-gone giants heaping up those great piles of granite for purposes unknown and unknowable.

Tring was driving. He had to slow to a near stop now and then while sheep made up their tiny minds whether to vacate the roadway in favour of the noisy intruder. The wild ponies had no doubts. They scattered at the Austin's approach.

Declining in the west, the sun painted the striated clouds in tones of rose and primrose. It could do nothing to brighten the grimness of His Majesty's Prison at Princetown, a stark contrast to the smiling face of nature.

"Poor devils," Alec observed.

"We put some of 'em there, Chief," Tom protested, "and not without good reason. Better than the long jump."

"I'm not so certain of that. Death can be a merciful release. Hanging is more of an offence against society than against the wretches we hang."

Tom, who didn't consider hanging an offence against anything or anyone, maintained a stubborn silence.

"We teach by example that violence is an acceptable solution. It fails as a deterrent, because most murders are committed in a moment of unthinking passion or panic.

Take the present case. Pettigrew, who was a large and in-
timidating man, made what was taken as a verbal threat,
and very likely waved the flint weapon in a threatening
manner. The murderer seized it from him. He probably
lunged forward to grab it back."

"And hey presto! He's dead," said Tom. "But that's
guessing, Chief, and any road, if you're right, Pettigrew's
words were taken as a threat because our man had already
committed a felony."

Alec sighed.

In the warm twilight, they drove down off the moor into
the little town of Tavistock. A Saturday evening queue was
moving into the picture palace, and the sound of voices
floated through the open doors of pubs. With a longing
glance at the nearest of these, Tom stopped the Austin outside the police station.

The sergeant on duty was expecting them. "We've found
him for you, zir," he reported in a slow, soft West Country
voice. "Waren't as easy as you might think, coming from the
city. There's a Westcott village, zame name as your man, up
north t'ard the Lyd valley, near Coryton, and a Rushbrook
Farm not far off. We did think as that might be the one."

"I take it, it wasn't," said Alec patiently.

"Nay, zir, and we found four more. Rushbrook, zee, isn't
an uncommon name for a farm in these parts, as could
be from a hillside stream rushing down, or could be a
meadowland stream wi' rushes growing."

"And which is the one we want, Sergeant?"

"Oh, 'tis Jack Trevinnick's place, over towards Zyden-
ham Damerel, down by the Tamar. Good, fertile zoil, and
the rushes to harvest for baskets and the like. You've may-
hap heard of our pannier market, here in Tavistock?"

Alec admitted he had not, nor of the October Goose
Fair, though he vaguely recalled that Tavistock was Sir
Francis Drake's birthplace. With weary courtesy he cut
short the sergeant's discourse on the town's history as a
mining centre since it became a stannary town in 1309.

"How do we get to Sydenham Damerel?" he enquired.

Tom wrote down the directions. Alec asked the local man to book them a couple of rooms for the night. Then he took the wheel, and they wound about the country lanes for six or seven miles, passing through several tiny hamlets. Sydenham Damerel was large enough to boast its own constable. Calling at his house for further directions to Rushbrook Farm, they learnt that ex-Constable Westcott had dropped in to introduce himself on arrival in Devon.

"And a good job too," said Tom as they set out on the last leg of their journey, "or it might've taken 'em a week to ferret him out for us."

It was all but dark when they pulled up in a cow-smelling farmyard, to be greeted by a volley of barks. On the doorstep of the whitewashed granite house, a plump woman appeared, silhouetted against the light within.

Hushing the two black and white dogs, she invited the policemen into a large, low-ceilinged kitchen, where hams and onions hung from the beams. An elaborately plaited corn-dolly, still green, was nailed up over the vast fireplace, and a kettle steamed on the hob.

"Fred's down the byre with my Jack and our Jed," said Mrs. Trevinnick, waving them to a wooden settle by the fire, and bustling about with teapot, kettle, and caddy. "They'll be up pretty quick now 'tis dark. Fred'll be right glad to zee you. He do miss his p'lice friends, but I can tell you, it's done him a world o' good to retire and get away from the city."

Alec made a noncommittal noise. Tom's eyes were fixed on the big white-wood table, where an enormous cake had joined teapot, best cups and saucers, jug of milk, and basin of sugar. They had stopped *very* briefly for lunch on the way.

"Well, stands to reason, doesn't it?" Mrs. Trevinnick chattered on. "'Tis not healthy living in a big town like that, all smoke and fog. And him on the beat all these years. Not that my Jack don't walk plenty, but country walking's not like pavements, is it? And even when they put Fred in that museum place, there was stairs up and stairs down and stairs all around. His knees hurt him zomething dreadful when he come, but they're a-getting better, bit by bit."

"I'm glad to hear it," said Alec truthfully, well aware that the lot of a lifelong beat copper was not easy.

"And his eyes! You wouldn't think of it, maybe, but I reckon 'tis that 'lectric light doesn't do them any good. 'Tis not natural." She glanced up at the pair of brightly polished brass lanterns, casting a gentle glow from their hooks on the central beam. "Give me paraffin any day, zays I to Jack, when he asks do I want the gas put in."

She supplied them with tea and apple cake, Tom's huge wedge reflecting her view of the appetite appropriate to his size. The men came in shortly. Fred Westcott, a thickset, grizzled old fellow, was not noticeably pleased to see his fellow police officers.

"We're hoping you can help us, Mr. Westcott," said Alec as the men exchanged mucky boots for carpet slippers and washed their hands. "If you would just think back to the beginning of July . . ."

"We'll go in the parlour, Betty," Westcott interrupted grumpily, picking up a hand-lantern the men had brought in with them. "This way, sir, if you don't mind."

Alec and Tom followed him to a small, bleak, excessively tidy room with cross-stitch samplers on the walls. The furniture was early Victorian, faded but otherwise like new. The vicar was probably the only person ever entertained there.

Tom took out his notebook as he and Alec sat down. Westcott stood before them, his hands clasped behind his back.

"I weren't asleep, sir," he declared. "Jest resting me pins a minute. The knees ain't what they was, see, and me eyes gets that tired."

"No one is accusing you of anything, man. You're not in

the force anymore. Sit down, for heaven's sake—or your knees' sake if you prefer—and tell me *when* you weren't asleep."

"Thirteenth o' July, when he come down the stairs. Leastways, that's what I reckoned, then, or from Lower Mammals. By the Nesting Birds, I were, see, the wrong side for Minerlology."

"Who came?" Alec demanded.

But Westcott had to tell his story his own way. "Never thought nothing of it, I didn't, not till it was in the papers how someone stole them jools. See, they knows in the village as I used to work in the museum, so when I went in with Betty Saturday to do her bit shopping, summun showed it me. And I started to wonder. I were on days for a couple of months before, see, so I knowed 'em all. What I arst myself was, what did a fossil man want with mammals, high or low, or botinny, come to that, at that time of night?"

"Good question. Which fossil man?"

"Or any time, come to that. It wasn't like he was fossil mammals, nor yet fossil plants, poor blighter."

Witt exonerated? Alec wasn't sure whether the "poor blighter" was the thief, or merely old Dr. Bentworth.

Westcott enlightened him, on that question at least: "Still, we all come to that, lessn we're in the grave. Which is where they ought to leave them monsters, if you arst me. Stands to reason it'll turn a man's mind, messing about with them dinysores."

"Steadman!" breathed Tom.

"Dinosaurs?" Alec said sharply. "It was the dinosaur curator you saw wandering about on the first floor, late at night, on July thirteenth?"

"Aye, sir. I didn't see his face plain, mind, but he's the only one tall and skinny like that, see, and I knowed his voice, too. It were Mr. Steadman all right. I'd swear to it."

"You may have to. Please describe exactly what you did, where you were, what was said if anything."

Fortunately, once it was a matter of making a straight-forward report, Westcott recalled his police training. Worry over his minor dereliction of duty had obviously impressed the incident on his memory, as well as stopping him wondering at the time what Steadman had been doing. The report was soon done.

Alec stood up. "We'll get a statement typed up tonight and bring it out for you to sign tomorrow. Thank you, Mr. Westcott. Allow me to wish you a happy retirement."

Mrs. Trevinnick, impressed by the speed with which Tom had devoured his piece of cake, and convinced that wholesome food was unobtainable in London, had packed a basket of provisions for them. She refused payment, even for the basket, which she had made herself. Alec managed to press five bob on Jack Trevinnick, who pulled on his boots to light them out to the Austin.

Tom delved in, by feel, as they drove out of the farmyard. "Aha, a great slab of cake," he said with satisfaction. "D'you mind a bit broken off, Chief?"

"Not at all. Hold on while I get my gloves off. Oh, right or left?" queried Alec, coming to a fork in the lane.

"Hold on, I'll have to find that bit of paper and my electric torch. Should've brought young Ernie with us. He'd know."

"There would be less cake for you."

"True! Just as well we left him behind. It's almost worth coming all this way for even if we hadn't got the answer out of Westcott. Left here, Chief, and . . . uh . . . right at the next crossroads."

"But we have no proof, you know, Tom, not even that Steadman's the thief, let alone that he's the murderer. Remember Mummery and the crocodiles. Steadman *might* have been studying parallels between dinosaurs and mammals. He could claim to have been comparing their necks with giraffe necks, say."

"The giraffes are on the other side," Tom pointed out.

"That was just an example." Alec racked his brains. "If

you're going to be fussy, something to do with rhinos, perhaps, or hippos. They're all built like tanks. And Steadman is noted for working late."

"Now we know where to look," said Tom, confidently though muffled by a mouthful of cake, "we'll find evidence, sure enough, or confront him and get a confession. Steadman won't hold out."

With Westcott's signed statement, they left for London early on Sunday morning. Today, ominous clouds hung low over the moor, so Alec took the main road via Okehampton. They kept ahead of the rain all the way however, and even came out into sunshine as they crossed Bagshot Heath.

But from Hounslow Heath, they could see ahead a sepia mass of fog crouched over the city like a hungry octopus, sending out tentacles to draw the suburbs within its grasp. Alec groaned.

"Maybe Mrs. Trevinnick wasn't as far out as all that," said Tom, a sad admission from a born Londoner.

The premature dusk closed down on them. Soot-spattered windscreen open, they crept through the empty streets to Westminster. At New Scotland Yard, a message awaited them.

"Just come in a couple of minutes ago, Gov'nor," said the duty officer. "D. I. Wotherspoon went home. I was going to ring him up."

Alec scanned it. "Great Scott! Telephone Chelsea and tell them I want a dozen constables sent to the Natural History Museum at once. Come along, Tom."

Without protest, if wearily, Tom came. Not until the Austin was crawling up Birdcage Walk through the thickening murk did he venture to ask, "What's up, Chief?"

"Steadman entered the museum at five to six. On a Sunday evening, Tom! I knew the jewels were still there, hidden lord knows where. Damn this fog. Can you stick your head out of the window that side and tell me if I'm going to hit the kerb?"

Driving as fast as he dared, Alec reached the rear of the museum at last. Two plainclothesmen were on duty there at all times, well concealed among the pillars of the arcade. A third, who had been following Steadman, lurked nearby. They converged on Alec.

"I thought I'd better telephone, Gov'nor, him coming this time on a Sunday, and in all this muck. . . ."

"Well done—Culver, is it? I'll remember you. Now, who has the key? Right, open up. One of you inside and one stationed just outside—Steadman is not to be allowed to leave on any pretext whatsoever. You can arrest him if he refuses to stay with you. There will be more men arriving any minute in case we have to chase him all over this damn pile. Tring, Culver, come with me."

They could have done with Piper to lead them to the nearest staircase, but with the aid of Tom's torch, they found it. Only when he saw the door at the top did Alec remember that it was kept locked to bar the public from the basement.

In the lead, Tom, his weariness forgotten now that an arrest was in sight, turned the handle. The door opened. Maybe Steadman had left it unlocked to facilitate his escape.

"Stay here, Culver," Alec ordered in a low voice.

He and Tom emerged into the North Hall and paused to listen. Not a sound. The massive building felt like a mausoleum—as indeed it was, for the corpses and bare bones of countless creatures.

"I bet Steadman wears rubber-soled shoes, Chief." No morbid fancies for Tom Tring, the ever-practical. "He'd never have got away with it else."

"Yes. Keep your eyes peeled. The dinosaur gallery's the obvious place to try first. I'm suspicious of that new skeleton he's been setting up."

"Salty puss," said Tom with a muted chuckle.

"You take this side."

The elephantine sentinel loomed through the fog-hazed twilight of the Central Hall. "The vasty hall of death": The phrase sprang unbidden into Alec's mind. Matthew Arnold, *Requiescat,* he supplied automatically. Someone's spirit "doth inherit the vasty hall . . . " Whose?

Strew on her daisies, daisies, and never a spray of yew. A girl, then. A nameless girl.

But of course it was roses, not daisies. Not Daisy. A prickle of unease shivered down his spine. She *couldn't* be here, not on a foggy Sunday night, her research finished, as she herself had told him.

Wise Tom, to eschew fancies. Yet that was why he'd never advanced beyond the rank of sergeant. In Murder Squad parlance, he hadn't the "nose." Alec had. Something was wrong.

Ahead, the electric light in the police post made a circle of cheer, though it would have been more cheering if any of the officers had been there. They must be on patrol somewhere about the place. Alec was not sure whether to hope they came upon Steadman or not.

As Tom joined him, he glanced at the panel which controlled all the lights in the museum—one could not have visiting children messing about with switches. It must cost a fortune to light the place. At night, he knew, only a few dim lights were used, because of the expense. Given the evening's early darkness, why had they not been switched on?

"I wouldn't mess with that, Chief." Tom might not have the nose, but he sometimes read Alec's thoughts.

"No, it's far too complicated," he agreed reluctantly, "and sudden light might warn Steadman. Let's go."

Though neither was an Ernie Piper, after studying the plans and reconnoitring the territory, they could have found their way in complete darkness. As they reached the arch to the reptile gallery, Alec whispered, "You go round through the cephalopod gallery, Tom. Remember Steadman has keys. He can get away by the door to the General

Library and those stairs to the basement. We may have secured the back door, but I'd rather not have to hunt for him down there."

Alec waited a couple of minutes to let Tom reach the connecting archway. Then he crossed the reptile gallery and peered into the dinosaur gallery. The far end was lost in shadows. Scanning the nearer part, he saw a dark heap on the floor some twenty yards away, with two whitish objects lying beside it.

As he moved to investigate, a scraping sound came from the other end. Tom's bulk flitted across the centre to a point between the source of the noise and the library door, then receded into the shadows.

Hurrying to join him, Alec stopped dead as the dark heap sat up and said with shaky indignation, in Daisy's voice, "The Grand Duke hit me!"

"Daisy, it's not . . ." Alec babbled, dropping to his knees beside her, "it can't . . . What the bloody hell are you doing here?"

From the far corner of the gallery came a crash—bang—thump—groan, followed by Tom Tring's boom: "James Steadman, in the name of the law, I arrest you for larceny. Other charges may be preferred against you. I must warn you that you have the right not to speak, but anything you choose to say will be taken down and may be used in evidence." Handcuffs clicked.

"It's not what it looks like," squeaked Steadman.

"The Grand Duke hit you?" queried Alec, his arms around Daisy.

"Everything under control here, Chief," Tom reported. "What's going on? Did I hear Miss Dalrymple?"

"She says the Grand Duke hit her."

"That's right," Steadman confirmed in a shaky voice. "It was the Grand Duke. I saw everything. I was just collecting the stolen jewels to hand over to the police."

"Are you all right, sweetheart?"

"Yes. Sort of. My head aches frightfully."

"Mine's beginning to. What happened?"

"We caught Rudolf Maximilian extracting the jewels from the dinosaurs' skulls." Daisy leaned back against Alec's comfortingly broad chest. "The others chased him, but I came back to make sure the jewels were safe. He must have eluded them and followed me, and hit me on the head."

"With this." Alec reached out for one of the white objects, long, heavy, curved, tapering. "A broken rib, if I'm not mistaken."

Daisy started to laugh. She couldn't help it, though it made her head hurt worse.

"My poor darling," Alec said tenderly, kissing her ear. "But this is no time to get hysterical."

"Shall I let Mr. Steadman go?" Tom called.

"No, not yet, though I can't see him breaking a precious dinosaur bone."

"I wouldn't," Steadman affirmed.

"But it's not!" said Daisy.

"She's concussed," Alec said worriedly.

At that moment the lights went on.

Over by Saltopus, a ladder lay on the floor. Steadman sprawled beside it, on his back, his hands cuffed before him. Tom stood over him, splinters of shattered Saltopus skull scattered about his feet. Amidst the shards, gems winked red, purple, and green.

"It's plaster of Paris," said Daisy, "like the Diplodocus rib. I think I understand now."

"I don't!" Alec and Tom chorused.

The unmistakable sound of police boots approached beyond the entrance arch. Sergeant Jameson appeared, followed by Constables Mason and Neddle, with a sullen, disconsolate, handcuffed Grand Duke between them.

"Miss Dalrymple!" cried Jameson, running forward. "What the . . . ? Oh lor', Chief Inspector Fletcher!" He skidded to a halt, saluting, then saw Tom Tring and Steadman. "Oh lor', what's happened?"

"The Grand Duke hit Miss Dalrymple over the head with a dinosaur bone," said Alec, without any great degree of conviction.

"I do not! Chentlemans not hit ladies. Only want mine ruby, de odders for police to find I was leave. I not never will not hit Miss Dalrymple," declared Rudolf Maximilian passionately.

"Can't've, sir, and that's the truth. We was chasing him, four of us, right up till he went up to the Upper Mammals on the second floor and we nabbed him when he tried to hide in with the chimpanzees."

"'Sright, sir," said Sergeant Drummond, coming in behind the others. "Had him in sight the whole time, if it was only his heels. What's been going on here, then?"

Alec, still kneeling with his arm around Daisy's shoulders, looked down at her and said, "Miss Dalrymple claims to know."

"Not *know*," Daisy demurred, "but it's more of an educated deduction than sheer guesswork."

"Pray tell," said Alec.

"Mr. Tring, those jewels at your feet, are they actually embedded in the plaster?"

Tom bent down and picked up a chunk in one massive hand. With the other, he hauled Steadman to his feet as he straightened, keeping hold of the curator's arm. "Yes, Miss Dalrymple, right inside."

"That settles it, I think." Her head aching like billy-oh, Daisy cut her explanation as short as possible. "Mr. Steadman stole the jewels and hid them in the dinosaurs' heads. Grand Duke Rudolf could conceivably have done so, but he couldn't possibly have moulded some into the Saltopus skull. I believe he overheard Sergeant Jameson and me discussing it, and decided to try for his ruby, but he must have missed our planning to search tonight."

"Was lots noisy pee-ople," said Rudolf sulkily.

"He must have come in here very soon after Atkins cleared the public out. Mr. Jameson and I found him here, assumed he was the thief, and gave chase. I hadn't considered that this was the logical time for Mr. Steadman to retrieve his loot, on a Sunday evening, when none of his colleagues would be working late."

There, that would have to satisfy them for now. Daisy's head was pounding and swimming at the same time, and she simply did not have the pep to go into more detail. As for the murder, she didn't even want to think about it. She had to leave something for Alec to solve.

"And now, please, darling, I want to go home!"

"Can you stand, love? Careful." He helped her to rise, steadied her when she wobbled, then swept her up into his arms. "Sergeant Tring, you're in charge. You can take both of 'em in. We have evidence and witnesses enough to hold them both."

The sun shone bright on Primrose Hill. The night's hoar frost lingered in shady spots, but the air was warm. Ginger pigtails flying, Belinda raced ahead with Nana on the lead.

"They make me feel old," said Daisy.

"How's the bump?"

"Still there. And painful to the touch," she warned as Alec unceremoniously pulled off her hat and ran his fingers gently through her curls. "No headache for the past three days, thank heaven."

"I could kill the brute!" Alec said savagely, then he sighed. "No, I couldn't. He certainly didn't intend to kill you, or he'd have succeeded. Weedy as he looks, he's actually quite muscular."

"From heaving dinosaur bones about, I expect. That is, I take it you mean Steadman, not Grand Duke Rudolf?"

"Oh, yes, it was Steadman who hit you, and who killed Pettigrew. Your educated deductions were remarkably correct in all essentials."

Daisy frowned up at him, indignant. "What do you mean, remarkably?"

"Pax, sweetheart!" Alec kissed her nose. "Just that you really were slightly concussed at the time you expounded your theory."

"Oh, right-oh. But that was all about the jewels. Did he confess to murdering Pettigrew?"

"In the end. Once we focused on Steadman, and asked the right questions, we obtained other evidence with which to confront him."

"Such as?"

"He told the assistants in the work room he was going to compare the bones he was working on with some in the reptile gallery, not leaving to go home, as he told us. We could have eliminated the Grand Duke early on, incidentally, and ffinch-Brown as well, if I'd taken note of the hammer shaft's being found in the basement. Neither had access."

"Gosh, I never thought of that, either," Daisy admitted. Seeing Alec on the point of asking who had told her about the shaft, she hurried on: "Steadman met Pettigrew in the reptile gallery purely by chance?"

"Yes. Steadman's claiming self-defense. With a good lawyer, he might get away with manslaughter, though the theft will count against him. He'll be put away for a good long stretch for that, I'm sure. The odd thing is, all he seems worried about is that we shouldn't think he stole the gems for personal reasons. He—"

"Don't tell me! He wanted to set up his own expedition to hunt dinosaurs?"

"Daisy, how the deuce . . . ?"

"You know my methods, Watson."

"He told you!"

"Yes, actually. Alec, what about Rudolf Maximilian?"

"We're dropping charges. He's dropping his claim to the ruby. There's some talk of a royal pension for his family."

"Oh, good!"

"Daddy! Aunt Daisy!" Belinda came tearing down the slope towards them, laughing as the puppy almost pulled her off her feet.

"Just one quick question, love, before they get here. I've been promised a fortnight's leave. Will you marry me right away? I'm afraid there won't be time to arrange an elaborate wedding."

"Spiffing!" said Daisy.

HISTORICAL NOTE

In October 1923, the trustees of the British Museum at
last gave final approval for a dinosaur expedition to Tan-
ganyika. "The costs were paid by the Trustees, the
Treasury and by a public subscription, which raised
enough to buy one motor lorry. . . . Overall the results of
the expedition were disappointing."

J. C. Thackray, *Unofficial Archives,* Jan. 1997.

Please turn the page for an exciting
sneak peek of Carola Dunn's newest
Daisy Dalrymple mystery

TO DAVY JONES BELOW

coming in July 2003!

The Fletchers did not get up early. By the time they appeared on deck, the *Talavera* had passed the Fastnet lighthouse and was ploughing through great Atlantic rollers. The south coast of Ireland was fading on the starboard bow. The weather remained unusually benign for mid-October, but Dr. Amboyne, taking the air, reported that quite a few passengers had failed to emerge from their cabins that morning.

"It always happens as soon as we move from the Bristol Channel into the Atlantic," he said with a heartless grin. "Some can't take even this calm. There's really nothing I can do for them except advise tea and toast and fresh air. Not many take my advice."

"Miss Oliphant said she has a remedy," Daisy reminded him.

The doctor laughed. "I'm not about to recommend witchcraft to my patients! The Captain would have me in irons."

Pluming themselves on their immunity to sickness, Daisy and Alec continued their brisk stroll along the boat-deck, circling the central massif of the bridge, funnels, masts, skylights, and mysterious machinery. The sun was warm, but it was after all an October morning so most deck-chairs were set out on the enclosed promenade deck below. There were plenty of other obstacles to walkers, however, in the shape of ventilation ducts and game players.

They passed Arbuckle, Gotobed, and Miss Oliphant—in purple bloomers—playing shuffle-board.

"The blooming bride's probably still doing her face," Daisy observed.

"Cat. She may feel games are beneath her dignity. People who feel inferior have to stand on their dignity."

"It raises them in their own estimation, if no one else's," Daisy quipped. "No, that was beastly of me. I must try to be nice to her. I wish I liked her."

"You can't like everyone, love."

"Why do I feel I shall very shortly dislike Phillip extremely?" she asked, as that gentleman hallooed and waved them over to where he and Gloria were playing deck tennis against another couple.

"Daisy, Fletcher, we'll take you on next!"

"Phil, you know perfectly well I'm hopeless at games."

"Gee, Daisy, that doesn't matter," Gloria assured her earnestly. "It's only for fun."

"As long as you don't chuck too many quoits overboard," Phillip teased.

With deep misgivings, Daisy allowed herself to be persuaded. On their next circuit, she and Alec stopped to play. The best that could be said of her game was that not a single quoit was actually lost, but she enjoyed it anyway.

A second game with Phillip partnering her and Gloria playing with Alec was more evenly matched. At the end, quite a few spectators were there to applaud, including Arbuckle and Gotobed. Turning over the court to a waiting group, Phillip picked up his discarded jacket and offered his cigarette case to Alec.

"No, no," interjected Arbuckle, "have a Havana." He opened his cigar case.

Alec shook his head. "Thank you." With identical gestures, he and Gotobed felt in their pockets and produced pipes and tobacco pouches, Alec's embroidered by Belinda with a wobbly "A. F." Phillip took a cigar.

Daisy was not going to wait around for clouds of tobacco smoke. Besides, she was dripping. (Her nanny's maxim: "Horses sweat, gentlemen perspire, ladies merely glow," had clearly not been intended to apply to deck tennis.)

"I'm going to change, darling," she said.

"Me too," said Gloria, who really was glowing, her golden curls slightly tousled but prettier than ever. "Daisy, have you figured out what you're wearing for the Fancy Dress Ball?"

"No," Daisy admitted. "What about you?"

Together they went down the forward companionway to the open area of the promenade deck, in the bows, where more deck games were in progress around the cargo-hatch. On each side was a door into the enclosed area, the glassed-in promenade encircling the public rooms. Here they parted, Gloria to the port door and thence down the port companionway to the Arbuckle suite, Daisy taking the starboard door and the stairs just within.

As Daisy moved from the door to the companionway, she caught sight of Mrs. Gotobed some way along the promenade, sitting in one of the slatted, wooden deckchairs. She was talking earnestly with the men in the chairs on either side of her.

The one facing Daisy was large and dark, good-looking in a rather flashy way. She rather thought she had seen him with the young American poker-player, Chester, going into the Smoking Room. The other was unmemorable, smaller, wiry, with thinning, mousy hair. Both sat stiffly, leaning slightly towards Wanda Gotobed, giving an impression of nervousness.

Hot and sticky, Daisy had no intention of going to speak to the blooming bride. She was about to turn to go down the stairs when Mrs. Gotobed raised one hand and touched the smaller man's cheek.

Daisy must have made some involuntary gesture which caught the other man's attention, for he stared straight at her. He said something which made Mrs. Gotobed look round and speak sharply. Both men at once rose and, with slight bows, hurried away.

Mrs. Gotobed waved to Daisy, an unmistakable summons.

Reluctantly, Daisy went over to her. "I was on my way to change," she said. "We've been playing a rather energetic game of deck tennis."

"Oh, games! So undignified. Mrs. Fletcher, I suppose you've heard I was on the stage?"

"Well, yes."

"I wasn't a fancy actress or anything, not a star, but I did have my fans," she said coyly. "That was a couple of them, just a couple of stage-door Johnnies, like they say. They recognized me and had the blooming cheek to come and introduce themselves, would you believe?"

"How . . . er . . . flattering."

"Well, if you want the truth, it was, and no mistake. Ever so disappointed they was when I told 'em I'm a married woman now and they wasn't to hang about. So I talked to them for just a minute, just to cheer 'em up a bit, like. Only Mr. Gotobed doesn't care to be reminded of what I was, so be a sport and don't tell, eh?"

"I wouldn't dream of carrying tales," said Daisy, trying not to sound indignant. "Now if you'll excuse me, I really must go and change."

If Mrs. Gotobed wanted to flirt with her admirers, it was none of Daisy's business, though it didn't make her like the woman any better. She just hoped Mr. Gotobed would not find out, since she did rather like him.

* * *

They all met at the group of deck-chairs reserved by Mr. Arbuckle, forward, where they would catch the afternoon sun as long as possible. Here the deck stewards served hot bouillon, Bath Olivers, and digestive biscuits. It was very pleasant with the sun shining through the glass, the vast Atlantic spread glittering before them. They were still close enough to land for a few seagulls to sail alongside the ship, peering in hopefully. Gloria persuaded a steward to open a window so that she could throw them crumbs. Swooping, they caught them in mid-air, to her delight.

The *Talavera*'s gentle pitch as she cut through the swells was cradle-like, soporific. Daisy started to drift off, only to be rudely awoken by the noon whistle.

Arbuckle jumped up. "Time for the mileage pool," he said. "I'm not a gambling man in the general way, but I wouldn't miss this for the world."

"Oh aye, it's like putting a flyer each way on the Derby," Gotobed agreed. "Almost a patriotic duty." He and his wife went off with Arbuckle to find out whether the distance the ship had sailed from Liverpool matched any of the numbers they had acquired in the auction pool last evening.

As half the take would go to seamen's charities, the others had each put a shilling in one of the lesser pools. Each drew a single digit to match against the last digit of the mileage. One of the stewards came round the promenade deck to report the result.

In spite of the one-in-ten odds, none of the four had won. However, a few minutes later Miss Oliphant came up to them, glowing with delight at her winnings of seventeen and six-pence.

They congratulated her and invited her to join them. She was a "nice old bird," as Phillip later remarked to Daisy.

Arbuckle and the Gotobeds returned.

"Nowt doing today," Gotobed reported.

"If you was to ask me," said the blooming bride resentfully, "that American Riddman rigged it with the stewards. I ought to've won, if he hadn't got hold of my number."

"You sold it to him, lass," Gotobed reminded her with a smile. "And I seem to remember you were right pleased with the price he paid."

After glowering at him momentarily, she switched on a blinding smile and squeezed his arm. "That's right, love; and after all, it was you bought the ticket for me in the first place. So kind he is to his little Wanda!" She mouthed a kiss at him, then turned her glower on Miss Oliphant. "Hey, that's my chair!"

"I'm so sorry," said the witch, flustered by the attack, and floundering as she tried to stand at the same time as retrieving her handbag from beneath the chair.

Alec sprang up to lend her his arm, and Phillip knelt down to fish for her bag.

"Don't go, ma'am," said Arbuckle. "We can easily get ahold of another seat."

"No, no, I really must go and tidy myself for lunch."

"Me too," said Daisy, trying—as were all the rest—not to look at Gotobed's red face. As she and Miss Oliphant walked towards the ladies' room, Daisy apologised. "My fault. I should have offered you my chair, or Mr. Arbuckle's."

"My dear, how could you have guessed that Mrs. Gotobed was so ferociously attached to that particular seat?"

"I couldn't, of course. After all, I only met her yesterday. But I'm afraid she seems to be rather on the lookout for slights."

"Only natural in her position," said the witch forgivingly. "Lavender, I think, to lift her spirits and calm her nerves. Perhaps even St. John's-wort. It must be difficult for her married to a gentleman so superior to her."

"Oh, but she's not," Daisy protested. "That is, Mr. Gotobed has lots of money now, but his antecedents are no better than hers."

"One cannot help but notice the influence of Yorkshire in his speech. However, I referred to his manners, not his birth."

"Only the most inveterate snob could hold his birth against him," Daisy agreed. "From all I've seen, he's thoroughly *nice.*"

"So I have observed. I do not believe him a weakling, however, except in having married a . . . No, I must not cast invidious aspersions! But if I were her, I should take great care how I behaved in his presence."

"He's no doormat," Daisy agreed, "or he couldn't have made his millions. You're right, he worships the ground she treads; but it wouldn't surprise me if he put his foot down if she carries on carrying on."

Mrs. Gotobed was quite subdued at lunch, so perhaps her husband had put his foot down. In fact, Alec told Daisy later that he had whisked her off willy-nilly to their suite on the specious excuse of changing his tie before lunch. She even invited Daisy and Gloria to call her Wanda, forcing them to reciprocate.

After lunch, Alec and Daisy attended the dancing lesson, the teacher adding the tango to the curriculum. Alec emerged confident of having mastered the fox-trot. Daisy hoped she'd be able to follow his lead.

She breathed a sigh of relief when he said apologetically, "I'm not sure I'm prepared to attempt the tango in public, not among experts like the Petries and the Gotobeds."

"Let's not," Daisy said fervently.

Next on the programme came the life-boat drill. Wanda didn't turn up.

"She said she wouldn't be seen dead in one of these hulking great things," Gotobed explained, as they tried on the clumsy life-jackets under the direction of the second mate, Mr. Harvey. "Leastways, she wouldn't be seen in one unless the alternative was imminent death."

"There are always a few who don't come," sighed Harvey. "Ladies who'd rather risk their lives than don anything so unfashionable, and men who refuse to be told what to do."

"That's why Chester wouldn't leave his blasted poker game." Lady Brenda, who had created a fuss at the next boat station until she was transferred to Harvey's boat, batted her eyelashes at him. *"I'll* do anything you tell me," she cooed, "but may I take it off now? It's frightfully uncomfortable."

With great solicitude, he helped her undo the straps. If Wanda had bothered to attend, she could have learnt a lesson about making the best of the most unpromising occasion.

Later that afternoon, Wanda did unbend sufficiently to join Gotobed and Arbuckle in a decorous game of shuffleboard, at which she proved surprisingly adept.

"Not so surprising," Gloria said when Daisy commented, as they watched. "Dancing in a chorus line, you'd have to make every move real precise, so your muscles and reflexes would get trained. I guess she'd be good at deck tennis, too, but I doubt she'll play. It might mess up her hair-do."

Daisy giggled, but said, "We really must try to be more charitable to the blooming bride. We have the rest of the voyage to get through, and then you'll be entertaining her at the other end, won't you?"

"Yes, Poppa invited Mr. Gotobed to stay before he married, of course; but he can't very well take back the invitation, let alone exclude Wanda. You're right, Daisy, I'll try to like her. Come and have a game of tennis now. You'll get better with practice."

"Not me! I've always been hopeless at sports, though I liked bicycling and climbing trees. Besides, what with playing this morning and dancing and everything, I'm going to be so stiff by tomorrow I shan't be able to move."

"What you need's a bit of gentle exercise to loosen up those muscles," said Gloria ruthlessly. "Come on, I'll coach you so when we play tomorrow you'll dazzle them all."

"A hot bath, followed by poplar-bark salve," came a murmur from behind.

"Miss Oliphant!"

"Sorry," said the witch. "I do endeavour not to push my remedies, and I promised Dr. Amboyne . . ."

"You're not competing with him," Daisy said, "since I wouldn't go to him anyway, not for stiffness. Your prescription sounds much pleasanter than Gloria's, though it doesn't seem likely that the shop sells poplar salve."

"I can let you have some," offered Miss Oliphant hesitantly.

"Spiffing! Gloria, if the salve works, you can coach me tomorrow, I promise; but it really is time I did a bit of work before I forget my first impressions of the voyage. Lead the way, Miss Oliphant. I'll stagger along after you."

In a third-class cabin shared with three strangers, the witch showed Daisy her medicine chest, a plain but well-polished teak box with a brass lock. It was lined with green plush, with dozens of blue glass vials and jars, neatly labelled, resting each in its own niche. Some of the labels were bright red, Daisy noted, perhaps those of dangerous herbs like foxglove which had both therapeutic and deadly qualities.

No wonder herbalists had been regarded as witches with mysterious powers for good and evil. She wouldn't want to get on the wrong side of someone with that sort of knowledge.

Luckily, Miss Oliphant was a good witch. She refused payment for the salve, saying, "You will not need a great deal. Rub a little into the stiff muscles and please return the rest."

"Of course. Thank you so much; it's very kind of you."

Daisy left the jar in her cabin and went to the writing room. One wall, or bulkhead as it was called by those in the know, was devoted to the ship's library. This was kept in glass-fronted cabinets, not because of its value—it consisted of all the books passengers had brought to read on board and not considered worth keeping—but to stop the volumes flying about in rough seas.

The several writing desks, like the swivel chairs in front of them, were securely fastened to the deck. Like school desks, they had holes to hold sunken inkwells, with the addition of hinged caps to stop ink sploshing about in a storm. At one of the desks, Alec was already intent on the stacks of information his superiors at the Met considered necessary to his job in Washington.

Daisy glanced around. All those reading and writing seemed to be minding their own business, so she kissed the back of Alec's neck, where the crisp, dark hair she loved turned into tiny, curly wisps. He jumped.

"Darling, I couldn't resist. How is it going?"

"Ghastly. Great Scott, they expect me to be a diplomat and a bureaucrat crossed with a don, not a policeman!"

"What a frightful miscegenation! But I know you can handle it, darling. You'll show Mr. Arbuckle's J. Edgar Whatsit what's what. I'll leave you in peace—I've got to get deck tennis and life-boat drills and dancing lessons down on paper, and the auction pool Mr. Gotobed explained to me. Not to mention fellow passengers!"

"I wonder if I ought to warn them?" Alec mused.

"Don't you dare! They won't be half so amusing if they

know they might turn up in a magazine article. Names changed to protect the guilty, of course."

"I hope so. The A.C. would have a fit if you were sued for libel."

They both stayed there for a couple of hours. Daisy did not have to go in search of tea. A steward brought it around, complete with triangular, crustless cucumber and gentleman's relish sandwiches, assorted biscuits, and those decorative *petits fours* which look so much better than they taste, as Daisy told herself firmly.

In due time, she went down to bag the bathroom they shared with three other cabins. Whether it was the poplar-bark salve or simply the hot sea-water, she felt much less stiff after her bath. She returned to the cabin feeling able to face an evening of dancing.

Under Lucy's critical eye, Daisy had bought two new evening frocks for the trip. Both were simple, so that their appearance could be altered with a coloured scarf or a length of the newly fashionable coloured glass beads.

The black she had worn last night. Tonight she put on the dark blue, silk charmeuse, the shade of the sky when the first stars come out. It consisted of a thigh-length tunic over a straight underskirt to just above the ankles, more flattering to her figure, according to Lucy, than anything with a belt around the hips.

Alec came in just as she put a long string of azure blue beads over her head.

"Just the colour of your eyes," he said approvingly, kissing the tip of her nose. "You look stunning, love. Every man there will want to dance with you."

"Oh, gosh, I do hope not!"

"Don't sound so panic-stricken. We'll tell them we're still honeymooning."

Daisy breathed a sigh of relief.

After dinner, they waltzed together to "Swanee River Moon," watched a tango, then tackled a fox-trot while the tenor warbled some sort of twaddle with a chorus beginning, "Stealing, stealing with your eyes appealing . . ." Daisy didn't think she utterly disgraced Alec, but in spite of his strong lead, she was so tense she was exhausted by the end.

Alec grinned at her as she sank into a chair. "They're playing Schubert and Dvořák tomorrow afternoon," he said. "You'll enjoy that."

"As long as I don't have to dance to it!"

"All you need is practise, darling."

"I feel such an absolute ass."

"We must practise in private. There's nowhere on board, but when we get ashore . . . In the meantime, suppose we go 'stealing' away to see what the moon's doing tonight?"

Up on the boat-deck, it was a little warmer than the night before. The almost balmy breeze came from the southwest, rather than the east, sending wispy clouds drifting across a haloed moon.

" 'Wrapped in a gauzy veil,' " said Daisy, who knew her English literature if she knew nothing else, "but it never looks to me 'like a dying lady, lean and pale.' More of a 'Goddess excellently bright.' "

"Mmmm," said Alec, putting a stop to Ben Jonson and Percy Bysshe Shelley alike in the most agreeable manner possible.

For some minutes Daisy was too busy to contemplate the moon or attend to her surroundings. Low voices, the scrape of a match nearby, footsteps coming and going barely impinged upon her consciousness, but she was jerked back to awareness by a sudden, wordless yell, followed by a splash.

"Man overboard!" someone bawled, and others took up the cry.

Alec sprang into action. Grabbing the nearest life-belt, he hung over the rail, peering down at the water. "There!" He flung the belt. "Damn, he's gone down again!"

Heart in mouth, Daisy leant beside him as a second life-belt spun down. In the moonlight, the bow wake was a white frill, losing definition as it spread. The water just below them was a dark, heaving mass, glimmering as it swelled and receded, with the white circles of the life-belts floating swiftly backwards as the ship steamed on. Daisy and Alec ran aft, along with an agitated group, trying to keep up with the receding circles.

Between the rings, something broke the surface. Arms reached upward, flailing, begging for help.

"The belt!" shouted several voices. "Grab the belt!"

As the drowning man floundered towards the nearest life-belt, Daisy discovered she was holding her breath. Suddenly she realized that the throb of the engines, the constant, unheeded heartbeat of the *Talavera,* had ceased.

"Fast reflexes on the bridge," Alec commented.

"I think he's got it," someone said. "Yes, he's got it!"

"Hang on!"

"Hold hard, fella, we'll get you out of there." That was surely Harvey, the second mate—and a dozen seamen had materialized on deck. "Here, men, this boat. Lower away, now! Ladies and gentlemen, out of the way, if you please."

They moved back, crowded to the rail a little further along. Someone was sobbing. Daisy clung to Alec, weak with shock and still tentative relief. Creaking, the davit swung the life-boat out over the side and began to lower it.

"Lights!" called Harvey impatiently.

"How the dickens did he come to fall?" a man wondered aloud.

"I saw it," a hysterical voice responded. "He was pushed!"

ABOUT THE AUTHOR

Born and raised in England, Carola Dunn now lives in Eugene, Oregon. Her next Daisy Dalrymple mystery, *To Davy Jones Below,* will be published by Kensington Publishing in July 2003. You can visit her website at: www.geocities.com/CarolaDunn.

Mickey Rawlings Mysteries
By Troy Soos

__The Cincinnati Red Stalkings $5.99US/$7.50CAN
   1-57566-408-9

__Hunting a Detroit Tiger $5.99US/$7.50CAN
   1-57566-291-4

__Murder at Wrigley Field $5.50US/$7.00CAN
   1-57566-155-1

__Hanging Curve $5.99US/$7.99CAN
   1-57566-656-1

Mischief, Murder, &
Mayheim – Grab These
Kensington Mysteries

Feel the Seduction of Pinnacle Horror

__The Vampire Memoirs
   by Mara McCunniff   0-7860-1124-6 $5.99US/$7.99CAN
   & Traci Briery

__The Stake
   by Richard Laymon   0-7860-1095-9 $5.99US/$7.99CAN

__Blood of My Blood: The Vampire Legacy
   by Karen E. Taylor   0-7860-1153-X $5.99US/$7.99CAN

Call toll free **1-888-345-BOOK** to order by phone or use this coupon to order by mail.

Name_____

Address_____

City_____ State_____ Zip_____

Please send me the books that I checked above.

I am enclosing $_____
Plus postage and handling* $_____
Sales tax (in NY, TN, and DC) $_____
Total amount enclosed $_____

*Add $2.50 for the first book and $.50 for each additional book.
Send check or money order (no cash or CODs) to: **Kensington Publishing Corp., Dept. C.O., 850 Third Avenue, 16th Floor, New York, NY 10022**
Prices and numbers subject to change without notice.
All orders subject to availability.
Visit our website at **www.kensingtonbooks.com**.

Western Adventures
From F.M. Parker